Joined

The Ashes of Eden Chronicles
Book 1

STEVEN DELONG

Preface

This piece of work could not be completed without the patience, encouragement and understanding of my good friend James Lengele. Bringing a sensitive subject like religion to the core of a fictional/magical realism novel is a lot trickier than it sounds. It means late nights, gallons of whiskey, tons of edits, and inexplicable frustration as these characters took on a life of their own and spun the direction of this book completely out of control!

I would also like to thank another friend of mine for dedicating the cover work for the novel Matt Delaney. You can find more of his work on his Instagram page md7photos (**https://instagram.com/md7photos**) make sure to follow him to see more great work!

Joined sets the foundation for a world that we are just scratching the surface of. I hope you enjoy and look forward to bringing you the next installment soon.

steveauthorthe@gmail.com

Library of Congress Control Number: TXu 2-156-679
ISBN: 9781086566093

Front cover image by Matthew Delaney.
Book design by Designer.

First printing edition 2019.

https://stevesavestheworld.wixsite.com/authorstevethe

Prologue

Age 6

The living room was small, the loveseat and sofa were crammed so tightly together there was no room to walk between them. The cushions of the couch were so aged they could no longer hold their shape. When you look at them, the word frumpy comes to mind. Cigarette burns and stains covered their entire surfaces.

The small television that sat on the floor had been broken, most likely for years. A layer of dust lay untouched, stuck to the nicotine that coated every inch of surface in the room. The once white walls were now a dull, sickening yellow.

Beer bottles, cans, cheap plastic gallons of vodka littered the floor of the living room so carelessly that only the truly despondent could understand. The odor of spilled booze, stale cigarettes, and human waste was thick in the air. The smell permeated the nostrils so thick the body's natural response was to flood the mouth with bile in an attempt to rid itself of the offending odor.

Past the living room, the hallway led to the bathroom and bedrooms. The once-plush carpet was now so severely matted that it felt like a sticky cement floor. Of the sparse picture frames that were still on the walls, none hung straight. Dirty clothes and moldy takeout food containers littered the sides of the hall, leaving only a few inches to walk through.

Inching past the debris, Father Michael looked into the small bedroom. The walls, once painted a deep blue, had faded. Tobacco stains had turned part of the walls a sickly green. On the bed sat a boy, his knees drawn to chest face buried, sobbing. He clutched a toy robot in one hand, which shook with each exhale.

He had mussed black hair and required a shower. His clothes were dirty; they had not been changed in days. Father Michael saw the boy had bags under his eyes from crying and staying awake for days. He had been crying since things got bad. No one could blame the boy for that. The boy lifted his face and Father Michael met his eyes, the bags were there alright, deep and pained from things he should never have been through.

"Will she be alright Father?" The boys' voice was timid and scared, but it didn't shake. The boy was brave.

"I don't know my Son, her demons are strong. I will do my best, God will prevail."

The boy laid his head back on to his knees, fallen silent again, but not quite resigned. The boy was trying to be brave. No boy should have to be this bold.

Father Michael made the sign of the cross and said a silent prayer for the boy, then for himself. As soon as the prayer was complete, Father Michael opened the door to the other bedroom. As soon as it opened, the screaming began.

Age 8

The boy (he had no name now, just boy) was one of many in the orphanage. Everyone here spoke Italian or Latin. It took some time to learn, but hunger was a good motivator. He was brought here once the Demon killed his mother. The boy was surrounded by those whose parents had been killed by Demons, either before or during their exorcisms.

When he arrived, the boy was taught to believe in Christ, to believe in the Church, and to believe he was going to exact revenge on those who took his mother from him. Father Michael said so. He didn't see Father Michael as often as he wanted though, and when he did The Father did not have as pleasant a demeanor towards him anymore, but the boy understood. Father Michael was here to teach, not here to coddle. It only took five lashes of the whip on his back for him to understand.

Everyone in the class was excited today, as they were each to see their first Demon tonight. Of the thirty, it seemed that only two or three actually remembered the face of the Demon who was responsible for making them be here tonight.

The boy was one who remembered. He remembered the face of his mother after the Demon took its toll on her. Of course, the boy thought his mother was beautiful, all boys did, but the lasting memory of his mother was that of the Demon. The Demon dehydrated her so that the skin of her face was split cracked, but refused to bleed. Black bags were under her eyes, her body was thin, her skin just thicker than wet paper. It wasn't the pretty mother that he remembered.

Not to say that she was ever a kind, nurturing mother. She always seemed distant, more like an observer of his life rather than a participant in it. The boy wasn't sure if he should blame the Demon inside her at the end, but he found that if he did, he could sleep better at night.

Midafternoon the children were summoned from the classroom. They had been learning about the three stages of possession. Infestation, oppression, possession. Briefly, one of the sisters spoke about the theory of integration but was interrupted by the calling to leave for the chapel.

The school they were in was an Old, Italian monastery constructed a thousand years before any of the children had been born. They were lead to the chapel, where Father Michael stood before them on the pulpit dressed in his best. He spoke to the children in Italian; the boy hoped that newer arrivals could understand.

"Tonight, children, you will encounter your truest of fears. You will come to see the face of the possessed. You will see the face of a Demon. Flee, and you will find yourself on the street to starve. Only the dedicated will walk this path. Cleanse your minds, children, for the Demon, will know your fears, and he will show them to you."

One at a time they were taken from the chapel through a doorway behind the pulpit. The boy sat for hours as the sun set and the night became full. The Boy was the only one left when Father Michael finally came to retrieve him. "Sixteen of your classmates chose the streets, thirteen chose to stay. I wonder, what shall you choose?"

He led the boy through the same doorway that all the other children had been lead. It was a dark tunnel, much smaller than a hallway. Torches were sitting in iron fixtures dug into the side walls. The torchlight made the tan walls look like a bright yellow that faded to an almost orange color the farther away from the torch it got.

They walked in silence for a time. The walls of the tunnel muffled every sound, even their footsteps. There were too many turns left, then left then right then left. The boy was more afraid of getting lost in the maze than facing the demon or facing the streets.

After a time, sounds began to come into the passageway. An almost moaning was followed by a clink of chains. As they walked along the sounds grew louder. There was moaning, cursing in languages that the boy both understood and had never heard before. The boy somehow knew that they were threats or pleas. Whatever was making the sound was a mix of anger, confusion, hatred, jealousy.

The tunnel opened to a large room. There were no windows, so the boy assumed they were underground. Torchlight guttered against the walls every eight feet or so, lighting the entire room. Except on the far side of the room, there was a space about thirty feet that remained unlit and pitch black. Several priests and nuns were walking about the room, some in prayer, and others in observation.

Father Michael pointed to the inky blackness across the room. "There are two lines painted on the floor. You will walk past the first but under no circumstances shall you walk past the second." He made the sign of the cross over the boy "May Christ protect you."

The boy walked across the room. He could see the lines on the floor. The first line was about eight inches from the second, and the second line was about six inches from the blackness, from the moaning, from the rage.

The boy crossed the first line, peering into the darkness looking for the Demon, but nothing happened. Nothing jumped or screamed or tried to tear out his throat. From the darkness came a chuckle, and peering into the blackness, the boy could see its face for the first time.

The eyes held the boy's focus. The irises were different sizes and colors, the left eye was larger than the right. The left eye had a yellow iris, and could not be mistaken as naturally human in any circumstances. The right eye had a thin brown iris, but the pupil took up most of the eye. There were blisters oozing puss on the Demons mouth. The mouth had cracked and dry lips. The Demon looked at the boy, the silence in the room was unnerving to the boy.

When it spoke, the demon almost had two voices. "Here another Exorcist comes." The Demon sounded almost childishly excited. "Tell me child, why you think you can overpower me? You couldn't save your mother, you can't save yourself. You will save no one."

The boy looked at the Demon "Is that what you seek, to be saved? Salvation? Redemption?"

"I will make my own Kingdom in Hell. I will make it with the souls of those I ride. One day I may ride your stinking soul into Hell, and then you can be with Mommy again."

The boy looked at the demon, "If you seek Hell so badly, I will take it from you. Demon, I say unto thee, God, the Father of mercies, through the death and resurrection of his Son has reconciled the world to himself and sent the Holy Spirit among us for the forgiveness of sins."

There was laughter to be heard throughout the room, maybe those gathered had never thought to absolve the demon, perhaps it wouldn't work, or perhaps it was just a trick of the Demon for his ears only. "Through the ministry of the Church may God give you pardon and peace, and I absolve you from your sins in the name of the Father, and of the Son, and of the Holy Spirit. Amen."

There was a strangled gargle followed by silence as the Demon looked at the boy. Suddenly, it was pulled back into the darkness by invisible hands. There were screams of pain and anger, a wind was suddenly in the room, despite it having no windows. The firelight was guttering, flickering and sputtering, throwing shadows and light where they weren't before.

The cries in the darkness became human sounds; a human sobbing that bounced off the walls of the room, and the boy couldn't tell where they were coming from. Priests ran around the room relighting the torches that had guttered out. As a priest moved to light another torch a bit of light fell on a human figure crouched, kneeling and sobbing in the darkness.

The boy inched forward to get a better look. It appeared as if the Demon was gone. The eyes were normal, and there were no more blisters, no more cracked lips.

The boy felt proud. "Come forward to be recognized and saved," the boy called.

There was a rush of wind and a snap of chain. In an instant, the Demon was close enough to almost touch the boy. The smell of the breath reminded the boy of his Mother. The smell of booze, cigarettes, and teeth that had not been brushed in months.

"Absolution only comes to those who ask for it Boy, and I have not, I will not. I am building a wonderful paradise in Hell. I'll be taking this soul with me now, and I'll be coming back for you soon." The Demon turned its head to the right as far as it could go. It closed its eyes in concentration, winced, and then the neck snapped. The body fell to the floor, the chains rattling.

Father Michael walked to the boy and led him back to the chapel, then back to the dorms in silence. The sleeping quarters was one large room with bunk beds in the center. The Boy could hear multiple children quietly crying in their beds, trying hard not to make any noise but failing. More than half were now empty.

The boy walked to his bed, made the sign of the cross, and got in. Once Father Michael left the room and closed the door, the dorm was dark. There the boy allowed himself to remember his mother, and he let himself cry in silence.

1.

She tapped her fingers on the steering wheel to the beat of the music. She was listening to her second favorite Japanese DJ Satoshi Tomii. The earbuds thumped with the bass and hiss of the techno music. She adjusted herself in the seat of the car, even in cool weather sitting in a car parked in a parking lot gets hot.

Her long naturally brown hair had been dyed black with bright blue highlights and tips. It had been pulled into a bun and then held in spikes by hair spray and gel. She wore dark makeup around her eyes and bright blue lipstick that matched her hair. It was in contrast with her almost alabaster white skin.

Her nails were not overly long, but they were fake, manicured and painted blue. Glitter was added to the polish to ensure they caught the light. The oversized t-shirt she wore displayed an anime character from a video game that never really found its footing in the United States, but it was one that she loved.

She was sitting in a mid-nineties Taurus four door. The faded paint and interior came with matching holes in the floor mats and a tape deck. The vehicle was so old that it didn't have a cd player, much less an axillary jack for her phone. It was paid for though and she could drive it whenever she wanted. In her eyes, it had no flaws.

Raz was parked in the parking lot of St. Michaels Cathedral in the sleepy town of Woodstock Georgia. Her brother and friends were inside the church partaking in communion and giving their confessions. The cleansing ritual was done every time before they began the rite of exorcism.

She was a practicing witch though, so different rules applied to her. At least that's what she told herself. She didn't worry about some long bearded grandfather figure in the sky that would wag his finger at you in disgust if you did the wrong thing.

To further her point God gave man (and woman) instincts and then set all the rules in direct opposition to those instincts. 'Desire to look, but don't touch. The desire to touch, but don't taste. If you taste, you're fucked.' She didn't understand.

Her brother and two friends emerged from the church. Her brother Gus stood about five foot nine or so. He had long sandy brown, almost boarded on dirty blond hair that fell to the base of his neck just above his shoulder. He was dressed in brown slacks and a light blue polo shirt.

Technically, she was adopted so he wasn't 'technically' her brother in blood. She came from Asian descent. More people had described her eyes as 'almond' than they had the color of her eyes. Generic ass hats, all of them. Granted her eyes were a light brown, but she would really rather have the color of her eyes described as light diarrhea after bad Mexican, before almond. Outside of the hair (which she took care of), they didn't match at all. His skin wasn't pale like hers, while he could tan, he would get skin cancer before he turned to bronze. She would blister and burn before she tanned. She was also short, maybe reaching five foot four if she were on her tiptoes.

Following behind Gus was Josh. He was the tallest of the group standing at six one, maybe six two depending on the shoes he wore. His hair was blond with black undertones. He kept the hair a medium length, off the ears and neck but otherwise messy. He wore a black t-shirt that was half a size too small.

She and Josh had a lot in common when it came to physical fitness. His body was very toned and well defined. He was very smart and always learning and doing research.

Josh had never been considered normal, his thought process was different and he communicated differently than anyone she had ever known. She wasn't sure if it was the possession that Preacher freed him from or if he was born with his different way of thinking.

Preacher came down last. He was taller than Gus, shorter than Josh. His freshly shaved head reflected the sunlight, as did his wraparound sunglasses. He wore a loose-fitting black t-shirt, black slack, shoes, and a belt. He was their friend and leader. He was confident even when he didn't know all the answers and she felt that made him a good leader.

Also, Preacher used to be a Catholic Priest. Maybe he still was, she wasn't sure. If he was still one, he didn't act like one that she had ever met before though. When she and Gus met him, he was going by Preacher, not Father. She never bothered to ask.

She knew that when the exorcism rite would take place he would look like any other Catholic priest in the ranks. He still had all his vestments and would dress to the nines to get a Demon back to Hell.

The group piled in the car. Preacher took the front seat as normal. She tugged the earbuds out of her ears, turned the radio up and turned the car on. The radio played the only rock station in Atlanta, oldies but probably goodies.

It only took a few moments to get back to the house they lived in. It was a raised ranch, four bedrooms, and three bathrooms. She parked in the driveway because the garage was full of shelves and workbenches.

The group piled out of the car and headed for the front door. As they entered Preacher turned to Raz "Have you completed the spell work for tonight?"

She shook her head. "Not yet, I'm going to finish this afternoon. When should I be ready to leave?"

Preacher thought for a moment. "The bar opens at one, we should be there when it opens."

Raz nodded. "It is easier to cast charms to keep people out than to make them leave. Sounds like a good plan to me." She turned and headed downstairs to her workspace. She had powders and ointments to make.

Preacher walked into the dining room and took a seat at the head of the table. Gus followed him into the dining room sitting to Preachers left. "You don't seem sure about taking Josh tonight. I think it's time, he's as ready as he will ever be."

Preacher was silent for a few moments. "I'm nervous. Making contact in the open is much more dangerous. Any hesitation could ruin all the work we put into finding and tracking this Demon down. We don't find the Joined easily. We only get one chance at trying to exorcise them."

Gus nodded. "I understand that, but he's got a personal score to settle. He was almost Joined when you exorcized the Demon that was dwelling in him. He'll do his part."

Preacher nodded. "Josh." He called out, he hadn't heard him go downstairs to his workspace. He was probably hovering in the kitchen or living room.

Josh came sheepishly around the corner like someone who just got caught eavesdropping. He walked into the dining room and sat opposite Gus.

"Josh," Preachers voice was smooth like a practiced teacher. "What are the stages of possession?"

"Infestation or manifestation is the first stage, then oppression followed by full possession." Josh paused, and Preacher looked at him expectantly not saying a word. "Infestation or manifestation begins when the Demon first comes into contact with its victim. It can be in the guise of a ghost or haunting, contact through a spirit board or something as mundane as nightmares."

Preacher nodded he wanted Josh to continue. "The Demon is weak in this world, not being able to fully manifest at this point. It feeds off fear, anxiety, and pain. As the Demon grows in power the infestation turns into oppression. It is the whispers in your ears and the movement out of the corner of your eye. It's the sound of footsteps in an empty room, scratching in and knocking on the walls."

"It can create sensations on the skin like spiders crawling on the arms or legs of the oppressed person. Maybe it is snakes slithering across the body while the victim tries to sleep. It can be something as simple as feeling a flea crawling or jumping on your body. Whatever the victim is scared of."

Preacher nodded his approval. "Knowing this do you know how the infestation started in or around you?"

Josh shook his head. "I am not clear on when it started. Only when it started to get really bad, which was the manifestation. The Demon can enter your dreams, move objects, and write on a fogged mirror during a hot shower."

Preacher nodded but remained silent again for Josh to go on.

"It can touch the victim, grabbing them or scratching them. It can manifest a physical form though usually only in dim light. Objects will fly across the room, lights will flicker, it can take the tone of other people voices. The Demon is more powerful and centered around a person, not just a place. It has focused on a target and works the person's weaknesses until the person stops fighting and the Demon gets into the body."

Preacher held up a hand and stopped Josh's regurgitation of information. "During your oppression Josh, what do you remember?"

Josh ran his hands over one another nervously. "The thing of nightmares. Every door I closed would open. Dishes I cleaned and put away were put back into the sink. Every chair I pushed into the dining room table was lying on its side the morning. I stopped sleeping under the sheet because I would wake up in the middle of the night pinned to the bed by a force I couldn't see."

Preacher nodded in approval. "At least you remember. That will help you to understand and empathize. Because you empathize it shows you believe. Because you believe the prayers will come easier and will have more effect because your faith is stronger."

The silence in the room became an abyss. Preacher looked at Josh, his gaze was unwavering. Josh was staring at the table, running his hand through his hair over and over.

"Josh, what is it?" Preacher asked.

Gus could tell from the tone that Preacher was asking more for academic reasons than personal ones.

Josh licked his lips. "Possession is almost a relief from the physical terror. The Demon enters you and it becomes part of you. Everything becomes an internal nightmare instead of a physical one. When the Demon or Demons have control, you can rest. It's like sleep, but watching yourself in the dream. When they don't you have to fight like crazy to keep them from taking control."

Preacher nodded. "The Demon is very powerful during a possession and can take over the body for extended lengths of time. The Demon can stay in control for hours at a time fighting the soul into submission."

"It uses the soul like a battery, eventually the Demon has to let the soul resurface to rejuvenate and recharge so it can be used again. The Demon cares little for the body it possesses, so it usually will not eat, drink or sleep at all for days. When the Demon allows the soul to resurface they are using suffering from several health problems and may die."

Josh paused for a moment, remembering some far off trauma. "I read that those that do survive this treatment for long often suffer from long term mental problems. It literally drives them crazy. While in control of the body the Demon can make the body move and contort in inhuman ways. It can exude disgusting fluids that stink to high hell from any opening on their body."

Josh paused for a moment looking past Preacher as if he were remembering something. Preacher wondered if Josh was remembering the stage when Preacher found him. Josh was lost to possession and close to death. Everything that he was describing he lived through, it was first-hand testimony.

Josh swallowed hard enough to be audible. "Integration, or as you call it, Joining, comes as the last stage if the person lives long enough. The Demon whispers sweetly of peace and sharing power. The Demon says it is a blending of souls. They take you into their own. They change you, but you also change them. The Demons call it a shared power. I think they are lying."

Preacher nodded slightly then asked, "What makes Joined different from the other levels of possession?"

Josh met Preacher's steel-like eyes with his own. "The Church doesn't believe it is real, at least not officially. They believe that possession ends once the body dies or the Demon is driven out."

"But there is a Joining. It is a rebirth that allows the Demon to be in control all the time. Once Joined, all the physical signs of possession go away. The dehydration, sores, bruises, anything, and everything is healed once the soul gives in and allows the Demon to take control." Josh looked at Preacher to see if there was anything else he wanted him to recite.

Preacher remained silent looking at Josh for a moment. "Tonight, we are going to confront a Joined Demon in public. It is more than simply dangerous. The last two times we have attempted this, the Demon killed the host before we could finish the exorcism. Remember your responses to the prayers. If I ask for something hand it to me quickly. Do not hesitate and do not listen to the Demons lies."

"The Demon will know that you were once possessed. It will recognize the marks possession has left on you. It will try to use that against you. Wrap your faith around you like armor. If you start to falter or fail I want you to leave. It is asking a lot to even bring you tonight instead of starting you on a normal possession and exorcism. It takes more to ask you to leave."

Preacher nodded at Gus. "Gus says you know your lines, and you will not fail. I trust Gus. Preacher looked over Josh, he looked younger than when Preacher first found him.

"I want to be clear Josh. I believe that you will be fine tonight. I believe that you will do the right thing when the time comes. But you're not tested yet, so I don't know what you are going to do in the moment. Understand that I am making the decision on faith, both in you and in God. Also, understand that finding this Demon has taken months of searching, researching, stalking, and a considerable amount of luck. Do not fuck this up."

Preacher stood and walked out of the room past Josh, patting him on the shoulder. It wasn't a great pep talk. Hell, it wasn't even close to good, but Preacher didn't really care. Josh would do his job and that was the important part.

Preacher checked his phone for the time. It was just before ten in the morning, which meant they didn't need to leave for a little while. He stepped into the kitchen and poured himself a glass of whiskey. He spent time in church this morning getting his spirit right, now he had to get his mind right and whiskey was the only way he knew how to do that anymore.

2.

There was a mix of hesitation and anxiety rolling through Josiah as he stood at the terminal of the small airport. He looked over the runway at the small one engine plane descending on the lone runway. It wasn't the first time he thought this mode of transportation to be odd.

Demons like him can just step into shadows and simply be somewhere else. It is one of the many powers that made Demons scary. Distance was certainly not an issue, so why someone would be flying in instead of shadow walking?

Josiah knew that shadow walking left a trail, like some kind of thread of consciousness. If someone knew what they were looking for they could follow it. There were those amongst the Fallen that could sniff you down like a bloodhound. Boogieman stories if you asked him.

And yet there he was, at a tiny airport in Kennesaw, Georgia watching this tiny plane touch down. As a human, he might be irritated by being sent out like an errand boy, but when Baba Doek tells you to go and bring someone back, you go and bring someone back.

Still, it would be nice to have some of his warrior brothers and sisters with him. Josiah was a deal maker, not a warrior. He wasn't as strong as a warrior, or as clever as a trickster. His gift was negotiations. Keeping Spiritus Vitae stocked for the area had made him very influential among his kind, but that wouldn't do him a whole lot of good if the Fallen descended on him.

Spiritus Vitae literally translated means Spirit of Life. While all Demons needed human souls if they wanted to stay powerful, dealers could literally take it from people they were not possessing and store it.

He stepped out of the terminal into the cool night air. At least it wasn't June. Even Demons dislike humidity. He walked over to his borrowed SUV and climbed inside. The small plane had taken its spot and the stairs were coming down.

Josiah navigated the SUV to the plane and left it running as he walked around to greet the guests. A tall, slender man was coming down the stairs. He had long black hair that was tied in a ponytail. He had a tightly trimmed goatee, and a black suit with a matching, narrow tie. The man was neatly put together, nothing out of place, walking with an effortless grace reserved for athletes. As he approached the last step he looked at Josiah, his eyes flashing a crimson red. He was a Warrior.

His counterpart, however, was the exact opposite. He came thudding down the steps wearing scuffed and worn work boots. He wore stained and tattered blue jeans with a chain wallet hanging from one side that swayed with every step taken by his tree trunk legs. Straining against his large stomach he had on a blue jean jacket with the arms torn off, a dirty t-shirt from an eighties metal band, which was also missing its sleeves. The fat man in a little coat also had a beard but it was bushy, unkempt and orange. This guy was just one pointy hat away from looking like the trashiest oversized yard gnome in existence. Glancing at Josiah his eyes flashed an emerald green of Tricksters.

The third being descending the stairs was surprising. She was young, no older than eleven or twelve human years. Demons generally avoid such young hosts because there was no benefit to it. The Demon could use a souls' energy to stave off aging for years. Taking someone so young posed no benefit unless there was something special about the host itself, perhaps a strong connection between host and Demon?

The girl was dressed in a simple, sleeveless, black dress that came to her knees. The light from the small airport bounced off her shiny black belt that drew attention to her slender figure. Black high heels tried to shape her legs like a woman's but her body simply had not developed that far yet.

Her dark brown hair was cut at shoulder length, bringing more attention to the youthfulness of her face. Heavy black eyeliner outlined her dark brown eyes, and a deep red lipstick was painted on her slender childlike lips. She was carrying a metal briefcase and part of Josiah was surprised that it wasn't handcuffed to her wrist. Her eyes appeared black in the night, and when they gazed over at Josiah they flashed an electric blue. So, she was a dealer – like Josiah.

The Warrior spoke first, placing a hand on his chest. "Malik." He nodded to the trickster, "Snyder." He extended his hand out to the dealer coming down the stairs and she took it with grace. Josiah could tell this was practiced, and this relationship was well established. The warrior was definitely her subordinate and had been for many years. "It is my pleasure to introduce Regent Balisk's emissary, Izabella."

Josiah bowed slightly, showing his deference. "I'm Josiah, I will be escorting you this evening." Josiah opened the back door as Izabella reached the pavement and she climbed into the SUV. The Trickster followed her and Josiah closed the door. Josiah walked around to the drivers' side of the SUV, letting the Warrior open his own door. Warriors are touchy about having things done for them that they can do for themselves.

For several minutes they rode down the Georgia interstate in silence. Through one construction zone to the next, by the baseball stadium. Never let it be said that Atlanta stopped trying to improve itself.

"How long?" The voice came from Izabella, thick with an eastern European accent. Her voice was deeper than Josiah had been expecting, coming from such a tiny frame.

Josiah looked into the rearview mirror at the Demon inhabiting a child's body. "30 minutes give or take traffic. This isn't my favorite mode of transportation but orders are orders." Josiah shrugged, hoping that would satisfy the Demon child in the back seat.

The ride in silence continued as they finally exited off the highway and into the city. Cars buzzed by them and they in turn buzzed by others. The skyscrapers of the city fell behind them as they made their way closer to their destination. Office buildings were replaced with trendy restaurants and fashion boutiques. The route took them to a point in the city that is called Little Five Points.

The neighborhood is named Little Five Points because there are five streets that intersect at a common red-light. Situated on one of the corners is a restaurant called the Vortex, the entrance to the restaurant is a large white skull with a gaping maw. Josiah always thought that it was ironic that people would walk through a skull, a face of death, to eat food that would bring them closer to death. Eating there once in a while was a delight as long as you treated your body correctly, but this was America, and gluttony, sloth, and laziness controlled most of the population.

A slight chuckle came from Izabella as they passed the iconic Atlanta landmark. Apparently, the irony wasn't lost on the visitor either. Josiah turned the SUV into a parking lot just down the street from the center of Little Five Points.

He pulled the vehicle around the back of the building, the tires of the SUV crushing glass beer bottles left behind the club. Josiah pulled up to a red door that had no doorknob. It was just a steel red slab with a single incandescent light glowing above it. Josiah got out of the SUV and walked around to the door. Hellion protection spells radiated power off the door. Josiah lifted his hand to the center of the door and barked out some of his own Hellion Hoodoo. The door clicked and swung inward a fraction of an inch.

Malik got out of the vehicle and opened the door for Snyder and Izabella. The three followed Josiah through the door and into a narrow hallway. Cinder block walls were illuminated by single lightbulbs hanging from power cables every few feet. The lights were dim enough that you walked through spaces of shadow and darkness before coming back into the light.

The sound of the music from the club was muffled by the concrete, leaving just the sounds of the bass reverberating across the walls and vibrating in your chest. With each thump of the bass, the lights in the hall shook, throwing shadows and light in strange and unpredictable ways.

Josiah led them to the end of the hall and opened a door obscured by the darkness. He entered the doorway and began walking down a set of stairs. The sounds of the music started to fade as they descended below the building.

As the group descended into the subbasement, the lighting grew red. They entered an antechamber, the walls lined with bookshelves stuffed full of dusty books and rolled parchments. The titles of each had long worn away with time and use. The antechamber was empty except for two menacing individuals, flanking the only other door in the room. Castor and Pollux.

Both were bald and wore all black. Their face wore no expression, deep shadows under their eyes only added to their menacing look. The one on the left was short, standing about five foot six. He held a long chain wrapped around his left arm and chest, dangling from the end was a spiked steel ball.

The one on the right was taller, standing about six feet tall. A baseball bat tipped with spikes rested on the ground, dangling loosely from his hand. Both were human, but each was pulled through the veil into Hell as children. Each spent what felt like years being tortured, then torturing damned souls until there was nothing left but loyalty to their master.

They gazed at the group as they entered the room. The taller one, Pollux?, turned his gaze to Josiah, "You're late." He looked at the trio behind Josiah and made a deep bow. "Your Eminence, welcome."

Pollux opened the door, and the four were allowed entry. Red, LED lighting ran across the walls casting the room in red light. The room was crowded. Twelve benches sat at an angle with an aisle breaking between them into sides of six. Beyond the benches was a semicircle, used for receiving and hearing guests. Raised by three steps was an elegant chair that could only be considered a throne.

Sitting on the throne was Baba Doek. Baba Doek took a host that was no more than twenty. Her brown hair was braided in a single long braid that fell over her left shoulder and came to just above her stomach. The host was pretty in the girl next door way and wore no makeup to hide it. Her sleeveless royal blue dress looked almost purple in the red light surrounding the room. She wore sapphire earrings, three small stones dangling from each ear with a matching three stone necklace on a silver chain that sat next to a thin golden chain. Whatever was connected to the gold chain fell inside the dress and could not be seen. Sitting high on her throat like a choker was a third necklace, a simple piece of leather dangling thirteen teeth.

Josiah led the group between the benches to the center of the circle. "My Regent, please allow me to introduce the Emissary, Izabella, and her companions Malik, and Snyder." Josiah took a bow and allowed the three to step forward. His job done he made his way to the back of the room.

Izabella handed the briefcase she was carrying to Snyder and took a deep bow. "Regent Balisk apologizes for his absence but sends his regards. He found the mode of transportation…. Unappealing, so he sent us three."

Izabella turned to Snyder and opened the briefcase. She removed a glass mason jar and approached the steps. "Sent from the Hungarian region, the eyes of twelve virgin children, baptized and dedicated to the church." She went to one knee as she presented the jar.

Baba Doek took the jar and held it up to view. There were murmurs throughout crowded room. Izabella returned to the briefcase and removed a thin leather-bound book.

"A Grimoire, the pages made of shittim wood, as was the Ark of Covenant, wrapped in leather made from the skin of uncircumcised children of Israel." Izabella again took to the steps to hand the offering to Baba Doek. It was accepted and placed on the arm of the throne without examination.

Izabella turned once more to the briefcase and removed a rolled parchment. She turned to Baba Doek, "This parchment was created by our finest Demons. A spell is attached to it. Once cast, it will show you the location of the item you most desperately seek." Izabella began her ascent to Baba Doek but was stopped short when Baba Doek held up her hand.

"It is not complete? Why flatter me with these gifts, if what I asked for is not ready?" The silence in the room was palatable. "First, your Regent doesn't come as invited, and then he sends a poor substitute and an unfulfilled request? Explain yourself."

"Regent Balisk sent me to implore you not to seek this goal. He is concerned that the outcome is not what you may have predicted." Izabella turned to the enclave opposite the throne. "I am told there are those here who share these same concerns. Let us speak together as one voice to stave off this madness."

Murmurs broke out amongst the room, Baba Doek silenced them with a raised hand. "Regent Balisk doesn't approve? What does he think my plans are?" Baba Doek allowed a laugh to escape her lips.

From the back of the room, someone spoke. "We all know. Baba, I am Nicolas, Regent from New York. We all know about your design. Your plan is flawed." Murmurs erupted from the enclave again. "The one called Preacher; he was contained within the church thanks to us. When he left, he lost the resources. He was content with leaving us alone until you took and kept that host. Now he hunts us actively, and none of us are safe."

Another voice sang from the back of the room. "In Hell, you are a King amongst us. But on the Earth, you are a Regent, and cannot act with impunity."

Murmurs erupted through the room again, the obvious discord was so thick you could almost touch it. Izabella looked at Baba Doek, "Unsealing the Seven Seals and bringing Armageddon is foolish. It has been tried, and because of it, the Clave was formed. The Clave has decided to not pursue such matters."

Baba Doek rose up from her perch and descended the stairs. A pair of serpent tattoos swam under her skin, one down each arm resting their heads on the back of her hands. The viper's tongues shot out of their mouths and off her skin, licking the air. She took the scroll from Izabella, and with her free hand, she cupped the Izabella's cheek.

"Your Regent knows nothing of my designs. I have no desire to open the Seven Seals." Baba Doek looked at Malik. "Tell Balisk his insolence has been forgiven, and his debt paid." From the hand cupping Izabella's cheek, a viper rose into reality and struck Izabella in the face.

The strike was so sudden it was hard to see. The viper dove back into the skin of Baba Doek and was nothing more than ink on flesh once more.

Izabella gave a small gasp but otherwise showed no signs of pain. Two tiny punctures on her cheek welled then began spilling blood. Malik lunged towards Izabella but was stopped short by Snyder, who was deceptively fast despite his large girth.

From inside the viper's wounds fire erupted from Izabella face. Izabella's scream of agony echoed off the chamber walls as the pain of the fire consumed her. Her scream silenced as the fire burst from her mouth and eyes. Her skin turned black, charred and cracked. The flames burst from them consuming her. It took less than a minute for Izabella to turn into a smoldering heap of ashes on the floor.

Silence fell across the chamber as Baba Doek ascended to her throne. "If there is anyone else who wants to discuss the futility of my plans, please let them speak." There was a moment of silence. "If there is nothing else, get out of my city. Tell those who will not obey what awaits them."

Castor and Pollux made their way to the center of the court. The baseball bat and chain flail were replaced with a broom, dustpan, and coffee can. Castor, or Pollux, Josiah still didn't know who was who, swept the ashy remains into the dustpan and dumped the contents in the coffee can.

Pollux, or Castor, who cares really, held the coffee can out to Malik. Malik made another lunge but remained restrained by Snyder. It took several seconds, but Malik seemed to calm down and relaxed in Snyder's grasp. Malik took the can containing Izabella and stormed out, followed by Snyder.

Castor retrieved the metal briefcase, and the two made their way to the back of the room. Josiah assumed that's where the flail and baseball bat were; the two were rarely more than an arm's reach away from their chosen methods of destruction.

Josiah watched the foreign dignitaries leave as quickly as they could. Usually, groups would break off to linger and play their social games, but not this time. The destruction of an Emissary hastened their departure.

It was not the first time that an Emissary's host had been destroyed. This was Demonic politics after all, but it was uncommon and taboo even amongst demonkind. Josiah wasn't sure how Balisk would react to his Emissary's host being destroyed, sending her back to hell, but he was pretty sure there would be no more aid from the Baltic Region coming this way any time soon.

Baba Doek was sitting on her throne watching the crowd leave. If there was disappointment that they were not fleeing for their lives, it didn't show. She sat like a statue watching them leave, the scroll and spell laying across her lap.

She laid a hand on the parchment and stroked it like a beloved pet. Once the Clave members left, she looked to those remaining in the room. They were thirty-three in number.

"What I will do shall marvel the world, but it will require much of us. Lay your ambitions aside. Until this task is complete, tributes shall be increased by half. Be cautious, as our Fallen brothers and sisters will no doubt put every effort into thwarting us should they learn of our plans."

Baba Doek dismissed them all with a wave of her hand. Many of the members stepped backward, finding the nearest shadow to step through. Josiah watched as members of the court faded out, becoming one with the darkness.

Josiah turned and stepped into the nearest shadow he could find. The Darkness touched him and wrapped him in its cold, silky tentacles. He allowed The Darkness to pull him into its solitude, the familiar cold womb of emptiness surrounded him and he felt at home.

3.

It always reminded Josiah of flying. There was no up or down in The Darkness. He felt weightless. It felt like a distant memory when he had physical form before the rebellion. But it was all taken away from him and his Brothers and Sisters.

Josiah banished the thoughts and emotions as he stepped out of the shadows. He came out in an ally, on the street known to the locals as Hooker Run. This part of town had more bars than churches, a rarity in the south, and at least two prostitutes and a drug dealer on each street corner.

For Josiah, it was a home away from home. There was always a hooker that was looking to get clean and off the streets. Who cares if the price for that is their soul? They aren't using it anyway. If tributes were raised by half he would need to collect one or two of them this week.

Each week, everyone living in Baba Doeks territory gave her an amount of Spiritus Vitae as a tribute. Most of the Demons in the area came to him to get it. He always had stock. Some were able to get their own or went to other dealers in the area. To meet the need he would need to get creative in getting these souls.

Josiah cast a glamour of obfuscation as he walked down the street. He would be seen, but not noticed or remembered as he walked to his destination.

Someone once said 'if you've been to one dive bar in this shit hole of a world, then you've been to 'em all'. Well, that may not be accurate when you take Whirlwinds' into account. The bar had all the hallmarks of being a dump. Low light, sticky floors, neon lights flickering in the windows, cheap beer and cheaper women. One of the two pool tables has the phone book from two years ago under one of the legs to keep it mostly level. But these people would still throw dollar after dollar into it just to have something to do.

The bell above the door jingled as he entered. Josiah has been coming here almost daily for the last month. There was something satisfying about being in this place. Josiah wasn't sure if it was because he has been successful here or if it was because the humans that came here reminded him of himself shortly after the fall. They were willing to listen to almost any promise of a better tomorrow while willing to accept life as it was.

Although the smoke inside Whirlwinds is generally so thick that you can barely see out of the windows, tonight seemed to be an exception. It was early, though, and the crowd was light. The crappy sound system was blaring out some mid-90s country song about a broken heart. It fits because in this place and places like it everyone is broken.

Scanning the room, Josiah can tell you the complaints and desires of all the humans in here. The old guy at the end of the bar, staring alternately at the lone television behind the bar and his beer – he wants to feel like he belongs somewhere. His friends have drifted away. His wife is distant simply because everything has been said and complacency has taken over. His dream job was owning a bar, but even owning Whirlwinds depresses him now. He doesn't have the money to fix things up and because he can't fix things up he can't make the money he needs.

He watches the football game on television and his team is losing. At this point, he has lost the desire to even care if they win or lose. He misses the passion he once had, the drive to be better than others, to stand out and be noticed. His soul is withering in his carcass, there is little of interest in this soul for Josiah.

Behind the bar was an unremarkable guy in his late twenties, with shoulder length sandy brown hair and eyes to match. The bartender was completely disinterested in everything and everyone surrounding him. He was wearing a tight fitting black t-shirt and black slacks. Typical bartender attire, typical boredom.

At the closest pool table, a young man shoots and misses. His eyes are glassed, his thoughts elsewhere. Iced blue eyes and dirty blond hair mixed with his youth gave him the look of an up and coming rocker. The only problem was this is Atlanta, not Seattle. He was wearing black jeans, boots and a red and black flannel shirt. He looked like everything that could go wrong in a fashion shoot for a grunge lumberjack.

Pool table guy glances at a woman sitting at a table near him and he smiles. He believes that he is still charming, but she sees through it. He moves to take another shot. The thought of being in his prime but not brave enough to talk to the girl chafes his brain and he moves to shoot again. He wants to be more charming, more attractive to women. Vanity is a worthy sin. But a base sin that grows boring after a while.

The girl, though, she was more complex. Her eyeglasses, shoes, and purse were expensive, but she came to a bar that sells two dollar domestics and hasn't improved its sound system since Pontiac was a major car company. She could go anywhere, and yet here she is sitting with an untouched vodka martini in front of her. Target acquired.

She didn't notice when he slid into the seat across the table, his obfuscation still intact. He sat there, observing her across the table. She was bored and looking for excitement. This would be an easy deal for him to make. He reached inside for that little spark he uses to trick the minds of the weak, the spark he used to walk up and sit there unseen. He would cause a flutter in the corner of her eye and when she looks back he would be there as if he appeared out of thin air.

Josiah reached down ready to cast his glamour, but the bar door opened, and she turned to see who was entering. He smiled, the power of souls wasn't infinite and saving every little bit was always on his mind. He allowed his obfuscation of her mind to dissolve as she was turned. When she turned back to him the oddest thing happened. She didn't flinch, she didn't startle. She smiled. Josiah knew there was something very, very wrong then his face exploded with burning fiery pain. He knew that he was in a lot of trouble.

**

Raz sat patiently, she could feel the creature eyeing her. It always made her uneasy when they were initiating the first contact in the open. It's one thing to have a mother, or auntie, or friend come up and contract for a house blessing. Maybe they think their special someone might be possessed. You can gather background information from them and have something to go on. Working in the streets, however, when you find one, there is no information to go on and that makes the rites of exorcism so much more difficult. She felt safe enough though, her brother Gus was behind the bar, Josh was at a pool table and Preacher was on his way.

The Demon had moved from the bar to sit across from her and according to the plan, this should be when Preacher walks in. She had charmed the designer knockoff glasses that afternoon with a fairly complex charm that would allow her to see things that did not want to be seen. So as the glasses sat halfway down her nose she could look through them to see the lower half of a person sit down in front of her.

The door jingled behind her and she knew it was going to be show time. She also put spell work on the front door of the bar, to make it unappealing for the normal person. They would look at the door and simply decide there was somewhere else they would rather be. It was a harmless little charm that would fade in a day or two. Tonight it would ensure that no one interrupted them or got hurt. Raz glanced over her shoulder and saw that Preacher had come inside, he was easy enough to recognize with this thrift store military surplus trench coat and black slack and a white t-shirt.

She could tell from his stride that he meant business and he was not happy. He walked in a direct path to the table, picked up the glass of holy water that she had sitting in front of her and threw it in the Demons face.

The Demon let out a scream and began clawing at his face. Holy water was like liquid fire to them. With enough time and preparation, they could fake like it didn't hurt very much. Take them by surprise however and you got to witness first hand exactly how much it hurt. A mixture of Hellion, a language, which sounds like guttural animal growling mixed with Klingon and curse words in English, Italian, German and Latin came spewing out of the creature.

Gus was already on his way to the door to lock it, and Josh was moving with the rope just as planned. Preacher clamped down on the Demons right arm securing it to the armrest on the chair. He removed a thick zip tie from his jacket pocket and secured the wrist to the armrest. Josh came right behind him and tied the thick rope around the Demons arm. The same was done to the other arm before the screaming ceased.

Raz walked behind the bar and brought out two gym bags and set them on the table in from of the howling Demon. One was black and worn with age, you could see where it had been mended and stitched over the years. The other was a neon pink Hello Kitty bag, which always made Raz smile when she saw it. She might be fighting Demons but she would never lose that sense of irony that helped define her.

Raz opened the Hello Kitty bag and took out a pair of scissors and a plastic sandwich bag. She walked to the struggling creature and grabbed a handful of hair and snipped it off. "Relax doll, it will grow back." She said to the grumbling creature.

Preacher opened the battered black bag and removed a small circular container. The gold caught the meager light in the bar and it shimmered. Even in the dim and dingy bar, the compact showed its age and beauty.

Preacher nodded to the old man still at the bar. The Demons screaming had died down to only a dull mumbling, no doubt it was Hellion spellcraft to relieve the pain. If he was already casting his magic, they needed to hurry. "Take Mr. Mallard to the back, make sure our charms are strong then come back. We don't have much time."

Gus nodded and went to get Mr. Mallard, and lead him to the back through a doorway. Raz had cast a powerful charm that left Mr. Mallard stuck in his own memories. He was reliving only his best memories. On the outside, he seemed despondent, depressed, and ready to make a deal. Mr. Mallard moved when guided and made no complaints. Preacher was hoping that Mr. Mallard had many happy memories. Once he ran out it would begin to loop and if he looped too many times the charm could weaken and break before they were done.

Preacher reached back in the black duffle and took out his vestment. He always had mixed feelings when he took it out. Like an old Soldier that would see his uniform hanging in the closet after being retired for years. The cloth would always be a part of you, like a second skin, but that didn't mean that you wanted to rip it off the hanger and put it back on and resume your duty.

Josh watched as Preacher removed the old army trench coat and laid it on the bar. The t-shirt was next. Preacher always wore two necklaces, a black rosary that he took off and placed on the bar and a half heart necklace. The kind you buy when you're a teenager in love. Josh was never close enough to see whose initials were on it and he never had the courage to ask.

Preacher was thin and pale, not albino white, but close. There was a thin scar on the left side of his abdomen below the ribs. It was jagged, pink and about 4 inches long. Josh had wondered about that too, and once asked Raz if she knew what it was. She just shrugged and didn't answer.

Preacher slid his clergy shirt over his head, placed his clerical collar in place and slid into his cassock. He lifted the purple stole from the bag, an embroidered cross lay in the middle, which he brought to his lips and then draped around his neck allowing it to fall over his shoulders. Lastly, he picked up his rosary from the bar and wrapped it loosely around his left wrist. Like an old Soldier, dressed for battle. Gus emerged from the back and gave a thumbs up sign. All good so far.

A peal of deep laughter came from behind Preacher. The Demon was laughing, "Stulti sunt…." You are fools. "Et Nos Unum Sumus" We are one. The Demons grinned at Preacher. "We are Joined, there is nothing that separates us."

Preacher made the sign of the cross. It caused the Demon, to wince just slightly. Good. The Demon was still uncomfortable. Preacher reached in his bag and removed a small vial of olive oil and he allowed a small smile to reach his lips. "Olive oil, from the Garden of Gethsemane. It is the purest oil in all of creation. I hear it hurts like hell." Preacher uncorked the small vial and tilted it over, allowing one drop to fall on the ropes holding the demon's wrists. He then placed a finger over the opening and allowed a bit of oil to touch his finger. He placed the stopper back into the bottle and returned the bottle to the bag. Preacher took his finger, wet with the oil and marked the sign of the cross on the Joined Demons forehead.

There was a sizzling sound of frying bacon where the oil caused the skin to burn. The Demon screamed in Hellion garbled with other languages. Curses and anger, the Demon was off balance. Preacher reached into the bag and removed a glass bottle, opened the top and sprinkled a bit of holy water on Gus, then Josh. "Josh, remember your responses, follow Gus' lead." Finally, he sprinkled himself, then sprinkled the Demon with the holy water and the curses began anew.

Preacher began the rite of exorcism, Gus and Josh saying the responses.

"Lord, have mercy on us." Preacher began.

"Lord Have mercy on us." Gus and Josh replied.

"Christ Have mercy on us." Preacher continued.

"Christ Have mercy on us." The two responded.

"Christ Hear us." Preacher started to feel like himself, it was like riding a bike. The movements were always the same, pedal and steer. Just a different bike path with each exorcism.

"Christ graciously hear us." The two were beginning to feel more comfortable. Their voices becoming more in unison and firm.

"God the Father. God the Son. God the Holy Spirit." The ritual goes on, calling on Holy Mary, Saint Michael, Saint Gabriel, Saint Raphael, Saint Joseph. The response is always 'pray for us'. The Demon writhed and the responses came with more fervor.

Saint Thaddeus, Saint Matthias, Saint Barnabas. The plea for all of them to pray for us. The rhythm picked up and became more intense. The responses coming with the passion that only comes with true faith. From every evil, deliver us, Lord. The response changes, their voices harden, their faith confirmed.

From the Demon came laughter and discouragement. It has always been that way. The competition of wills between the evil entity and the exorcist. In a normal possession, the Demon does not have access to the soul. The power of the exorcist's faith is enough to eventually drive it out. The Joined, however, have been invited in, the human soul and the Demon have bonded and essentially a new being is created. Plain faith has never been enough to unjoin a Joined Demon.

Minutes tick by, one by one, five by five. Exorcisms are not quick, sometimes they can take months. Attempting to separate the Joined may be an impossible task. Winding down through the Litany of the Saints, the first round will be a tie with neither the priest nor the Demon gaining an advantage.

Preacher ends the Litany, with the Lord's Prayer, "Our Father, who art in heaven. Hallowed be Thy name. Thy kingdom come. Thy will be done. On Earth, as it is in Heaven. Give us this day our daily bread and forgive us our trespasses as we forgive those who trespass against us. And lead us not into temptation, but Deliver us from evil".

Everyone responds "Amen."

The ritual has begun and would continue. Fortunately not everything was scripted and for that Preacher was thankful. He held the rosary in the face of the Demon who began laughing. Its tone a mixture of human and hellion sounds. "The power of Christ compels you, unclean spirit. Christ compels you to give me your name Demon."

"Give me your name, human." The Demons tone was an octave higher than it should have been, mocking the group. Another deep chuckle "Hunters. You silly little vermin. You read a book, or watch a movie and think that it is easy." The Demon looked over the pack of hunters, focusing on Josh. "You remember, don't you. The power that we wield as we ride your stinking meat suits. It's a shame boy, that you didn't give in. The feeling is immense."

"Josh." Preachers voice was firm, but not condescending or menacing. It was parental, and Josh looked to him as a boy would a father "The Demon will give you enough truth to make you believe in its lies. The best lies always start with the truth. Ignore the creature or leave." Preacher turned to the Demon and sprinkled the foul thing with holy water. The Demon gave out a yell and began to squirm against its restraints.

"Josh, this creature before you is something unique, did you know that?" Preacher has gone into teacher mode. His voice is calm but he is on alert waiting for the Demons attack. They always attacked. Usually, they started mentally or emotionally, but they would kill you quickly if they got the chance. "Unlike when I found you, and you were struggling through the possession, trying to retain your soul, this creature gave in and the Demon and human soul became one. They are Joined. And that means this Demon can use that soul like a renewable everlasting energy source."

Preacher thrust his rosary back into the face of the Demon, "It's the power of Christ that compels you. It is God the Father that compels you." Another sprinkle of holy water, another scream from the Demon. "It is your name I wish Demon, it is your Name that God Commands"

There was a sudden gust of wind in the bar. The lights flickered and the power of the wind began to pick up. The chair that the Demon was tied too began to lift into the air slightly and began slamming into the ground. So, Preacher thought, the Demons attack would start psychologically. Small manipulations of the environment combined with a little levitation, and suddenly you are dealing with something that you think you can't beat. Once you start thinking that you are going to lose, you lose big.

The Demon threw its head back and began laughing like a maniac. The Demon thought it was getting the upper hand. Which meant that Gus, Raz, or Josh were starting to think they were going to lose. Fucking Josh, the newbie. Preacher made a note to talk to Gus, he was the one that insisted that Josh be here tonight. Preacher knew though, that it was a possibility and had prepared for it.

Preacher reached into his black bag and removed a red water balloon. He opened the golden case and took out a communion wafer. The Demon was laughing with its head thrown back with its mouth open wide. Preacher dropped the wafer in the Demons mouth, shoved the water balloon in after it with his left hand. With his right, he delivered a surprise uppercut.

The water balloon popped instantly, and holy water flooded down the Demons throat. Some went into his lungs, some into his stomach, hell some even ran out its nose. The Demons eyes bulged to the point they looked like they would explode out of his head. The Demon sputtered and gasped for air. Each breath fueling an invisible fire. The wind rushing around the room came to a complete stop. The levitation of the chair quit. Nothing quite like a holy water uppercut to change the rules.

4.

The Demons chin dropped to its chest. It was heaving, struggling to breathe.

"The power of Christ compels you, but my methods may motivate you a bit quicker you filthy shit-bag. You've heard of me, haven't you? Think real hard about how you want to answer me next because I don't have time to play these little games." Preachers' voice was forceful, with undertones of anger.

A low growl came from the Demon that slowly turned into a chuckle. "Nunc te cognovi" Now we know you "Preacher" Another bit of laughter. "You're smart enough to know we are here to stay. There is no power in your pitiful religion to separate us. Sending me back to the pit will only destroy this soul."

Preacher reached into the duffle bag once more and began digging around blindly, keeping eye contact with the Demon. "I COMMAND thee, unclean spirit, whosoever thou art, along with all thine associates who have taken possession of this servant of God. That the mysteries of the Incarnation, Passion, and Resurrection, and Ascension of our Lord Jesus Christ, the descent of the Holy Spirit, but the coming of our Lord unto Judgment. Thou shalt tell me by some sign or other thy name and the day and hour of thy departure."

Preacher pulled from the bag a dull set of iron knuckles. Brass knuckles were perfect for use against normal people. Iron packed just a little bit more of a punch to Demons.

When the Demon saw what was on Preacher's right hand its eyes grew large. Ever so briefly there was a flash of blue that crossed his retinas. It would have been too fast for most people to notice, but Preacher was looking for it.

"I COMMAND thee, moreover, to obey me to the letter. I who, though unworthy, am a minister of God. Neither shalt thou be emboldened to harm in any way this creature of God, nor the bystanders, nor any of their possessions. Now Demon tell me thy Name!" Before the Demon could respond Preacher swung a right hook and hit the Demon full on the left cheek.

The impact sent the chair and the Demon over on their side. Guttural growls, and other languages that came spewing out of the Demons mouth. Josh and Gus moved to set the chair upright once again. The Demons cheek was split open and a few teeth were left behind on the floor. Once he was upright he looked at Preacher. "Josiah Scelus is who I have become. You cannot excise me Preacher, but perhaps there is something else that you would like to have. Let's make a deal."

The gash on the Demons cheek was already beginning to heal. "I would say it's a pleasure to meet you Josiah Scelus, but I wouldn't want to be marked a liar." Preacher looked to the back of the room to Raz, ensuring that she was ready. "You made a good point a moment ago Josiah. There may not be enough power in my religion to separate you from this hosts soul, but ya see, Raz over there, she's Wiccan. Her religion is a lot older than mine."

Josiah laughed. The wound on his cheek was fully closed now, only a faint pink line remained of the gash. "No witch has ever separated the Joined." Josiah spat and chuckled again. "Witches, after all, are the brides of Satan. That is in your little handbook, isn't it? Thou shall not suffer a witch to live."

"She's not going to try and unjoin you. See, she's going to summon that human half and tuck it away safe and sound. I'm going to excise the demonic half, and we are going to see what happens." Preacher shrugged. "Call it an experiment."

Raz was two tables away, the contents of her hello kitty bag were laid out before her. An old tanned leather mat with a pentagram on it lay flat in front of her. Four black candles were placed in the four cardinal directions of the earth, one on top, bottom, left and right of the pentagram. Dozens of small jars and oils arranged neatly to one side because you just never knew when you would need the toes of a salamander or some eye of newt.

Raz took a match and struck it, she lit the candle to her left and began the invocation "I call upon the Guardians of the Watchtower of the East, Lords of the Air, I summon thee to witness this occurrence, to protect this circle and to guide this vessel." Another match was struck, the next candlelit, "I call upon the Guardians of the Watchtower of the South, Lords of Fire, I summon thee to witness this occurrence, to protect this circle and to guide this vessel." Another match struck the next candle was lit.

Preacher looked back at Josiah, glad to see he looked a little nervous. "We got this idea from an old journal, whose author read about this in another journal, whose author read about it in another journal, so on and so forth. Turns out that this type of ceremony was used back in 1185 a.d to successfully Un-Join a few of your kind. When Pope Lucius III heard that witches and priests were joining forces to destroy your kind he turned a blind eye thinking that it was for the greater good."

"But someone was upset that he didn't condemn the act and the Pope mysteriously died later that year. The next Pope blessed off on the Inquisition and the ritual was all but lost as thousands of witches were killed over the next 300 years. So our methods are trial and error at best."

Preacher paused letting his lesson sink in. "Last time we tried it didn't work quite right and the host exploded. Bits of blood, bones, and brains, splattered all over the room." Preacher smirked at Josiah "I needed a new collar." Preacher cleared his throat and pulled out a big leather-bound family Bible from his bag. This was a large print, illustrated, and hardback. This type of Bible weighs forty pounds and has been in the family for a couple hundred years. Literally, they didn't make Bibles like these anymore, they are too heavy and expensive.

Preacher looked at Raz, who seemed to have finished her incantation. Her eyes were focused on something he couldn't see. She was staring at something that was right in front of her and a thousand miles away at the same time. There was a focus in her eyes that Preacher always admired. Raz relied on a structure to assist in her faith. She lived in a world that revolved because A plus B was always C. He heard her begin her spell work. As she began he could feel the lines of power being drawn into the air around them.

Preacher made the sign of the cross and began with Psalm 53. The passage was always recommended at this point and Preacher didn't see any reason to stray from tradition. If you counted an unsanctioned exorcism, on a Joined Demon, being conducted in conjunction with a witch, inside a dive bar, on hooker alley, in any way shape or form traditional. He finished the passage and began the Prayer portion.

Preacher looked over to ensure that Gus and Josh would be ready with the responses and saw the Josh was trying to hide the note card in his hand, the kid had a cheat sheet. Preacher wasn't sure if he should be proud or ashamed of the kid. At least he was trying.

Raz had her spell work crafted out and was waiting on Preacher to finish the prayer. The tricky part is when Preacher commands the demon to Hell and Raz calls the spirit to her. Last time they tried it wasn't as big of a mess as Preacher described, there was only a bit of blood but the host wasn't alive in the end. There was no telling what happened to the Demon. The theory is that the Joined use the soul's power to remain on this side of Hell. Burning through the souls' energy in a matter of hours, either finding a new host or existing without a physical body.

There were changes in the Demons demeanor now too. It was sweating, thrashing against its restraints. Its low guttural hellion language was barely audible. It was casting its own spell work. Countering their craft with its own. The Demon was using a lot of the host soul's power. Its lips begin cracking and bleeding. Its eyes began to sink into the skull, and the hair began to thin. The Demon was losing its hold and the body began to look like one that was normally possessed, not Joined.

Preacher continued his commands with force. The Demon began thrashing in the chair so violently that the front two legs were lifting off the ground and slamming into the floor. A cut opened on the Demons cheek and pea green pus began to ooze from the wound. The slamming began to slow as the front legs of the chair stayed in the air longer and longer.

The eyes of the Demon turned almost solid white and the pupils and retinas lost color. They were the eyes of the blind and soulless. The eyes were unseeing and uncaring. The Demon leaned to the right as the chair was in the air and balanced it on one leg. Slowly the chair began to spin in a counter-clockwise circle. The rotations began slowly but quickly picked up the pace.

Preacher's commands from the Lord were being ignored. The Demon was collecting power and self-confidence as it turned the chair faster in circles. The wind came again, threatening the candles that Raz had lit for her ceremony. The volume of the Demons chanting grew until it was hard to hear anything but the Demon. The sound became deafening.

Preacher threw holy water onto the spinning Demon but it had enough time to prepare and focus, the fucking thing didn't even flinch. The Demons arc began to widen; the chair was tilted back at almost forty-five degrees as it spun in its circle. As the Demon passed Preacher and came around for another spin Preacher did the only thing that he could think of. He slammed the big Bible closed and swung it as hard as he could at the Demons head.

It wasn't as loud as a baseball bat would have been. The forty-pound book was not aerodynamic in the slightest. But it was heavy, solid, and ironically enough, the word of God being swung at a Demons head. The result was impressive. The counter-clockwise motion of the chair ceased immediately and reversed. The chair actually spun clockwise twice before planting all four legs back on the ground. The wind ceased immediately and there was a silence that fell over the room.

The Demon sat with its chin to its chest sucking in the air. Preacher wasn't sure if it was the strike of the Bible that took the wind out of it or if the Demon was just starting to tire on its own.

According to the lore the Joined got lazy after a while, and they would quickly get winded. Having the renewable energy of the soul meant that the Demon didn't have to fight and over time would lose its stamina. Also, according to the lore, there was no known way to separate the soul from the Demon once they joined. This method was barely more than a forgotten rumor.

A strained groan came from the Demon. When it looked up there were black tears forming in its eyes, and starting to run down its cheeks. "Stop" It croaked. A tear fell from its cheek but once it left the body it suspended in mid-air hovering. A second later it evaporated. "Wait" It choked another word out, then coughed. When it coughed a handful of black mist came from the mouth and hung in the air for only a few seconds before it too evaporated.

Preacher wasn't sure what he was seeing in the air, but somehow, he understood that this was the unjoining and he was going to see it through. He began the next prayer through the exorcism rite John 1:1-14.

"Josh, get me a spirit trap." Josh moved to Raz's hello kitty bag and got a spirit trap. A spirit trap is basically an average everyday empty jar that had some major spell work done to it. It's a complex spell designed to catch and hold harmful spirits. Preacher wasn't sure if he could trap whatever was coming out of the Demon but why not try.

Preacher kept reciting the passage, and he could hear Raz in the background using her summoning spell. The air was getting humid, Josh and Gus sat in observation, ready to give assistance where they could.

"Preacher…." The Demons voice was deep and guttural, unsure if that is because the Demon had completely taken over the host or if the human soul was being pulled across the room. "Stop. I'll die."

Preacher was near the ending of the verse when another puff of – evil mist? – came out of the Demon. Preacher leaned in close and opened the spirit trap. Instead of evaporating the mist entered the jar and Preacher sealed it.

"I can help, Preacher" the Demons words were just a breath above nothing, it was almost over. "I kn…. know, Baba. Where she is. Baba…… Baba Doek." Preacher froze. "I know Baba Doek."

5.

"Raz stop." Preacher said.

"The Demon is weak." Gus was by Preachers side. Preacher didn't see him move. He was distracted, was he so easily distracted by a name? "We can finish this, it was working."

"Remember Demons lie," Raz was behind him as well, standing next to her brother. "Just enough truth to convince you of the lie."

The Demon groaned "He's right, it was working. She's right, I lie. But you want to know don't you." Josiah finally lifted his head, his face was wrinkled, eyes completely white. Its mouth drooped at the corners revealing crooked yellowing teeth. "As much as I hate to admit it, I'm not on the same scale as those like Baba, she's a King of Hell, and she's got the juice of something powerful."

Preacher cut him off with a look. "What do you mean by something powerful? Explain yourself."

"There are seven Holy Relics that unlock the power of Heaven. Well, the Lord said On Earth as it is in Heaven. There are seven Keys of Hell that unlock all the power of Hell. They are straight power, the more you have, the more power you wield over all the creatures of Hell. She has one of these."

"Myths and lies. We need to finish this Preacher." Raz seemed insistent, and part of Preacher knew that she was right. This was a slippery slope that could lead him down a dark path.

"Raz, can you bind his lies? I'd be interested in seeing if this is true."

Raz walked back over to her spirit board "This is bad juju Preacher. I don't know if this will work on a Demon." Raz went to her bag and removed a plastic container with several sections, each with its own lid. People who do crafting call them bead boxes, she opened a lid and lifted a lapis lazuli gemstone, and began her chant. A simple truth spell, so the holder can see the truth of the situation. It took Raz a moment to complete the magic and charge the crystal. She walked to Preacher who held out his hand for the stone.

"I only made one. Only the holder will know a lie from the truth. It's not perfect. It can be fooled. If it sounds too good to be true, then it probably is." She placed the stone in Preacher's hand hoping that he would be strong enough to avoid being tricked.

Preacher looked down at Josiah, the wound on his cheek was still oozing puss, though the flow had slowed. The Demon appeared to be weakened from the ceremony. However, Preacher knew the Demon could be faking. He put the iron knuckles back on just in case. "Start with Baba Doek. How do you know that name?" There was a focus in Preacher's voice that was usually absent.

"Baba Doek, as she is known now, I know as Damballa. Creator of voodoo, strong and old and proud." Josiah laughed "And she holds a Key of Hell." Preacher listened with an ear that would tell him of a lie, Josiah took a deep breath and looked at Preacher "I'll tell you what I know, but we need to make a deal."

Preacher hauled back with his right, ready to make another impression on Josiah. "Wait! Hear me out!" There was something in the voice that made Preacher hesitate. "All I want Preacher, the only thing I ask, is to walk away. I'll tell you all I know, and you let me leave."

There was nothing in Josiah's voice that made Preacher disbelieve. He knew that he should unjoin the soul. The anger in him was rising, and he wanted to strike, but there was a nagging hesitation that he couldn't explain. There was a very primal, a very sinful and very broken portion of himself that needed to know about Baba Doek. "Talk"

"Preacher, don't be ridiculous. You can't be thinking about making a deal." Gus sounded strained, and there was a nervous tone in it.

"He is right." Raz chimed in. "Let's get this done and over with and get out of here."

Preacher raised his hand for silence and looked back to the Demon. "Talk."

"A couple of years ago Damballa crawled out of the pit and got herself Joined. She's been building power ever since. She is powerful on her own, but since she's been out and gotten her hands on one of our Keys, she is practically unstoppable."

"So if I get my hands on a Key, could I use it to unjoin her?" Preacher asked.

Josiah chuckled, "No, it would be suicide to try to get a Key. You wouldn't make it within a mile the way you are. You stink of God, faith, hope, and desperation. Besides every time a human has come into contact with a Key the power consumes them. You need to get one of the Holy Relics your team plays with."

"And you just happen to know where one is I bet." Gus' voice came across dripping in disbelief, "Preacher, we need to excise this demon now, he is getting his power back." Preacher could see that the skin was smoothing and the hair was thickening. Slowly the Demon was returning back to its normal state.

"All Demons know where one is. I am surprised that you do not. Exorcisms take days, or weeks, and sometimes months. But one of your Order can do it in mere hours. Didn't you ever stop to wonder why that was? Not because he is most favored, or because his faith is strongest.... it is an iron bracelet on his wrist. Four links of iron that were forged in the fires of Old Rome, and used to keep St. Peter in prison. It seems like Father Michael did not tell you everything that you needed to know before you parted ways did he, Preacher."

"The chains of St. Peter are on display in the Vatican. The church wouldn't put such a powerful Relic on display when it could be used to drive the scourge of the Earth back to Hell." Gus's voice cut in like a knife. There was an echo in the voice that should not have been there. Preacher instinctively knew that there was falsehood in what Gus was saying. This was indeed a neat little charm. The Church would put something on display to bolster faith and give something to the people to believe in. Every organization that was run by man has an interest in its continual growth – the Church was no different.

Gus' voice grew louder; he was getting too emotionally involved. "Preacher can exorcise demons in a few hours. I've seen it happen. We almost separated you. That hasn't been done in almost three hundred years. How do you explain that? He doesn't have a Holy Relic. Preacher, please let's finish this ritual!"

Preacher held up a hand to stop Gus. "He's not lying. But neither are you. Josiah Scelus, with the Power of Christ, I COMMAND thee to speak the truth. How can I do the things you say are impossible?"

"We don't know, and that's why we fear you most of all Preacher. You're the one who does the impossible without the power of the Church behind you. We thought you a fluke, an unfortunate accident, a demon's boogeyman. But you left the church, and nothing changed." Josiah took a breath and looked away from Preacher "I would have left the city if I knew you were here."

"If I'm so feared, why are you telling me this? Why not just go back to Hell and climb back out of the pit like last time? The Joined can use the power of that soul to remain here and not even experience Hell."

"You don't send us to Hell Preacher. We don't know where we go, but it isn't Hell. Most believe that we simply cease to exist. You wink us into oblivion or a prison that we cannot escape from. There are some that think you absolve us and allow us back into the Kingdom and will seek you out if they are ever to escape The Pit." There was no echo, no sense of falsehood. Nothing he said resembled a lie. Preacher wasn't sure if this stone would work on the Demon, and without the stone, he couldn't tell if any of this was true. Josiah was looking almost healed, time was running out.

It felt like a truck hit Preacher in the chest. He was off his feet and sailing through the air before he knew what happened. He heard a cacophony of sounds as he landed hard on the table behind him. He heard a scream bitten off from Raz, but he couldn't see her. He was laying on his side, looking at Josiah's feet when he saw the ropes binding the demon fall to the floor. Time was over.

The voice came different now, full of a power that wasn't there before, "You should have listened to your lackeys Preacher. You should have sent me to wherever you send us." Josiah stood, they were in trouble and Preacher knew it.

"Lord Have Mercy on us!, Christ Have Mercy on US!" fucking Josh….. he didn't know enough to shut up when he was forgotten about. "Lord Have Mercy on US, Christ Ha…" his voice strangled off. There was a thud.

"No one will have mercy tonight. You made a deal with me. I walk out. I never said anything about you living. I fulfilled my end of the deal, I've told you all I know about Baba Doek and how to unjoin her. Unfortunately, I didn't say that you would live to see it through and you didn't make that stipulation."

Josh made a choking sound. The world swam in Preacher's vision. He was on the floor in pain. Pain is good, he harnessed that physical pain, it helped his vision steady. Preachers hand felt empty, the iron knuckles were gone. He brought himself to his hands and knees and tried to draw breath but couldn't. One of his hands slipped as his bag slid a few inches on the floor. His bag.... There were only two items left in it, he reached in, and found what he was looking for.

A kick to the ribs sent Preacher sliding across the floor. There was more than physical force behind the kick. Inside that kick was an infernal... heat maybe? Preachers vision swam again, but he saw Gus suspended in midair on his left, clawing at his throat and Josh across the bar doing the same.

Fortunately, Preacher held his grip, and when he turned, he pointed the small double-barreled shotgun at Josiah. The Demon only had a second to look confused before Preacher pulled the trigger. The blast sent Josiah flying back over tables and chairs. The sound of the shot was deafening but had the desired effect. Josh and Gus fell immediately to the floor gasping for breath.

Josiah writhed in pain on the floor, his curses a mix of Hellion, English, and other languages. Josh and Gus were on their knees disoriented, Preacher walked to Gus. "Check Raz" It didn't need to be said, but he felt better saying it anyway. He looked to Josh "Gather the gear." Choking he nodded and started moving.

Preacher walked to the writhing demon, who looked up at him "What the fuck is this!" More growling and Hellion came afterward, unintelligible gargling of the damned.

"Rock salt. Made from the water of the Sea of Galilee". Preacher reached down and grabbed the demon by the hair. "Is Raz alive?"

"She's breathing, but we need to get out of here."

"I am going to allow you to live, lest I be labeled a liar, but you shall live in pain. If what you said isn't true I will hunt you to the ends of the Earth, and you shall wish for oblivion when I find you again." Preacher straightened, ripping a handful of hair out, and aimed the shotgun at the Demons stomach and pulled the trigger.

6.

It only took Josh a few moments to gather all of the gear. Everything including the shotgun was shoved in the two bags haphazardly. Raz was awake and able to walk without assistance. That also meant she was able to talk, complain, and yell at Preacher. Which she was doing with the full fury of someone who had just been thrown across the room by a Demon. Preacher let the sound wash over him but didn't pay attention to the words.

Josiah was writhing in pain, grunting and whimpering. There was no way he would be able to follow them. Hell, Preacher didn't think he would be able to walk for at least a few hours. Something on the floor near Josiah shimmered in the light and caught Preacher's attention. It was the lapis stone. Preacher picked it up and put it in his pocket. Never know when that thing will come in handy.

The group walked out of the bar in silence. Being on the street was odd after what had just happened. No one expected the ceremony would work. Not really anyway. But it had started working, and then Preacher lets himself get talked out of it. Well, that was downright insane.

The group walked in silence to an old beat up early 90s four-door sedan. Josh opened the trunk so Preacher and Raz could put their bags in. Closing the trunk, Josh took a moment to settle his nerves. Everyone was already in the car waiting for him. He admired their bravery and hoped that he could learn to be as brave when it counted. Preacher sat in the passenger seat staring out of the window lost in thought. Josh started the sedan and merged on the road. Traffic was light for a Saturday in Atlanta.

The silence was humbling as each of them interpreted the night's events. Preacher knew that eventually, Baba Doek would resurface and that he would have to face it again, but that didn't make it any easier. No one in the car knew about Baba Doek except him. He wasn't sure if he was ready to explain.

A small giggle broke the silence from the back. It was hearty childish laughter that was welcomed in the somber confines of the car. Gus was giggling like a thirteen-year-old school girl who just got a selfie from their movie star crush.

"Lord have mercy on us," Gus said mockingly and began laughing again, followed shortly by Raz. "This was full Hollywood Exorcist, and this guy wants to start a Litany of Saints…." The laughter broke through his voice. Preacher glances at Josh who looks embarrassed enough and joins in the laughter too.

"You should have shot him" Preacher finds himself laughing harder "Shit, you should have shot me too."

Josh has slumped down in the driver's seat so far, it was impressive he could see over the steering wheel, which makes Preacher laugh even harder.

"What was that?" Raz's voice is a mix of amusement, confusion, anger, and fear. "What the hell is a babajoke? And why didn't we separate the host?"

"Baba Doek, not joke." Preacher corrected. "Baba Doek is the most powerful entity I have ever come across. If we can separate Baba Doek from the host, it is worth all our lives."   Preacher turned, looked sideways at Josh. "Let's go to Lucky's. After tonight I need some whiskey." Preacher tugged at the clergy collar, and it came off quickly enough. He definitely needed a stop at a liquor store. If he had been thinking earlier, he would have grabbed something from the bar.

"I grabbed two bottles of Bulleit Whiskey from Whirlwinds if you want whiskey." Fucking Josh… Doesn't remember to shoot the Demon, but remembers to bring home some whiskey. Bless his heart.

Raz began to laugh hysterically, "I'm going to call you PJ from now on."

Josh looked over his shoulder, "PJ?"

"Preacher Junior" more laughter from the back "memorize the litany of saints and whiskey of choice." more laughter. Josh turned on the radio and turned the volume up, but it didn't completely drown the laughter out from the back seat.

They drove north for twenty minutes and were out of the city. Then they drove another twenty minutes until they were safely tucked into an aging neighborhood with affordable rental housing. It wasn't great, but it was something that Preacher had been able to afford to purchase. They parked in the driveway and headed inside. Walking under the opening garage door, they dropped their bags in the makeshift workshop the garage had turned into. Post exorcism rituals started once they were inside. Preacher poured himself a drink, which is to say he poured half a glass of whiskey into half a glass of ice.

While the house was larger than most in the area, it certainly wasn't a mansion. There were four bedrooms and three bathrooms. Gus and Raz were already in the hall and basement shower, so Preacher allowed Josh to use the master shower. Preacher sat the bottle of whiskey on the dresser listening to the water running in the house.

It gave him time to compose himself for the story he would have to tell. Preacher stripped, placing his vestment into the wash. Once naked he slid on a pair of shorts to be comfortable in. Besides the bed, there was only a papasan chair in the bedroom for sitting, and Preacher took it, sitting cross-legged on it. Sipping on the cold whiskey Preacher wondered once again if he did the right thing letting Josiah go.

Josh came out of the master bath wearing basketball shorts and a towel draped over his shoulders. Preacher looked at Josh. "Ask Raz and Gus to join us please Josh." Josh nodded and left Preacher in peace for another moment.

Preacher didn't like to talk about his childhood. Being raised by the church without a family isn't exactly happy memories. There was always a sense of abandonment that was never filled. His eyes flooded involuntarily with tears, and suddenly it was hard to swallow. Preacher could hear the group coming down the hall and got himself under control by doing the only thing he could think of. He drank the glass of whiskey, all of it. He took a breath and refilled his glass.

He didn't wait for the three coming in to get comfortable in his room before he began the story. "My first memories are of my mother. Not happy memories filled with picnics and candy and movies. She was a drunk. I remember a lot of empty bottles, filth and yelling. Sometimes she was yelling at me, other times herself. She was possessed for as long as I can remember her."

"It wasn't like she was cruel in a physical sort of way. I ate twice a day; she drank all day. On Saturday I would have to clean the liquor bottles out of the house. She would be drunk all day most of the time. She would sometimes yell in tongues but mostly in white trash slurs. She was the scariest when she was quiet. When the demon would take control, it would just stare at me watching. It wouldn't speak, just stare."

"Father Michael came and tried to get the Demon out of her. He told me that the Demon snapped her neck before he could get it out. I was taken to Rome, sent to a special school to be trained as an exorcist by the Church."

"It was an improvement but not much of one. Neglect was replaced by abuse. When you're being raised to get demons out of others, you are expected to be perfect. Perfection was literally beat into you with whips or paddles, belts… whatever was handy."

Preacher drained his glass and filled it again. He was going to need new ice soon. "Father Michael was the closest thing I had to a father. I wanted him to be my father. Over the years he taught me everything that I know about exorcism. Once I graduated from seminary, he took me as his personal apprentice. I followed him into the field as his second for years, then he tested me and sat as my second."

"It took three exorcisms before he released me on my own. Three exorcisms in ten days. Then he became a distant father figure as I worked my cases across the globe. I completed over sixty exorcisms in my first two years."

"I spent seven years sending the cursed back to the pit. Over time though it seemed like I was brought back to the American Southeast more and more. The lay lines here cross at more angles, it makes the veil thinner or something. The Church offered me a position as a Cardinal here in Atlanta, but I turned it down. Putting me behind a desk would send fewer Demons back to the pit, and I wasn't ok with that."

"That's when the Church started denying my requests for exorcisms. No matter what I submitted, the Church always wanted more evidence. I could see the Demons riding these people. I could feel the evil. But the Church demanded more proof. Sure, I ran across fakes and schizophrenics. They became easy to spot. I knew the people I needed to help almost as fast as I saw them.

"I was sent to Cincinnati Ohio where I met with the local bishop and was taken to a young girl's residence. The locals were convinced that she was being ridden. I was sent to confirm and rid the evil if I found it."

"The Bishop drove me from the airport into an overcrowded subdivision. Yards were stacked on one another, separated with a four-foot fence if you were lucky enough to have a fence."

"It was spring, and almost all the yards had clothes hanging from clotheslines in the back yard. The wind was cheaper than paying for the dryer. That was a luxury reserved for winter when wet clothes would freeze on the line."

"On the way, the Bishop explains that Allison was an honor roll student three months ago, but she had changed. Her personality had turned menacing. Her language had become vulgar, she had stopped being herself. He told me that when you were with her, you could simply 'taste evil in the air'"

"When I entered the house, I could smell it. It was no different than any Demon I had found before. I met Allison at the dining room table. I did the Church mandated test, and she didn't meet the criteria. But I knew, I felt it. Once that kind of evil has entered your life you know it."

Preacher looked to his team. They all knew what he was talking about. It was a smell you couldn't smell, a taste that you cannot describe. It is a taint that you feel with your senses and not something that can always be quantified by tests. Gus and Raz knew because their mother was almost ridden into the grave, like Preachers. Josh knew because he was the one ridden.

"The Church denied the exorcism, against my objections. I was sent to Michigan to another case, but I appealed to Father Michael. There was something here that I could help with, and I thought he would understand."

Preacher took a small drink, which was half his glass. How did his liver deal with this?

"I thought Michael would understand. He told me to move on. Of course, like a good Soldier, I did. I went to Michigan. To a bogus case, something that we should never have been involved in. The Demon in Allison wasn't done. It cut her parents throats the night after I left. Then in front of the news cameras, it slit Allison's."

"I did some digging after that. Six of the last ten exorcisms denied to me from the Church made the news. Dead parents, families, dead children. There were a lot of bodies piling up at the Church's doorstep. I refused to be told no again."

"It wasn't pleasant when I told Michael I was leaving. It was like telling your parents that you are moving to California to be in the movies, but you are going to refuse to show your tits so it would all be okay. It went over like a submarine with a screen door."

"Father Michael yammered on about untapped potential and yadda yadda yadda. In all honesty, I quit listening. That was probably short sited because we have not spoken since. He retired a few years ago to North Carolina."

"Tomorrow I'm going on a road trip to get answers on this stuff and you three have research to do. Dig into every book, every scroll, and every contact we have. I want to know about these Keys of Hells and these Holy Relics. I want to know everything I don't know. Chase rumors, hints, clues whatever it takes."

"Shouldn't someone go with you? We are stronger as a team." Gus asked with curiosity in his voice Preacher didn't normally hear.

Preacher shook his head no. "I'm going to see Father Michael and get the answers that I should have been given years ago. It's my task, I promise that I will need your help more here."

With that statement, the decision was made. One by one the group left. Gus to start research and Josh to assist him. Raz would boot up her laptop and start researching on the web, gathering more data than the two combined.

Preacher poured more whiskey and drank. It was his way to cope, and he did it well.

7.

The Church like other man run organizations has a retirement plan for its clergy. Like most, it is terrible. After service, most priests must find their own place to live, pay their own rent and are generally forgotten until it comes time to pass the plate on Sunday. Father Michael was no exception. He lived in an "active adult" community just outside of Ashville North Carolina.

Preacher moved through the tiny one-bedroom apartment, looking at its sparse furnishings. There was no television in the living room, only a recliner and a table that housed an old AM/FM radio and record player combination.

There was a small kitchenette with a table and two chairs. A hutch sat against the wall that had a few bottles of liquor and small glasses on it. Score! Preacher poured himself a glass of whiskey.

The bedroom had a twin bed, a dresser, a chair, a writing desk, and several bookcases. The books on the bookshelves were all religious. Some were old texts others were new. Everything here is what Preacher expected, except there was no Father Michael. And of course no bracelet.

It was almost sundown, Father Michael was probably eating the early bird special, or playing bingo. Preacher was sure that he wouldn't be gone long.

He grabbed a bottle of whiskey and went to the bedroom. He sat his glass on the nightstand and went to the books. He avoided looking at anything that had a publishers binding. Anything mass market was, as a rule, garbage when it came to fighting Demons. Sure, you can fight "personal demons" in the self-help section of the bookstore, but if you needed to combat actual demons that crawl out of the pit, you needed something that would never be released to the public on the mass level. There were occasional exceptions though, but Preacher already had those.

There were several leather-bound books with no titles on the binding. They were together on the bottom shelf, and that is where Preacher started. Preacher recognized Father Michael's handwriting immediately, it was a journal. The first entry was from 1955. Michael had just entered the Seminary. Damn Michael was old.

The next two journals were the same. Coming from seminary to serve in Rome blah blah blah priest shit. The fourth though started with Michael's induction to the Order of Exorcists. Preacher settled into the armchair and began reading.

Preacher had only made it through the first few pages when he heard keys in the door lock. So far the entries were boring everyday priest business. There was no mention about the artifact or even Demons for that matter. The door opened then closed. He heard shuffling in the living room, then a record was turned on. The music of Simon and Garfunkel came through the tiny apartment, The Sound of Silence. It was barely audible. Preacher could still hear the shuffling of Father Michael as he entered the kitchen.

Preacher heard the clink of a glass followed by the sound of water coming out of the tap. Preacher stood and put the journal back. He was thinking about borrowing it and several others before he left, but he didn't feel the need to advertise his larceny. There was always a guilt-inducing speech when a Catholic got caught stealing by a priest.

Preacher refilled his whiskey. He put the bottle down and felt there was something wrong. The awkward shuffling in the other room couldn't be heard anymore. Preacher sat the glass of whiskey on the end table in front of him. Was he really getting this sloppy? He closed his eyes to focus himself. The room temperature had risen two, no three degrees. Simon and Garfunkel were singing on the radio. Once the pattern was recognized Preacher could hear the breathing in sync with the beat of the music. Michael hasn't slowed down a bit. He was about four feet behind Preacher.

Preacher was glad that Michael was a priest. He knew what he would have if someone were breaking into his house. Preacher turned around slowly pretty sure Michael wasn't going to shoot him, but he had been wrong once or twice before.

Cold water hit Preacher in the face catching him off guard. He sputtered and coughed as water went up his nose. "Water? Not exactly the home defense choice of the year Father." He tried to force a grin. The Preacher tasted salt and realized it wasn't water. It was Holy Water. Was Michael was worried about Demons breaking in?

Father Michael did not return the grin. Instead, he raised the hand that did not have the glass and took aim with a Taser. "You?" Preacher heard a pop as the cartridge exploded outward and the prongs found purchase in Preacher's chest. He felt the pulse of electricity before he heard the crackling of the line and instantly lost control of his body. He fell awkwardly to the side, landing half on the bed and half on the nightstand.

Electric crackling filled his ears, then was drowned out by the sound of his pulse. There was no pain exactly, but he wasn't able to move any of his limbs. Soon panic began to set in. He started to feel like he would not be able to breathe, was he holding his breath? He couldn't tell. Preacher tried to force a breath in and couldn't. So he decided to push breath out, and it came out in a groan.

Preacher was able to roll his eyes up to look at Michael, who was staring down at him, a familiar scowl across his face. There wasn't malice in his face precisely, just his usual lack of compassion. Another groan escaped.

It seems like an eternity before the crackling stopped. The silence was deafening, as the sound of his pulse lowered to an average volume. The ability to move his body at will came as a blessing and surprise. Preacher flexed his hands as a test and took a deep breath to make sure that he could. He looked down and saw the two prongs sticking from his chest.

Another round of crackling began from the Taser as Preacher inhaled. His body froze again. As a rule, Preacher did not believe in violence against the elderly, but at the moment he really wanted to knock Michael out.

Preacher tried to calm himself, ten Mississippi, nine Mississippi, eight.... This was an eternity. Three Mississippi.... When would this stop? Negative One Mississippi. Negative two.... Michael definitely deserved a punch to the face.

Michael stepped forward as the cracking quit. He pulled a prong from Preachers' chest. Preacher took a breath, and Michael pulled the second out. That was uncomfortable, to put it mildly.

"Father Brandon?" Michael's voice was shaking, he was unsure. It was not a position he was used to being in. He was hunched over Preacher like he was seeing him for the first time all over again. "What are you doing here? My son, I'm sorry, I thought..."

"Preacher. They call me Preacher now. You know that already though." Preacher used the bed to stand and straighten himself. "Twice? Why twice? You were always a bastard, but damn." The shock from the stun gun left his hand shaking.

Michael sat on the foot of the bed his hands in his lap "I was sure you were possessed. Why else would you seek me out, other than for revenge? As for the stun gun, Demons react poorly to them. The electrical current disturbs them, it will make them weak. It is something that we wanted to use, but the Church forbade it. They thought it was cruel and would cause problems in the press if word got out that we electrocute those we thought might be possessed." Michael shrugged "It's not very elegant, but it is effective."

Preacher looked at Michael, he was older than he remembered. Time had withered his body down. Exorcists were never meant to make it to old age. Michael showed all the reasons why. He was all skin and bones. He looked sinewy, staring at his own feet. "I am here for answers. Long overdue answers."

Preacher dropped into the chair in the bedroom letting out a sigh. "Let me start with this. Why did you never mention Holy Relics in any of my studies?" Michaels' head shot up. Maybe there was a fire in him yet.

Michael looked at Preacher with shock in his eyes, he seemed vulnerable. It was another thing that Preacher had never seen. "You know about them?" There was shame on Michael's face. This was a day of firsts for Preacher. Vulnerability, shame, probably a bit of fear. Michael had never acted this way before.

Preacher looked over Michael. On his wrist laid a bracelet of four iron links. Preacher nodded at the bracelet. "I know about that one."

Michaels gaze fell to the links in question. "How? What do you think you know? You know nothing."

"I almost Un-Joined a Demon last night. Instead of going to Hell he wanted to talk about your magic bracelet. He said something about seven Holy Relics and how that one there let you exorcise Demons in a matter of hours instead of days and weeks like everyone else."

"Brandon. Did you come here because a Demon filled your head with a fairytale? You are getting sloppy then. Demons lie, it's the first thing I taught you." Michael made a waving motion with his hands as if he were dismissing Preacher from the room. "You have forgotten too much. There is nothing special about this bracelet. It's a family heirloom" There was a faint echo in Michael's voice. Preacher tapped his pocket and felt the lapis stone, thankful that he brought it with him. He pulled it out holding it in his closed fist.

Preacher shook his head, "We both know that's not true. For the sake of time let's just pretend that I already know every lie you're going to tell me. Just go for the truth first, and we will be done before your bedtime." Preacher pointed at the chains "Where did you get that?"

Michael looked at Preacher. "I received it from my mentor when he retired. Just as he received it from his. From master to apprentice it has been passed for almost twelve hundred years."

"Until now. Why didn't you hand it off? Why did the Church let you just walk off with one of the most powerful relics in the world? Unless the Church never knew you had it to begin with."

"The Church was too busy trying to fill seats and protecting its reputation to pay attention to a priest in the Order of Exorcists and his little iron bracelet. If the Church does know about it, they didn't ask for it back. They would have placed it behind glass on display in the Vatican, and it would have wasted away."

"Why not pass it down. Surely you would rather see it put to use rather than waste away here in a retirement community. And why didn't you tell me about it?"

Michael wrung his hands nervously. "I was going to when the time was right. I was going to pass it to you, but you were impatient and left the Church." Michael shrugged "What was I to do?"

"Michael, you trained me to save lives and fight the enemy. Not let innocent people get ridden and die without trying to help them. It was not my duty to stand by idly, let people die and demons go on living amongst us."

"Yes, and can you imagine how reckless you would have become if you had something like this? You would have tried to be a one-man army against all of Hell. The Church would have noticed, not only you but the bracelet. You're not exactly subtle now."

Preacher didn't need the lapis stone to know that was not a lie. He felt like a one-man army until he found his crew. Even when he was with the Church, he felt like he was on an island. Even the other exorcists kept him at arms-length.

"Tell me, Brandon, excuse me… Preacher, why are you here now? You said you almost Un-joined a Demon last night. How did you do that? You were always very talented, but even for someone talented like you that should be impossible."

"I'm working with a team now. We found an old copy of a journal from a Priest in Germany. He copied another journal, tracing history back to the late eleven hundreds. Witches and the Church working together to Un-Join Demons. How did you phrase it…. not very elegant, but effective."

"Witches? Preacher, what are you doing? What is it that could send you down this path? It is insane! Witches are the devils' whores. They are not to be trusted."

"It is because of love Michael. After I left the Church, I made my way by helping those the Church refused to help." Preacher looked at the floor and frowned. "It's all because of a girl."

8.

Preacher looked at Michael. He didn't know where to start this story, so he started at the beginning.

"I was doing freelance work, cleansings, and exorcisms. When the Church refused to help, I would get a call. It was about two years after I left the Church. I got a call from a girl that called herself M.C. She thought her friend was being ridden by a demon and found me online. I came to investigate."

"She had brown hair that came just past her shoulders when I met her. It was fine hair, the kind that would take hours to brush because it could get so knotted. She had these green eyes with flakes of gold, brown and black. They could just melt away all your defenses if they wanted to." Preacher refilled his whiskey.

"Anyway, her friend was being ridden hard. She was almost Joined by the time I got there. I performed the exorcism, the host was fine, I got paid, and it was time to leave."

"But when I got to the car M.C. was there. She had the girl next door look when she wasn't wearing makeup. When she was wearing it, she had the supermodel in the swimsuit edition look. Anyway, she hugged me. I can't quite explain it, but there was a fire that was born in that hug. She pulled away slightly and then we started kissing."

"I remember thinking that no one could kiss me like her. No one could mirror what I wanted exactly as I wanted it until her. This was the first kiss, keep that in mind, every other kiss only got more intense. Before that kiss was over, I knew I was in over my head."

"What we had was way more than a fling. As it turned out, we had lived in the same areas, been to the same places and even knew some of the same people. I took on more jobs, and she would travel with me. The whole thing fascinated her. She wanted to come to watch some exorcisms, but I never let her in the room. I wanted to keep her away from the evil. She was always good with the families, so we made quite a pair."

"She was from Savannah, so we spent a lot of time down there. We spent so much time down there I bought a house. Six bedroom house on an island. Rumor is that Savannah is the most haunted city in America. I'd say that's pretty close to true. There is some kind of Hoodoo going on out there in the swamps that allows the veil to be thinner than in other places and it seems like an easier place for Demons to cross."

"So, I took a lot of jobs down that way. When I wasn't performing exorcisms or cleansing houses we were on the beach at Tybee or laying around the house listening to old vinyl. We'd dance in the kitchen listening to Sinatra's My Way. It's the closest thing to living the dream a guy like me can get. We lived in this bliss for a few years."

"We came up to Atlanta for a job. Some poor souls Auntie had called us about a haunting. This poor kid was the trifecta of fucked. Poltergeists were packed into this place. Lights were flickering, the wind was blowing inside the house. The television was changing channels, the whole nine yards all at once."

"All of this was going on when I got there and didn't stop when I walked in. I started with a cleansing ritual and blessing, pretty standard stuff. It didn't work, in fact, I think it made it worse. I began feeling this strange draw that I'd never felt before, and have not since."

"Of course this pull led me straight to the basement. Dealing with ghosts and Demons isn't scary enough in the living room or bedroom with the lights on. Nope, let's add cobwebs and spiders and darkness."

Preacher stood and refilled his whiskey. "I had sent Auntie Whats-her-name and M.C. outside. Picture frames were flying around the house, mirrors coming off the walls. It was dangerous. But I hadn't found the possessed, and I didn't know what was drawing me to the basement."

**

The steps to the basement were the standard creepy steps that did not have a solid back. The kind where someone would be walking down them and then something would grab their foot from behind and trip them. The stairway light was flickering like every other light in the house, creating a strobe light effect.

The piece of the basement floor that could be seen was concrete. There was just enough room at the bottom of the stairs to break your neck in a fall and have your death look accidental. For a moment he thought about just setting the place on fire and calling it a night. The was too easy though, besides he still hadn't found the girl he was called to help.

He could hear chanting coming from the basement. Some kind of ceremony that resonated with power. Preacher took out a flask of Holy Water and took his first tentative step down the stairs. When nothing grabbed him, he relaxed slightly. He went down the stairs as quietly as possible and made it to the bottom without incident.

The flickering ceiling lights cast shadows on the grey cement walls. The rumbling chant was coming from his left. There was a fireplace down in the basement, fully ablaze even though it was over ninety degrees outside. Sitting in front of the fire was the kid he was called to help.

She was on her knees in front of a coffee table, her hands were on the table in front of her. She had a kitchen knife in her right hand and cuts on her left arm that were still bleeding. The fire reflected off a bone necklace the girl wore. She rocked gently to the rhythm of the chant forward and back. Candles were holding down a leather parchment with a pentagram on it. Preacher knew that if the star of the pentagram pointed away from the user, it was usually a white magick, no harm - no foul magick. When the star pointed at the witch, like it was in this case, the energy was dark and unpredictable. For the novice it was uncontrollable.

The very air was a buzz of vibration and power. The heat was oppressive and had turned the girl's long stingy hair into a black wet clump that fell around her face as she stared down at the board. In front of the girl, between the table and fire, there was a shimmering ball that seemed to float in the air.

The girl was speaking in a language that sounded like Arabic, but Preacher wasn't sure. The volume was barely above a whisper. Preacher made the sign of the cross and brought the rosary to his lips for a kiss out of habit. It was barely audible, but somehow the girl heard.

Slowly her head turned over her shoulder. Her head was bowed with hair falling across her face. Her neck reached the point of breaking and Preacher was worried for a moment that it would. The head kept turning though with no popping, cracking, snapping. The young girl didn't fall over dead. But it should have, the head was turned entirely backward on the body.

Her head snapped up, causing the hair to sweep from her face. The girls face lacked all signs of regular possession. There were no bags under the eyes, no blisters or sores on her skin. Her eyes were completely white like no color had ever been present. Preacher understood then that he was looking at a summoning spell and she was bringing something powerful.

The girl's voice was not hers. "You're too late Priest, My Master has arrived."

Preacher reached into his pocket and slipped on the iron knuckles. "You'll have to forgive me if I skip the Holy Water." Before he could throw a punch, a roar of triumph spilled into the room from something floating in the air. The girls head completed its three-hundred-and-sixty-degree turn.

There was a ball of shimmering light floating behind the girl. Light from the fireplace gave it the color it had. The center of the sparkling ball rolled from bright, clean energy into a dark flash of light, then back to clear. The ball strained and surged and began to lose its form. It almost seemed to melt down on to the floor where it puddled. It was the most fascinating and terrifying thing that Preacher had ever seen.

The thing slowly rose from the puddle taking form but also remaining shapeless. The thing stood, its attention focused on the one that summoned it. The heat in the basement was quickly dissipating. It was becoming cold. Preacher could see his breath forming in the air when he exhaled.

"Unworthy." It wasn't a sound; it was a feeling. Telepathy, extreme empathy, Preacher wasn't sure. The girl's body flew backward over a couch, rolling into darkness. The attention of the thing came full on Preacher.

It was instantly inside his head. There were no secrets from this thing. It was in his mind, his memories, it was a part of him. Tiny bugs were crawling on his skin, in his mind, through his memory. He heard footsteps on the stairs.

"Preacher? Everything stopped up here, did you finish already?" M.C. came down the steps and froze. "Preacher?"

"Unacceptable" Preacher was in the air before the thought was completed. The attention was off him. He hit the ground and rolled.

M.C. stood frozen on the bottom step. She was staring at the thing that wasn't there. She was being judged, Preacher crawled to his knees and flicked the flask of Holy Water at the shimmering nothingness.

Some drops made contact and began sizzling, like butter being tossed on a hot pan. But the scream of pain didn't come from the creature. It came from the girl, and from M.C. Preacher pulled himself to his feet and stood in between the shimmering nothingness and M.C.

"Acceptable. Let Me In." The creature urged.

Preacher threw more Holy Water. The screams came again. The chorus of screams died, and a different cry came from beside him. It was a scream of anger and frustration. The girl slammed into Preacher, driving her knife into his side. She took him to the ground. The pain was exquisite. It blocked out everything else in the world. He was laying on his side, his vision a blur.

The girl stood between M.C. and the thing now. She was screaming at the shimmering thing. Preacher couldn't tell what she was saying, he could barely breathe. M.C. was suddenly beside him, trying to get him up. Every touch sent pain through his body. She was pulling and crying, couldn't she see he was hurting?

His focus was fading, he looked beyond M.C. to the girl standing there. Suddenly her head spun around neck snapped. The girl's face went slack, and she fell into a crumpled heap. Preacher remembered the shimmering thing, that's why M.C. was pulling. Preacher tried to sit up and almost blacked out. M.C. wasn't helping anymore.

She was still facing him, but her eyes were looking left like she was listening to something. She shouldn't be listening to the thing. Preacher tried to tell her, but he just choked and spat up blood.

She was nodding. She shouldn't be nodding. The shimmering shapeless thing exploded and flooded over M.C. like a swarm of bees attacking from the hive. But instead of stinging, they were entering her. Through her eyes, nose, mouth, ears, they were flooding into her.

It took only seconds, but it seemed like an eternity to Preacher. Once it was done M.C. looked at Preacher. He looked deep into her eyes, and he saw the green and black flecks that he had memorized disappear one by one. Her pupils grew larger.

"Mon pauvre garcon" M.C. reached down and pulled out the knife. Fire burst through Preachers stomach. "It is not your time to die, Preacher, she made sure of that." M.C. giggled and placed a hand over the stab wound. She muttered something under her breath that Preacher couldn't quite hear. A hot and burning sensation came over his body that built in intensity until he almost passed out. Suddenly the feeling was gone, and Preacher was able to breathe easier, it felt like the bleeding had stopped.

M.C. lifted her hand covered in blood and stuck her finger in her mouth sucking the blood off the finger. "It's coppery Preacher, your cholesterol is too high" M.C. giggled. "Your girl is gone, Preacher. She and I have Joined, and all it took was for me to save you. You will want to seek us out, don't. No good will come of it for we are one. We are Baba Doek."

Preacher leaned back against the wall and suddenly tired. Baba Doek placed her palm on his head "Sleep now. It will all be better when you wake up." Baba Doek stood and walked to the girl that lay crumpled on the floor. She removed the bone necklace from her twisted neck and put it on. She stepped over Preacher and looked at him, just before he passed out she winked.

**

"When I woke up, Auntie Whatshername was laying upstairs with her neck broken. There was no sign of Baba Doek. I've been looking for a way to Un-join Demons ever since." Preacher drained his whiskey glass and filled it again.

Michael looked at Preacher for the first time with compassion. "Why the name Baba Doek? During the joining the Demon and human blend, the name comes from that blending. I don't understand the name."

Preacher's eyes glossed over, in that thousand-yard stare that people get when they are remembering something from long ago. Painful things. "We called each other Doek. I sent her a text, meant to call her a dork but misspelled it. Called her Doek. Misspelled it three times, doek, doek, doek. It stuck. The Demon chose it to mock me."

"Or because M.C. is strong in there. Maybe M.C. can still be saved." Michael had a tenderness that was new, to Preacher.

Preacher felt his lips start to tremble, that tremble that signified a cry was coming on. One of those sloppy, sobbing cries that come from the pain in the soul. Preacher took another deep drink to try and stable himself.

"Maybe. And I'll find out. But Baba Doek has a Key of Hell, and I cannot combat that without your fancy, make-believe bracelet, Michael."

Michael stood and patted Preacher on the shoulder. "Let's not get ahead of ourselves. There is still much to tell you. You still have much to discover." Michael took the glass from Preachers' hand, and the bottle off the nightstand. "We will not find it here, or in the bottom of a bottle. Come. Let's go visit a friend of mine."

Father Michael led him to the living room where he slipped on an old pair of sneakers. They went out the front door to Michaels Oldsmobile 88'. Not a lot of muscle under the hood, but all the luxury that 1999 could muster.

9.

It should have been a short drive to Ashville, but some stereotypes are there for a reason. Father Michael kept their speed a solid five miles an hour under the speed limit and never turned off his left blinker.

They were almost in the city when Michael broke the silence. "I am sorry you have found yourself here. It was not supposed to turn out this way."

Preacher grunted. "I'm no expert, but I'm pretty sure that no one knows how things are supposed to turn out."

"You speak more truth than you know. You have been in a war since you were born. A hidden war that has been kept from mankind since the beginning of time.

"I've heard. Something about the battle for souls, Heaven and Hell. I think I read about that in the Bible." Preacher sighed "If you were going to start my lessons from the beginning then you could have let me finish the whiskey."

Michael gave a chuckle. "You are still the boy with all the answers. While you're not wrong, you still do not fathom the depth." Michael turned right off the street into a shopping center, his left blinker still on. "We will talk more about this after our visit."

They had pulled into a traditional looking shopping center. A Barbershop, Mexican Restaurant, a niche clothing store, a psychic, a golf shop…. A Psychic? Maybe retirement was too much for his former mentor.

"Do you remember your lessons on King Solomon?" Michael raised an eyebrow. Preacher wondered if he got the answer wrong if he would get lashed again.

"King Solomon ruled over Israel in the time of David, and it's believed that he regularly communed with Demons to gain his power and wisdom. The Lesser Key of Solomon was written with a list of Demons in the order he met them. Does that count?"

Michael nodded. He handed Preacher a pad of paper and pen that was stuffed in the side of the door. "Number seventeen. Write his name and symbol. Tell me who he is and why he can help."

Two things struck Preacher at the same time. The first, he didn't know who the seventeenth demon was. Second, it sounded like Father Michael wanted to summon a demon. He looked at the old man next to him "Are you insane? Are you seriously thinking about summoning a demon? We don't summon, we send them back to the pit. Have you forgotten your own lessons, old man?"

Michael smiled slyly, "You do not remember. You act like the boy with all the answers, but you still do not possess them. You are correct that Priests do not summon demons. You left the church, and you don't let people call you Father. You're called Preacher now, remember? I am retired. I am not a Priest. The answers you need are there. Now, remember your lessons."

"I haven't thought about the Lesser Keys for years, give me a hint." Preacher submerged himself in memory, back to the monastery. There were seventy-eight demons in total, each with their own sigil.

Michael snatched away the paper and started to scribble. "You will need to know your allies as well as your enemies in the days to come. I will not always be here to teach you the things that you should know." He handed the paper back to Preacher, and on it, he saw the sigil.

Michael got out of the car and walked around to the trunk where he started rummaging through the contents. Preacher looked down at the paper in his hand.

Preacher recognized the symbol, literally because it was beaten into him. Botis. Michael wanted to bring forth Botis. Michael wants to bring forth a demon in a psychic's office, inside a shopping center. This was either going to be an epic success or a colossal failure. Michael was walking towards the office with a small black bag in his hand when Preacher caught up with him.

"Are you out of your mind?" Preacher asked.

Michael paused a moment, looking off into the distance over Preacher's shoulder. Maybe he was reconsidering. "Botis tells all things past, present and to come. He reconciles both friends and foes. You need knowledge, and you have both friends and foes that you wish to reconcile with yes?" Ok, maybe not. He was out of his mind.

Michael tried to walk past Preacher and into the store, but Preacher grabbed him by the arm. "Michael, we cannot summon a Demon here. This is ludicrous. You really have lost your mind."

"Are you still going to act like the boy with all the answers?" Michael lowered his voice not to be overheard. "All Demons are Fallen Angels yes?"

Preacher nodded.

"But that's not the whole truth, is it? Not all Fallen Angels are Demons, and some truly wretched human souls turn from being tortured into Demons as well. You only know what you were taught, since you have left we have continued to learn, remember that you do not know everything."

Michael continued. "It is the war I mentioned earlier. There are those that did not forsake God after the fall, they are known as The Fallen. The Fallen want to get back into the grace of God. They fight and thwart the Demons where they can. They have helped us in the past and will help again in the future."

"So, Botis is a Fallen Angel, not a Demon." Preacher clarified.

Michael shrugged

"And you think he'll help us?"

"Mhm" Michael nodded

"What in the Hell makes you think that?" Preacher was getting exasperated.

Michael reached up and pinched his cheek. "My son, Botis helped me find my Grandmothers cheese soufflé recipe. I'll have to make it for you one day, it's delicious. For now, stop questioning me and let's step inside and see what we can discover."

"You want to give me shit about working with a Wiccan, and you're over here summoning Demons for a fancy way of making scrambled eggs. You're the one who has forgotten his way."

The slap came out of nowhere proving Michael was still spry. "I started in the church in 1955. I have exorcized more Demons than you can fathom. You come to me for help, but instead of giving thanks, you demand I help in the way you want."

Preachers face stung from the slap as Michael continued. "You disapprove of this, but you ran from the path that I had laid out for you because you disapproved of that too. You harbor impatience and fail to listen. Just like you did when you were eight years old. You come to me crying because I didn't tell you about my bracelet or this war. However, you fail to look at the world like it is and demand that it bends to how you want it."

Michael poked Preacher in the chest. "Grow up. Listen with not just your ears, but your heart. You'll know the truth when you hear it. You won't need that stone anymore. Now, listen and obey. Learn from this. You have too much to learn and not enough time."

With that Michael turned and went inside, leaving Preacher no choice but to follow. A little bell jingled as the door opened. Immediately Preacher was greeted by the scent of overpowering sticks of clove incense. Nothing like the smell of damp fake weed. They were in a receiving room that tripled as a gift shop and bookstore.

A beaded curtain separated the front from the back of the store. Preacher could see five different sticks on the incense burning in the front of the store alone. Michael placed his bag on the counter next to prepackaged cones of incense. Preacher walked to the nearest stick of incense and rubbed it out, and started moving to the next one.

The rustling of the plastic bead curtain took his attention from the incense. He turned to see the proprietor of the shop. It had to be. If he were looking at a patron, he would be leaving immediately. She stood about five foot six, she was plump but not fat. Her skin was wrinkled, from a combination of age and too much sun, but she wasn't old. She was wearing sandals, her toenails were painted a deep red. She wore a light blue and gold gypsy costume. The kind that you would see on Halloween.

The costume came complete with cheap beads worn around her neck and waist. A light blue and gold bandanna to make the outfit complete. The top was a size too small around the bust, probably done on purpose. She stood with her hands on her hips and smiled at her guests.

Her voice was deep but it seemed practiced and not natural. When she spoke her accent could be placed somewhere in the eastern European region. It was a blend of terrible, wrong and Disney movies. "I think maybe, you have come to have your Tarot read?" She glanced at Preacher, "Maybe is future to be told, hm? Through the leave of tea? Maybe through the palm? Hrm?"

She glanced at Michael "Maybe you come to speak to wife yes? Is she gone on? Come inside Madam Katya help connect you."

Michael nodded suddenly in agreement. He looked back at Preacher "I told you she was good. Come on, let's go talk to Mom." Preacher raised an eyebrow but didn't argue. He followed through the beaded curtain to the other side.

It was larger than the reception area. There was a round table with a table cloth on it. A deck of tarot cards laid on the table, and there was a real-life crystal ball in the middle of the table.

Madam Katya had circled to the far end of the table and sat down. Father Michael took a small velvet pouch from his pocket and opened it. He poured a finely ground powder in his hand, raised it to his mouth and blew it into Madam Katya's face.

Madam Katya sputtered as the powder coated her face. Her eyes widened, "Oh, my" She sounded dreamy, distant and happy. "What was that?" She giggled. Her terrible hack of an Eastern European accent was gone, replaced with a natural southern born accent that was actually a little charming.

Katya's eyes slowly closed and her head fell to the table with a thud.

"What the hell was that Michael?"

"Little bit of sleeping Hoodoo. Gypsum, vanilla, dill weed, ketamine, it will help her sleep while we set up. We should not summon Botis without a protective circle."

"Thought you said that Botis was a friend. That he was Fallen, not a Demon. Why do we need a protective circle for a friend?"

"I implied that he was Fallen, but he will help. Quickly help me move this table. We don't have long. The powder will wear off soon." They moved Katya to the floor. They set her next to the wall and then moved the table. Michael retrieved his bag and removed a chunk of charcoal. Michael began drawing the summoning circle whistling some old show tune or another as he worked.

Michael made quick work of the intricate circle. He nodded over at his bag. "Pour a circle of salt around the circle." Michael shrugged "Just in case." Preacher raised an eyebrow. "It repels Demons. This is going to take all night if I have to explain everything, hurry."

Preacher went to the bag and found an unopened container of salt. When he turned back, he saw the Michael had moved Katya to the center of the circle. Michael had his back turned to Preacher, he was moving stray hair out of Katya's face.

"What are you doing? Get her out of the circle."

"Botis will speak to us better through a vessel. She will not be harmed." He moved another strand of hair and tucked it behind her ear."

Preacher chuckled. "How did I miss it? Who are you? You're not Michael. Offering answers and kindness." Preacher took a step forward and was suddenly seized by paralysis. Michael turned his head over his shoulder, his eyes glowing a deep golden color. Suddenly Preacher was flying back against the wall, and the world went dark.

10.

Michael completed the circle of salt. The sign of Botis was on the floor with Katya laying in the center. Michael began a slow chant in a language Preacher didn't recognize. Preacher was an American Priest, English and Latin were all he spoke unless he was ordering a beer or asking where the bathroom was.

After a moment, Michael began saying words that Preacher recognized. Correction, names that Preacher recognized. "Osurmy, Delmusan, Atalsloym, Melany, Botis, Person, Omot, Dragin. Come forth Botis."

Preacher did not realize he was holding his breath until he let out a gasp. Katya stirred and drew herself up on all fours. A groan passed her lips. She looked up at Michael, and then glanced over at Preacher crumpled on the floor. Confusion was in her eyes. Of course, getting a face full of ketamine dust could do that to anyone.

A strangled gargling noise came from her throat, and her eyes went wide. A crimson color began seeping into her eyes and slowly filled them. Her head dropped as a growl came from her. Something animalistic and beastly. The sound of nightmares made flesh. Her upper body rocked forwards and then upwards, as invisible strings pulled her and she stood awkwardly balanced on the tips of her toes.

Her arms hung at awkward angles, as if she were being held by her armpits, her hands curling into fists, slowly pumping and then releasing. She began to move forward without taking a stepping, dragging her toes on the floor towards Michael.

Katya looked from Michael to Preacher, and a roar split the deafening silence as Botis came to the edge of the sigil. Katya's mouth grew ever wider, disjoining and becoming unrecognizable. Something poked its head out of her mouth, its forked tongue flashing in the air. The viper emerged from her mouth, circling first around her throat then slithering down her body. It was longer than any viper should have been. It wrapped twice around her body and touched the floor before the body fully emerged from the mouth.

Once free of the mouth the viper moved to the center of the sigil and curled onto itself. It must have been twenty feet long. Katya's body fell to the floor with a thud.

"I provided you a means to communicate Botis. If you wish to show your power and take form do so quickly. We are on limited time." Michael placed his hand behind his back taking on an air of patience and control. The viper began to writhe and slide over itself. The viper started to rise in the air, taking on a pillar-like shape. The pillar rose about four feet into the air when it split in half, shifting and melting onto itself resembling legs.

A torso began to build, and long, strong arms formed as the serpent split and split again. The chest was muscled, defined and without blemish. A neck rose from the torso followed by a face. Strong neck and jaw muscled became visible, a strong angular nose formed. Olive-shaped eyes developed closed with long eyelashes. Brown hair sprouted from the head, and grew shoulder length, wavy and shiny.

It was very distracting. Botis opened his eyes, and the crimson glow filled everything but the black pupils. He smiled revealing long, predator teeth, white and shimmering. He shook his mane revealing two pointed horns at the top of his skull. Preacher could see where the horned images of demons came from. The horns were clearly weapons. Not simple decoration to show the world their wickedness, but weapons used to gouge their enemies when all else failed.

Botis stood over six feet tall, he wore loose fitting leggings and sandals. Leather crisscrossed his chest, attached in the middle by a metallic disk with his sigil engraved in it. He reached over his shoulder and unsheathed a sword held on his back.

He spoke with a melodic voice, deep and soothing. There was not a trace of anger or hate that Preacher was used to when dealing with demons. "Father Michael returns. Speak your purpose priest."

Michael did not move or speak; he stood there and allowed Botis to look him over.

"You are not alone Michael, come forward brother and speak."

Preacher laid as still as he could, he saw Michaels' eyes flash golden again. Someone was definitely getting a punch in the face when this was over.

Botis Smiled "Hashmal it is well to see you brother. However, you have me at a disadvantage." Botis lunged forth with his sword in a stab, but the blade stopped short of Michael/Hashmal. Angry red flames burst at the end of the sigil where the sword struck, keeping Botis at bay.

"Hashmal Vindex precisely. I have business with you, let us dispense of it quickly. We both have more important things to do this day."

Hashmal turned his head to look at Preacher. It felt like there were a thousand lights on him at the same time even though nothing became brighter. Preacher could not pretend that he was not awake. There was nothing to do but rise to his feet.

Preacher stood clumsily. It was almost as if his body were half-asleep and just now coming back to life. Nevertheless, he managed to rise and forced himself to look at the body of his mentor.

Hashmal's gaze turned back to Botis. "You remember the last time this person came before you yes? He has lost much and needs to find it." Hashmal looked back at Preacher, "Come here, no harm shall come to you. It is time to set things right." There was compassion coming from Michael's voice again. It was getting a little irritating.

Preacher walked forward tentatively. Mentally he went down the list, no cross, no holy water, and no iron knuckles. He swore at that moment that he would never be unarmed again. He was walking toward a possessed Michael who had summoned an actual Demon. Said Demon was only being held at bay by a barbeque requirement and condiment. He had never found himself in a worse situation in his life.

Preacher looked at Botis, "I need to know what Baba Doek is planning. I need to know what I need to separate her from her host." Preacher didn't mean to sound needy or weak, but he did.

Botis looked over Preacher. The weight of judgment was heavy. Preachers knees felt like they would buckle. The pressure eased, and Preacher could breathe better when Botis looked back to Hashmal.

"Is this the boy your host brought before me all those years ago? Does he seek to be whole? Tell me, Brother, does Father Michael think the time of reckoning has come on us?"

Hashmal nodded "He is the same. He will need to be restored for the upcoming trials before him. He will need the location of the one that can tell us how to find Baba Doek. Only you can provide what we need. That is what we came for."

Botis looked at Preacher. "You were a boy when I took part of you and hid it inside yourself. I did it because it was the right thing to do. I will not ask forgiveness for that I have done, I was right to do it. However, I will ask your forgiveness now, as this will be most... unpleasant."

With a glance from Botis, Hashmal seized Preacher by the throat. There was an incredible strength in the old man's hands. Hashmal lifted Preacher off his feet with supernatural power. Preacher clamped his hands around Hashmal's wrist to keep breathing. Someone was definitely getting a punch in the face when this was over.

Hashmal lifted Preacher over the ring of salt and into the sigil that contained Botis. As Preacher crossed the salt line, he had the sensation like being covered in angry fire ants. One instant they were crawling and biting his flesh, the next they were gone. Hashmal felt it also and dropped Preacher unceremoniously into the circle on top of Katya's unmoving body.

Preacher struggled to his feet unwrapping himself from the unconscious body under him. He stood and found himself face to face with Botis. The eyes of the Demon were now completely taken over by the crimson glow. Saliva streams were hanging between the rows of sharp teeth as the Demon smiled at Preacher.

"From this day onward, you shall devise your own demise. The one they call Preacher, you shall be made whole. Understanding of much is coming, I hope you do not crumble under the weight of it all." Botis reached forward and grabbed Preacher's forehead and skull in his hand.

Searing pain manifested behind Preacher's eyes. He tried not to cry out and failed. It was a pitiful scream, held while half awake and half-asleep. Sigils, symbols, and runes flashed before his eyes. Many he understood, others he didn't. Fatigue settled on him, and tears filled his eyes. The world was broken, but yet whole. He was whole, yet broken. There was light, and darkness. Then the Darkness consumed him, and there was silence.

He fell to his knees gasping for air. Everything and nothing made sense at that same time. Preacher felt like his head was going to explode.

"What did you do to me?" Preacher was gasping out of pain. His body felt like a million ants were alive and crawling under his skin. At the same time, his skin felt like a stone made flesh hardened and defined in a way that it was not before.

Botis growled and barked in Hellion as he stood over Preacher. He knelt beside Preacher, "It will all make sense soon. If you manage not to go insane."

"I must already be insane." Preacher barked. "Michael is possessed and summoning Demons. My mentor tossed me in this circle with you." Preacher looked up at Botis towering over him and stood in a fluid motion.

"It's working already. Most excellent." There was almost a prideful sound in Hashmal's voice.

"What's working already?" Preacher asked.

"Don't you realize Preacher? You are speaking Hellion." Michael's voice said. "You will find that certain gifts come with your condition, like being able to speak and understand different languages."

Botis smiled at Preacher, showing rows of sharpened teeth. "Let us go down, and there confuse their language. Therefore, it happened. Angles however still understand. It is part of you now."

Another round of searing pain shot through Preachers head, and he fell to his knees. The pain was blinding. It felt like a migraine on steroids having a bout of roid rage. Preacher closed his eyes and blackness enveloped him, and suddenly there was nothing.

11.

She stood barefoot in the kitchen. The tiles felt cool on her feet. There was a breeze gently flowing through the open windows causing her sundress to dance across her legs. She looked out the window to the birds singing and allowed herself to smile.

She carried her empty plate to the sink and set it inside. She took off her engagement ring and placed it on the counter. The small diamond sparkled in the sunlight as she picked up her plate.

After running water over it, she gently washed the dish with a sponge and soap. Setting the plate in the sink to dry she looked out the kitchen windows, past the small trees in the yard and out to the ocean. She used a towel on the counter to wipe her hands and put her ring back on.

She could not imagine a happier life. Everything had gone so terribly wrong and been bad for so long it was hard to believe all this was really happening. She walked from the kitchen through the living room. The house was simple in its design, the light hardwood floors reflected light back onto the off-white walls.

A soft microfiber couch and matching recliner were set next to a fireplace. It gave the home a nice cozy feeling. A small entertainment center sat next to the back door, holding a record player that was flanked by vases of fresh flowers. One vase was filled with purple lilies, the other carried a dozen roses of various colors. Jim had put in pink and red and purple roses this time. He said fresh flowers kept the room smelling fresh. Combined with the sea breeze coming in the windows, it made for a little slice of paradise.

There was a familiar scent in the air that she could not readily place. It was a musky manly scent, but it was also sweet on the nose. With the scent came a nagging thought of a memory she couldn't remember. A memory of wearing her favorite house t-shirts, oversized an comfy. The kind you only wear around the house.

She took the handle of the glass patio door and began to open it, but stopped when she saw her reflection in the glass. M.C. looked into her own hazel eyes, flecks of gold and green caught the sunlight and shimmered.

She marveled at how spotless Jim kept the house. There was never a trace of dust or dirt. There were always fresh flowers, but she never saw him bring them in. She never needed to worry about cleaning laundry or putting it away. It was almost too perfect.

Even in the cleanest of homes, there was always a place that mail was placed to collect as clutter. Not in this house. There was never as much as a shoe out of place. The more she thought about it, the more it seemed too good to be true. She felt her pulse start to race and her breath quicken in panic. She closed her eyes to try to calm down.

She used the breathing techniques shown to her by Dr. DuChamps to calm down. She took a long breath through her nose and held it once her lungs were full. Slowly she released it through her mouth and imagined relaxing.

She felt a tension release in her shoulders that she didn't know she had. Slowly she opened her eyes. She was staring at her feet that were covered in dirt and sand up to her ankles. The sand was spilling in from the open patio door.

Her eyes darted around the room. The flowers in the vases were wilted and dead. Spider webs clung between the few pedals left. A black widow walked on the front edge of the record player.

The couch that was pristine a moment ago had lost its shape. Rips were in the cushions that a second ago showed no signs of wear. The previously white curtains that were flowing in the breeze now hung still, dingy brown and tattered.

M.C. turned back to the open patio door and saw her reflection in the grim covered glass. There were bags under her eyes, which were now brown and dull. Her hair was stringy and needed washing. Her lips were dry and cracked. The sundress she was wearing was faded and frayed.

She looked past her reflection to the outside. The sandy beaches were still there, but storm clouds had taken over the once blue sky. Clouds rolled over the sun and completely blocked it out. The light faded from the home leaving her in near darkness. She was looking at the sky and dirty glass door when she saw movement reflected over her shoulder, but she was the only one home.

M.C. spun around and saw nothing but the dingy home. The paint was peeling from the walls, sand, and dirt covering the floor. There was no movement, nothing there. She felt eyes watching her, another presence was in the house, but she couldn't see it. The hair on the back of her neck moved as something blew on the back of her neck. The putrid smell of rotten meat accompanied the breath.

She turned back, but she only saw the open patio door. She did the only thing that she could think of, she ran. She flew out of the house and onto the beach. The top layer of sand was hot on her feet, but she refused to notice. She ran down to the water, broken shells littered the beach cutting into her feet.

She spun in circles, looking for signs that something had followed her. She only saw her footprints in the sand. The sky lit up in angry shades of purple as lighting rippled above her head. Thunder rolled in the sky above like a thousand angry monsters trying to break out of a cage. The smell of the ocean was missing, replaced with the musky scent of cologne that she smelled in the house.

Lighting broke from the clouds and struck the beach instantly charging the sand with electricity. The ends of her hair began to lift from her shoulders because of the charge. Large drops of rain began to fall violently from the sky stinging her skin where it hit her.

She ran for the pier to escape the lightning and the rain. The sand quickly began turning soft as the rain pounded it making each step more difficult. The sand started to open beneath her feet like quicksand, trying to swallow her.

Deeper angry growls came from the sky overhead, and lightning struck again. This time it was closer. Panic took over, and she tried harder to sprint to safety. She was only feet away when her foot sank into the sand passed her ankle. She fell forward and started crawling towards the pier, but something held her leg in the sand. She rolled to her side and tried to use her leverage to begin pulling her foot from the sand, but the grip would not let her go.

The remaining light fell away casting the world into darkness. Strong arms wrapped around her waist and pulled her free from the sand. Someone drug her the last few feet to safety under the pier.

Whoever was dragging her to safety fell backward into the sand behind her. They pulled her upwards, so her head was resting on their chest. Both of them were breathing hard from the struggle. M.C. nuzzled her face into her savior's chest. There was something familiar about how this body felt against her. The smell of the cologne was recognizable now.

He brushed away a wet loose strand of her hair and tucked it behind her ear, just as he did so many times before. M.C. began to tremble, even though she was not cold. She had to be dreaming, it was the only explanation possible.

"It's okay Doek, you're safe now. I've got you." His voice was soft and patient like she remembered. She felt him kiss her on the forehead. The slight roughness of his unshaved stubble was scratchy and made her forehead itch a little. His cologne was in the air and on his skin, and she remembered him entirely for the first time in a long time.

A wave of horror flooded through her. He couldn't be here holding her. He died. M.C.'s eyes shot open, and she pulled away and sprang to her feet. The temporary bliss she felt turned to a cold piece of ice that chilled her to the bone.

She looked down on Preacher as he sat in the sand. He was the same as she remembered, with short hair and an unshaven face. She watched as he slowly stood up,

"This can't be happening. You're dead. You're dead, and this is a dream!" She pressed her hands to the side of her head – a relaxation technique that Dr. DuChamps taught her. Pressure on her temples had always helped ground her in reality since she learned it. When she opened her eyes though, he was still standing on the beach under the pier.

He was looking at her with a puzzled look on his face. It was the look he had when he didn't understand her but wanted her to think that he did. Even two years after his death, his platitudes annoyed the hell out of her.

"I'm not dead Doek. You saved me." His tone was a matter of fact. The words sounded rehearsed and came off the tongue smoothly. "You saved me, and I'm trying to find you so I can save you."

He took a step toward her, and she recoiled. Lightning struck behind her casting him in the light. He was exactly as she remembered.

"I'm happy now! I am going to get married!" M.C. shouted at her nightmare. Dr. DuChamps taught her about controlling these dreams, these hallucinations. "You died! I watched you die." She raised her left hand to show her ring to this dream intruder. Instead of an engagement ring on her finger, a baby viper rolled around her finger. It was swallowing its own tail causing her to scream again.

Lightning struck again, bathing the pier in its light. M.C. saw movement in the corner of her eye and spun towards it. Instead of a frightening monster standing beside her, it was a little old man dressed as a priest. He was walking towards her, hands clasped in front of his body, the perfect model of patience.

She looked from the priest to Preacher and back. The priest looked at Preacher "You shouldn't be here. Be gone." With a dismissing hand gesture, Preacher flew backward from under the peer as if he had been struck with a great force. Once Preacher was back in the rain, he could no longer be seen anymore, and the smell of cologne was gone.

M.C. looked at the priest, it was strange, but she knew that she was looking at something more than an old priest. His dismissal of her former lover didn't scare her as it should have. He didn't seem to be a threat to her at all. The priest touched her forehead with his index finger. "Sleep," he said.

The world faded to black as she fell on the soft sand. Gently on the breeze, she heard the words "And Forget."

She stood barefoot in the kitchen. The tiles felt cool on her feet. There was a breeze gently flowing through the open windows causing her sundress to dance across her legs. She looked out the window to the birds singing and allowed herself to smile.

She carried her empty plate to the sink set it inside. She took off her engagement ring and placed it on the counter. The small diamond sparkled in the sunlight as she picked up her plate.

After running water over it, she gently washed the dish with a sponge and soap. Setting the plate in the sink to dry she looked out the kitchen windows, past the small trees in the yard and out to the ocean. She used a towel on the counter to wipe her hands and put her ring back on.

She experienced the strangest sense of déjà vu as she walked into the living room.

In the distance, she thought she heard her name being called out. She turned to look for the source, but the house was empty. "M.C." She heard it again, louder this time. It sounded like Jim, but it was too far away to be sure.

The sound of the ocean filled her ears, and she felt water rushing on her feet. She looked around for the source of the sensation and found herself under the pier. Jim was next to her gently shaking her shoulder.

"M.C., what are you doing out here?" He sounded concerned or maybe amused. There was something in his voice that told her something wasn't quite right. Her nightmare came flooding back to her, and she hugged him and clung to him.

"What's happening to me?" She asked bewildered.

12.

The world blurred back into focus, accompanied with all the glory of the worst hangover ever felt by man. Preacher groaned and looked around. He was back at Michaels, laying in the bed of the single bedroom. Michael/Hashmal stood in the corner of the room watching Preacher.

"You still snore like a freight train." Michael stated flatly.

Preacher sat up, and the world spun again. "What happened?" His words came out slower than he thought they should. His tongue felt thick in his mouth. "Wanna explain yourself?"

"I should. But first I should explain what you are, in your entirety." Michael took the bottle of whiskey from the nightstand where Preacher left it, poured a glass and handed it to Preacher. "Your mother, rest her soul, was Joined before she gave birth to you. Your birth was a test to see if Nephilim could be created."

"You are part human, part Angel. You are an abomination. Hated and feared by both Heaven and Hell. When I discovered that you were Nephilim I took you to Botis and had your Celestial side locked away in a cell deep inside you."

Preacher slung his feet off the side of the bed, and the world went spinning again.

"After the Rebellion against God, Angles still had a physical form. It was not until the end of the Nephilim War that the Fallen were forced to forsake their bodies and live as spirits."

"Nephilim War?" Preacher shook his head and blinked rapidly trying to clear the cobwebs. "I don't remember reading about that in the Bible, or any other book." Things were starting to become easier to focus on now.

"Genesis, chapter six, versus four through seven. The Nephilim were on the earth in those days and also afterward when the sons of God went to the daughters of humans and had children by them. They were the heroes of old, men of renown. The Lord saw how great the wickedness of the Human race had become on Earth, and that every inclination of the thoughts of the human mind was only evil all the time. The Lord regretted that he had made the human beings on the Earth, and his heart was deeply troubled."

"Before God destroyed the Earth he found favor in Noah and let him build an Ark. What's not written in the Bible here is that the hybrid of human and celestial was more powerful than anything ever created." Michael looked Preacher up and down "Some say they became more powerful than God, but they were half human and tied to their human body. That's the only thing that stopped them from traveling to and taking Heaven."

The headache was subsiding now. Preacher was able to move his head without it feeling like it was going to explode.

"As these Nephilim developed, some grew benevolent and wise. They made beautiful things and strived to make life better. Others, however, became driven by base desires and grew twisted and evil. Every legend, of every monster, sprang forth from these creatures. Vampires, Werewolves, the Boogeyman, all of it."

"See, the power of the Nephilim is also a curse. If you do not take care of your soul, the power twists you into something terrible, the very thing nightmares are made of."

Preacher nodded, the understanding that this was truth flowed through is body naturally.

"The Nephilim became so powerful that even the hosts of Heaven could not defeat them in battle. To prevent a war Heaven might lose, God sent a flood and destroyed them."

"The Fallen bodies were all going to be destroyed too, so most hid their bodies away to live as spirits. Others tried to keep their bodies and live through the flood, their bodies were destroyed, and they soon withered away to nothing."

"The hosts of Heaven took the opportunity to seal the physical bodies in a place called Tartarus. Effectively trapping them, and there they have stayed ever since."

Preacher looked at Michael "You're telling me a lot of facts, but not a lot of why. I'm not concerned with a history lesson right now. What did you do to me?" Preachers voice was impatient anger was seeping into it.

"In short I saved you. If the Church knew what you were they would have destroyed you, or worse. If the Fallen or the Demons had gotten their hands on you, they would have twisted you to their own ends. So I hid you."

Michael shrugged and sat in the chair. "It's the only thing my conscience would allow me to do."

"Tell me about Hashmal and the Fallen." Preacher asked.

Michael thought for a moment, the silence was thick in the air.

"I have cancer. It had started in my prostate then spread to my liver, lungs, and brain before I even felt sick. I was given eight months to live. I told my superiors at the Church, who were now much younger and far less experienced than I was, and they retired me. No medical care, no hospice, no medicine."

Michael sighed. "I was put out to pasture with nowhere to die. After over sixty years of service to the Church, I was expected to crawl off and die in silence." Michael scoffed and frowned. "At first Hashmal came to me in my dreams. Eventually, facing death, I let him in. He keeps my cancer at bay, and we share the body, knowledge, and power."

"There is something more important to discuss at the moment, all of this we can discuss at a later time. We need to talk about where you were a moment ago."

Preacher took another sip of his whiskey. It needed ice. "I was dreaming. It was more of a nightmare than a dream though. I was seeing M.C., but she couldn't see me at first. It seemed like her life was perfect, then it all changed. I don't want to talk about it."

Michael sighed and leaned forward in the chair. "You were dream walking. It is something that Celestial beings can do. You went to her inside her dream. It is an efficient way to communicate over long distances assuming the person you want to communicate with is sleeping. In this case, it is imperative that you stay out."

"Baba Doek has her locked in a living dream. A dream world in which you died, and she moved on. Your presence there disturbed the dream. If Baba Doek notices changes in her dream, ripples from your appearance there she could change the dream. She could change it from a dream to torment. Demons will not copilot a body like the Fallen. As long as the soul stays submissive Baba Doek will not care. If it starts to try and rise she will do whatever she has to in order to stay in control."

There was a slight tremor in his hand as Preacher drained his whiskey and nodded. The dream had seemed too real not to be. Anger rolled beneath the surface of his skin, but he swallowed it down and stood up.

"I need to get her out of there Michael. Her possession may fall on my shoulders, but if I knew about all this Nephilim shit before now, she never would have been in danger. That falls on you."

Preacher walked to the kitchen, refilled the ice for his whiskey, and poured himself a glass of water. He said a short blessing over the water making a weak version of Holy Water. Not as effective as saturating in salt and letting a crucifix rest in it for a few days, but it should work in a pinch.

He walked back to the bedroom and refilled his other glass with Whiskey. "So, I am half Angel, and that makes me a threat. How do I use that against Baba Doek to have her release M.C.?" Walking back into the bedroom he was starting to feel like himself again. "Where do I go from here?"

"First you need to learn your capabilities. Learn how you can throw hoodoo and survive in a Celestial fight. There is no need to run off and kill yourself quickly." Michael leaned back and closed his eyes. "Then we track down Baba Doek and thwart her plans and get your girl back."

"I will learn as we go Michael. I am not interested in thwarting her plans. I am interested in sending Damballa back to Hell and freeing M.C. for good. I need your help though, I need you to come with me for a little while. Help me figure this out."

Michael chuckled. "Yes, you have made that clear. I will come with you. Please do me a favor, don't ignore my advice every time?" Preacher nodded his assent to the request. "Let me gather a few items, and we can leave shortly."

Michael walked to the bookshelf, removed some scrolls and books. He laid them on the bed. "After you passed out, Botis was kind enough to point us in the right direction to discover Baba Doeks plan."

Preacher grunted. "Does it involve summoning another Demon? I can't handle another summoning."

Familiar laughter came from Michael. Preacher remembered the cruel laughter from his childhood. "No. We do not need to summon this time. This Demon managed to possess a body over a thousand years ago. He is extremely old, extremely powerful, and he is apparently very insane. It seems that a steady supply of souls has become inefficient in sustaining his needs and he has started finding celestials and consuming them as well. He will eat Demon or Fallen, it is that spark of the divine that he is looking for now."

"So, we are going to go back to your people, and then you my boy, are off to see a Demon." Michael turned to the bookshelf and began placing other books on the bed.

"Me? Don't you mean us? You're the one with an Angel riding shotgun." Preacher seemed insistent.

"No. I mean you. You wouldn't want him to eat me, would you?" Michael said with a hint of humor in his voice.

Michael pulled an old trunk from under the bed and opened the lid. It was almost full of books and scrolls already. He topped it off with what was on the bed and closed the lid. As he turned to say something to Preacher, he received a face full of Holy Water.

Michael sputtered and coughed a bit as the water hit the back of his throat. Preacher was standing before him with a crucifix that he had borrowed from the wall. Preacher was beginning the Litany of Saints, the standard opening for an exorcism.

Michael's coughing turned to laughter "You really are a silly boy. Holy Water doesn't work on the Fallen, and neither do objects of faith. It is what separates them from the Demons."

Preacher smiled broadly. "I figured so, but I needed a distraction." Preacher hauled back and hit Michael in the face as hard as he could. The force spun Michael around, and he fell on the bed out cold. Preacher glanced at the body and saw the rise and fall of the chest. He was breathing, and alive was good. Preacher assumed that supernatural strength was part of his arsenal now.

He picked up the trunk and headed to the car. Supernatural strength was definitely there, this trunk should have been a lot heavier.

13.

The drive back to Atlanta was mostly in awkward silence. Preacher was still wrestling with the new identity that he found himself saddled with. Fortunately, Preacher was the one driving, so the car was able to travel at or above the speed limit without turn signals on.

Michael for his part sat in silence pouting about the whole knock out thing. Michael would later claim that he allowed his protégé time to digest all that was dropped on him in the last few hours.

In truth, Michael was relieved that Preacher did not have a psychotic break when he learned everything and his Nephilim side was unleashed. There was nothing in any written text or in Hashmal's memory of this ever being performed.

Michael had certainly never seen it before. Even Hashmal could only offer a guess. It had been so long since Hashmal saw a Nephilim born. No one had never seen it done this way. Nephilim are the product of the physical union of the Celestial and humans.

Being born from a Joined Demon was a first in all of known history. There must have been something going on with the way the stars were aligned, or something special with the father. Once word spread about the rebirth of Nephilim Demons were going to start trying to make an army of them.

Finally, Preacher broke the silence. "How do I not remember? You brought me in front of a Demon, and let him stuff part of me in a box and hide it. I remember my mother, the observations, the neglect, the alcohol, but not the ceremony to summon a Demon."

Michael looked out the window, then back at Preacher. "I had anticipated this question since it was done. The answer still shames me. I asked Botis to take your memories of it. I had him hide it from you because I thought it was best. I couldn't have you arrive in Rome telling everyone that I summoned a Demon to suppress the fact that you were Nephilim, now could I?

"Do you think that justifies what you did? It was in my best interest?" Preacher scoffed at Michael. Preacher was acting like the boy that still couldn't see past the nose on his face.

"If I did not hide you, you would have been killed or worse. It would have only been a matter of time." Michael stated. This was not an apology from the old priest.

Preacher fell into silence again. He was brooding, but Michael knew that he would soon turn his thoughts to the future and the problems before him. All he had to do was wait and have patience.

"Which Demon am I paying a house visit too? And how am I supposed not to be eaten? If you and Hashmal are frightened, how am I expected to survive?"

Michael shrugged "Use holy water, iron, and salt. I imagine you are very clever when it comes to battling the forces of Hell. Also, Hashmal can teach you to throw a bit of your own Hoodoo. Also because you're Nephilim you're faster and stronger than before."

"I'll be faster and stronger than this Demon? A Demon that's been in a body for over a thousand years?" Preacher scoffed again. He was wearing sunglasses, but Michael could hear the boys' eyes rolling beneath them. Michael liked to believe that it was his Nephilim side that made his so stubborn but he wasn't convinced of that. Sometimes Preacher was just a jackass.

"Maybe not yet, but maybe he won't even try to eat you." Michael tried to sound hopeful.

"Do you believe that?" A flat, non-sarcastic response. Now that did take Michael by surprise. He didn't think that Preacher would be so logical so quickly. Preacher had only punched him in the face once.

"No. I do not, but I have been wrong before." Michael reached to the floorboard and pulled out a notebook and pen. "I'll just jot down some ingredients, and directions and your team will get them and help keep you safe."

"What are you writing down? And why do you think my team will help you?"

Michael resisted the urge to roll his own eyes. Years ago that tone and insubordination would have resulted in a backhand across the face or lashes to the back. There were privileges to being old, but fragile bones were not one of them. Michael wasn't sure if Hashmal would heal a broken knuckle if he backhanded Preacher in the face.

"Don't you trust me?" Michael asked.

"No, not particularly. Not anymore. You're smart enough to figure that out though. So just answer my questions, what is the name of this Demon?" Preacher said forcefully.

"Bolfry is his name. King Solomon summoned him because he could turn anything into gold with only a touch. During the banishment spell, something went wrong, and Bolfry was freed from the pit. He has remained free ever since."

"So, this Demon has been around for just over three thousand years and has kept such a low profile that no one knew he was walking the Earth. Three thousand fucking years? And what, we know where he is now? Am I just going to knock on the door and act like I am delivering a fucking pizza?" That was the outburst that Michael was waiting for.

"No. You're going to shadow-step into his living space and confront him. You're going to discover the plans of Baba Doek then stop her. I really shouldn't have to come up with all the plans myself, you're smart too." Michael smirked.

"What the fuck is Shadow Stepping? Goddamn it Michael. You're making me feel like a kid that doesn't know up from down all over again. Stop talking in riddles. I am not a child for you to scold anymore."

Michael made a tsk sound, sucking his teeth like he would do when chiding a young kid.

"Language." He scolded. One step forward, two steps backward Michael thought. Preacher's emotions were seeping back into play. His childhood was difficult. Being raised by a Demon that observed him like an experiment. Having no father in his life at all. When the Demon wasn't in control of his mother, she remained drunk. Michael was sure that his treatment of the boy in Rome was better, but not by much.

"Listen to me, Brandon. In many ways, you are indeed my student again. Hashmal and I have a lot to teach you and not a lot of time to do it in. Your goals have become our goals. I can advise you on somethings and Hashmal on others. We both know that whatever Baba Doek is after, it is not for the betterment of human civilization."

Preacher grunted. He didn't want to take on the mantle of the student again. He was the teacher now in his own circle. Michael understood.

The ride went on in silence for the rest of the way with just the occasional change to one hard rock station to the next.

The house that they pulled up too looked normal enough. Michael wasn't sure what to expect, but the commonness of the structure made him a little sad. Preacher parked in the driveway next to another mid-nineties four-door sedan.

"I've asked the team to look into Holy Relics and Keys of Hell. Let's see what the team has discovered. Maybe you and Hashmal can fill in any gaps." Preacher paused staring at the house. "Oh, and let's keep the Fallen Angel you've got riding shotgun under wraps for now. I don't want the team to get sidetracked or spooked. We'll tell them when the time is right. And, don't mention Nephilim either, not yet anyway."

Michael nodded. "Take a bit of advice, secrets will break a family as quickly as sticks and stone can break your bones. Make sure you do not wait too long."

Preacher nodded, and they headed inside. Josh and Raz were at the dining room table. They had books and scrolls piled haphazardly on the table cluttering what little workspace there was. Raz had barely been able to find room for her laptop, and she was busy researching cyberspace as well as the hardbacks in front of her.

Josh looked up from the book he was reading when they walked in. He looked tired. Preacher wondered how long he had been digging through old texts looking for the answers he asked for. Josh's eyes moved over to Michael. If he was surprised that Preacher brought company home, it didn't show.

Gus walked in from the kitchen. He was carrying a tray with a craft of coffee and four cups. He paused when he saw Michael. "I didn't know we had company," he glanced at Preacher, "or I would have cleaned another cup."

Gus sat the tray down on the table then walked over to Michael and extended his hand. "I'm Gus. That's my sister Raz, and that's Josh." Michael took his hand and smiled.

"I am Michael. I am pleased to meet all of you." Michael smiled "I don't drink coffee this late in the day so don't bother yourself with another cup. Tell me, what does this guy have you looking up? If there isn't a book on the topic here, there should be in the trunk of the car. I didn't exactly pack lightly."

"We are looking for Holy Relics and the Keys of Hell. It's riveting stuff, let me tell ya." Raz sounded irritated. Which seemed unusual because she was wearing a t-shirt with a unicorn farting a rainbow on it, and her hair was in pigtails. She looked playful and flirty, Michael should have known better than to judge her by the way that she looked.

"Actually, it's quite interesting. We think we have tracked down two." Josh sounded pleased with himself. "Well three, if you count the one he is wearing." Josh nodded towards Michael's wrist.

"That was fast. Good job. Tell me what you have found." Preacher seemed eager to establish the chain of command with his old mentor here. Gus started pouring coffee for the others as Josh began talking.

"The first one we think we located was a piece of wood from something. We think it was the Ark of Covenant. Rumors have the Knights Templar bringing back a lot of lost religious treasures after the Crusades. Whatever it was, was being stored in a church in England just before the Second World War. When the Nazis were bombing England, The Church lost track of it along with almost everything in Europe." Josh paused to shuffle some papers, looking for something he had written down.

"Turns out that what we think was the Ark was smuggled back to what became Israel. It was damaged from a bombing, and a piece broke off about a meter long and was left. The church was demolished from a bomb, but this piece was found years later during reconstruction. It was put in a frame and mounted on a pillar, saved as a reminder of the devastation that war brings."

"Here is what we caught on to. The residents that attend this church live an average of four to six years longer than those in the area do. Living or working within a mile of the church seems to have a similar but diminished benefit."

Raz continued with the briefing. "The second one we found is being marketed as a nail from the crucifixion of Christ. It is reported to have healing powers, and is very very expensive." Raz sounded firm in her conviction of the authenticity of the item. "I can trace the sales back for the last 60 years, each person that purchased it either had, or knew someone who had a fatal disease. They all recovered within days, being hailed as miracles."

"Its currently in Hollywood being rented for 30 Million Dollars a day. Before you ask, I checked for cursed items, the people that seem to be affected remain healthy, happy and live a full life." Raz sounded pleased with her report.

Preacher took a sip of the coffee offered by Gus. "Good job. We are halfway there." Preacher glanced at Michael and made eye contact, but didn't say anything. "Did we find anything on the Keys of Hell?" Preacher turned his gaze to Gus. Michael suspected that Gus would look into it before he let his sister look into it.

"Nothing concrete, or worth chasing down. Anyone with an imagination could make this stuff up. There is only one lead I am willing to chase down, and it is for the Crown of Thorns." Gus gave a shrug in disbelief in the article.

"What did you find? This could be something to chase down." Michael tried not to sound overeager, but this was an actual Key that he and Hashmal had debated before.

"Scripture states that a crown of thorns was placed on Christ's brow before the crucifixion to mock him and left during the burial. But when he arose, no crown was ever mentioned. I have made inquiries, but I have little hope of having anyone call me back."

"Did you call Bobby? He seems to be the end all, know all when it comes to this stuff." Preacher sounded almost irritated that he had to bring it up.

"Yeah, he's going to call me back. So he says." Gus took a sip of the coffee he made and smirked a bit. "How was your trip? Any cool discoveries on your end?" Michael knew Gus would be one he needed to watch, this one was cle

14.

Sitting in the waiting room for Dr. DuChamps was usually uncomfortable and awkward for M.C. But the hallucination that she had was so powerful and real she didn't notice how calm she was being. There was a window in the waiting room that was open. She felt a cool breeze coming in bringing with it the smell of the ocean.

Jim had found her asleep under the pier, covered in sand, wet and terrified. There was no sign of the storm that had ravished the beach. Only her footprints could be found on the beach. Apparently, there was only one explanation, and that was she had a setback. She had a vivid hallucination.

M.C. looked at the open windows set in the wall. The curtains were blowing in the breeze coming in. A blue dragonfly had landed on the windowsill and fluttered its wings. M.C. smiled at the little creature, her mother had once told her that butterflies and dragonflies were Gods little messengers. You could whisper them a message, and they would fly for hundreds of miles to deliver it.

As a child M.C. would sit in the back yard of her home after school and would whisper "I love you" to each and every one that she saw. She would watch them fly away wondering who they would land on and if she would ever meet them.

M.C. remembered a time in Preachers back yard on the island that a dragonfly landed on her leg. She whispered, "Love you" out of habit. She didn't think about it at all. The dragonfly took off flying, she watched it bob and weave. It zigged and zagged, it came back toward her then darted over her head and landed on Preacher's arm while he lay in the hammock napping behind her.

It astonished her that the dragonfly flew and landed on him. M.C. didn't know how she felt towards Preacher. She was always in the debate of if he was Mr. Right, or just Mr. Right now. She knew that she cared, but it wasn't until he died that she really understood how much she did care.

Dr. Duchamps allowed her to grieve and showed her how to do it healthily. Finding Dr. D had helped her immensely. Shortly afterward she found Jim and fell in love with him. She was fortunate. She walked over to the window and leaned down looking at the dragonfly. She thought it was only blue, but when she got close, she could see emerald and yellow flakes along its body.

She pulled her long hair to the side, to prevent it from falling in her face as she leaned in close to the insect. "I love you" she whispered. Instantly the creature took flight off the window ledge. Childishly M.C. wondered if the creature would fly off and find Jim to let him know. She wished that she could follow to see where it would go.

"What were you doing?" M.C. spun around and saw Dr. DuChamps standing in the doorway of her office.

M.C. must have been rooted in thought not to hear the door open. Being caught whispering to insects in front of your therapist was usually frowned upon. After all, she was there to learn how to get better, not show off childish antics that she should have let go of long ago. M.C. felt her cheeks flush a little with embarrassment.

"Something silly that my mother encouraged as a child. It's nothing really." M.C. tucked her hair behind her ears in a swooping motion. It was a nervous tick that she knew she did and hated. Preacher had pointed it out to her one night as they played cards for chores. It was an intense game, with three weeks' worth of laundry folding on the line.

Dr. DuChamps nodded and stepped aside to allow for M.C. to enter the office. M.C. tried to banish the thought of Preacher from her mind, there would be enough talking about that in the session today. She took her usual chair across from Dr. DuChamps. The proverbial couch did not exist in this office and M.C. was thankful for it.

"So," Dr. DuChamps started, "Jim tells me that he found you under the pier unconscious. The back door of the house left wide open because you had an episode. Tell me, what started it all?" Dr. DuChamps voice was patient and kind.

M.C. tucked her hair behind her ears and swallowed hard. "I noticed a smell. Preacher's old cologne was in the air. I didn't recognize the smell at first. I knew it, but I couldn't place it. I smelled it for almost two years straight through, it should be as familiar as the scent of flowers."

M.C. cleared her throat before she continued. "But after I smelled it things in the house began to change. Flowers that were alive were dead. Anything clean became dirty. I could feel something in the house with me. I ran into a storm that came out of nowhere, and the beach tried to swallow me up. I was stuck in the sand, and something was pulling me down trying to keep me from the pier. The rain came in hard, I heard strange screeching and screaming. I was pulled free and drug to safety. I was laying on Preacher, he was comforting me, but he is dead." M.C. blinked away tears and wiped her face. It sounded absurd.

"I told him he was dead, that he couldn't be here because he was dead. Then it all went black, and Jim found me under the pier asleep."

Dr. DuChamps offered a box of tissues to M.C., who touched her cheek and found them wet. She didn't realize that she had been crying. She took the box of tissue and dried her cheeks, and began staring at her feet ashamed.

"Did he say anything to you? Did he say why, after all this time he came back?" There was a firmness in Dr. DuChamps voice that was usually subtler, and kind.

M.C. shook her head. "I don't think so, I don't remember him saying anything. I passed out after I shouted at him." She felt fresh tears rolling down her cheeks.

"I cannot help you if you lie to me. You have never lied to me before. It is important that you do not start now. So, think about it and tell me what he said." Dr. D was firm with her tone, making M.C. think that maybe she was lying.

M.C. stared from her shoes to the floor. Her vision was blurring from the tears she couldn't control any longer. "It doesn't matter what he said. He's gone. I don't know why I imagined him at all. I have moved on, I don't understand." M.C. was close to panic.

"That is what we are here to do. We are here to understand. Now please, the words he spoke. What were they?" Dr. D almost sounded angry. She had never spoken to M.C. like this before.

"I can't remember. I'm sorry, I want to remember so I can tell you. I swear it" M.C. pushed her memories hard but as soon as she saw him everything became fuzzy. It was like trying to watch a movie while having your head underwater in a murky pond. She could tell that there was something there, but she wasn't sure what it was.

"Relax, let it come. Did he say he was coming for you? Did he say he knew where you were?" Dr. D urged.

M.C. shook her head that didn't sound right. "He is dead, how can he know where I am?"

Dr. Duchamps shook her head, "It is your subconscious I am trying to decipher. I am only trying to save you from yourself, dear."

M.C.'s head shot up. "That was it. He said he was going to save me. But what does that mean? Save me from what?"

**

Baba Doek let the conversation with Dr. Duchamps keep going while she turned her attention to the present. She thought that she felt something with her host. It was like hearing the buzz of a mosquito in your ear. Once swatted at, it goes away and should be quickly forgotten.

However, there was something that stuck with Baba Doek. Her host was being erratic and trying to resist the dream she was in. Baba Doek needed to know why. She was close to casting her spell and needed to stay focused.

The Duchamps persona allowed her to maintain control of her host with minimum effort. It gave her the ability to manipulate the human side in the dream. It had proven to be extremely useful.

There were only two possibilities for what was happening. Either this human loved Preacher so much she could not completely let go. When she introduced Jim to the dream, she thought that would take care of the Preacher distraction.

The other option was that Preacher made his way in somehow. He should not have been able to do that. It's possible perhaps that he learned of the war and was working with The Fallen. Even more farfetched he learned to astral-project, though that gift was excessively rare. It could be a fluke, but Preacher hunting her down was not a stretch of the imagination. She knew that eventually, he would come after her. But after two years he still wasn't close to catching up with her.

It was one of the reasons that she kept this body. Once she was inside, she knew everything the host knew about Preacher and what he could do. Baba Doek knew that Preacher would never harm this host. His power and skill made him the only one good enough to give her a challenge. After all, every Savior needs an Adversary, why not allow him to be hers?

15.

Preacher was sitting on the front porch of the house sipping a hot cup of coffee watching the sunrise. He had not seen a sunrise since before he lost M.C. He didn't like thinking of her as lost, but there is something about the taste of coffee and watching the dawn that brings truth to mind in an undeniable way.

Preacher let himself understand that even if he were successful in unjoining the Demon, their relationship was over. In her dream life, she was screaming that she was getting married. Before he tried to make his presence known to her, her dream life looked ideal. She was living on the beach, happy and safe. She had what she deserved out here in the real world.

All of that happiness was going to be ripped away from her once this was over. She was going to come back to a world that was cold and uncaring. With an effort, Preacher pushed the thought from his mind. He was relieved that she was in a positive dream state and not being tortured. In the end, though, that still didn't mean he liked it.

Last night was the first time that he thought about what life would be like once M.C. was free. He lost himself in those thoughts, and before he knew it, the sun was starting to come up. He made coffee out of habit. Surprisingly enough, he was not tired. He wasn't sure if that was part of being Nephilim, or if the thought of life after revenge scared him a little.

Preacher felt a small tickle on his arm, and looked down and saw a dragonfly had perched on his elbow. As soon as he saw it, the dragonfly took off and around the side of the house. It was the first insect he had seen this year. It was still too cold for most insects to be out.

The front door opened and Michael stepped out holding a cup of coffee of his own. He walked to the edge of the porch and looked out toward the sunrise.

"It's nice seeing God's blessing in the form of a sunrise, isn't it?" The usual smugness that Preacher associated with Michael was not there.

"Good Morning Hashmal." Preacher was pretty sure it was Hashmal anyway. "Is sleep an option for me now? I didn't sleep last night."

"It is possible that you don't need sleep. It's also possible that you just had a restless night." Hashmal looked at Preacher with no emotion on his face. "You are the first of your kind in thousands of years. There are merely rumors about your abilities and physical condition. Most of those who knew the Nephilim are gone. We simply do not know."

Preacher nodded. "Why wait this long to try to make Nephilim? If we are so powerful, why bother making more? Without your bodies, you would be easy pickings for a Nephilim, right?"

Hashmal gave little more than a shrug. "Do you believe that you could defeat me in combat at the moment?"

Preacher thought for a moment. "You are in the body of someone that I care about. No. I don't suppose that I could. But I might be able to drive you out of the body, and that's just as good as a win."

Hashmal nodded. "I see your point, and yes, it is similar to victory. Unfortunately, though it is not a victory. If you do not smite the Demon, it can and often will return. Some Demons are very territorial, and will return to the same host over and over again."

Preacher nodded, he had heard this before but had never personally seen it.

"There are things that I need to teach you. We should get started before the others awake. If they were to discover my nature before you tell them, their reaction would probably be, unfavorable."

Hashmal walked down the steps of the front porch and headed around towards the back of the house. Preacher took another sip of the coffee and followed. Michael may have been an ass of a teacher, but Hashmal was dismissive in an entirely different and more annoying kind of way.

The backyard was heavily wooded. Pine straw and fallen leaves covered the ground. Broken branches and the remains of fallen pine trees littered the back yard. Shadows fell along the yard as the sun began to hit the pine trees.

"If it has not yet started, you will soon begin to see things differently. Your Celestial side will start to manifest. Colors will emerge you have never seen before. Sounds you have never heard will be louder than ever. You will soon see the world as God created it." Hashmal turned and looked at Preacher.

"You have been human your entire life. The last Nephilim on this world was born as Nephilim. I have no way of knowing when or how your Celestial side will manifest." Hashmal looked around the backyard.

"Tell me, Preacher, do you know why humanity fears the dark?" Hashmal paused and let the question hang in the air. "It is instinctual to fear what you cannot see. Have you ever thought why?" Hashmal stood near a fallen tree truck. The shadow was mingling with those trees still alive and the ivy that was growing on it. It created a deep darkness often ignored in the daylight.

Hashmal continued. "It is because there is nothing in the darkness. Not just the absence of light, there is a nothing. It's a void, a forgotten place where nothing and everything is connected. It is frightening for humanity because the space between nothing, is nothing." Hashmal looked at Preacher and then at the shadows that lay crisscross by his feet. "Nightmares about creatures in the closet, under the bed, behind the door, everything is possible here. Through this nothing, we can travel. It is called a Shadow Step."

With a small movement, Hashmal was gone. He did not dissolve into nothing or fall into the shadow. Instead, he just simply was not there anymore. He just vanished from sight. The only hint that he was ever there was rippling in the shadows that would have gone unnoticed if Preacher had not been looking at Hashmal when he disappeared.

A slight rustling in the woods behind Preacher caused him to turn. There, standing next to a tree was Hashmal. "It is an effective form of travel, as long as you know where you are going." Hashmal moved through the backyard effortlessly and without making a sound. He walked back to the spot he was standing at before. Hashmal looked at Preacher and nodded to the shadow.

"When you step, think of the place that you want to go, make sure to hold it in your thoughts. It makes sense that we should try somewhere familiar first. So, think of somewhere you are comfortable, somewhere safe."

Preacher walked to stand next to Hashmal. Somewhere safe and comfortable, somewhere familiar. A few places crossed his mind, but he banished them all as quickly as they came. He thought about the house sitting behind him, the old house that he lived in with M.C., his childhood home. He denied all of these locations. Finally, a place came to mind that he knew by heart. He knew every square inch of the place. The feeling of the floor under his feet and how it dipped down slightly when you first walked in.

Preacher stepped into the darkness of the shadow, the icy chill of nothingness swept across his legs. Instinct made him want to pull back and step out of the darkness, but curiosity kept him in place. A coldness swept across his body. No, not coldness, coldness implied that there was a sensation. This was nothing, no gravity, no air, no light. His skin searched for sensations of the world. Searching for a feeling and finding nothing created a searing pain. Like motivation, false sensation seemed better than no sensation at all.

It must have taken a split second, yet felt like years. Preacher's feet were on solid ground, his left foot settled in the small dip in the floor. He knew that Hashmal was behind him, though he didn't hear him follow. Smiling to himself Preacher took in his surroundings, and with pleasure, he knew it would irritate the shit out of Hashmal.

Liquor bottles lined the walls set on shelves and racking. Boxes of liquor set the foundation for displays of discounted booze and special sales.

The air inside was stale, it was the smell of dust in the air that was familiar. The slow-selling merchandise had not been dusted in a few days. In these early morning hours, the lights were off. The dim daylight coming through the little window space that was not covered by posters and neon signs was more than enough to work with.

"You cannot be serious," Hashmals voice showed all the signs of irritation, bordering on angry. "You feel safe and comfortable here, inside of a liquor store? You couldn't step us to your bedroom, or basement, or another place in the woods behind your home?"

Preacher smiled and took a few steps forward. He took two bottles of whiskey off the shelf and thrust them into Hashmals hands. He then turned and got two more. "I have prayed for help, I have spent countless hours on my knees in church praying. I have called out to God for comfort, for guidance, and for peace of mind." Preacher scoffed and rolled his eyes.

"Do you know what helps me sleep better at night Hashmal? This. Drinking helps me sleep. It helps me to numb the pain that I feel. I have seen too much, I feel too much, and this helps me to stay objective."

Preacher looked at Hashmal and for the first time Preacher seemed to let down his defenses. "There was too much I wanted to fix, and the Church wouldn't let me. After I lost M.C., I turned to drinking. I drink, and I drink a lot. You might be looking for a teaching moment, but I'm looking for some booze." Preacher reached into his pocket and removed his wallet. He dropped some money on the counter, after all, thou shalt not steal.

"This is a place that I am not judged or lied too. Things here are never hidden from me, and I am never critiqued. I don't lose anything here, I always know exactly what I am going to get." Preacher nodded to the shadow. "Now let's get back so I can learn some more."

Preacher stepped through the shadow leaving Hashmal to follow without a word.

16.

The alarm was going off. Again. It was such an annoying device. Yelling at you when to wake in its own annoying way. Sure you could pick the annoyance, but that didn't really make it any better. This morning her annoyance was one of her favorite tracks. Ken Ishii was playing live at the Loft in Barcelona Spain.

She smiled to herself thinking that she may just lay in bed for the entire track. This particular track lasted three hours. After drowning herself in research for the last two days straight, it was really the least that she deserved.

Besides, it was warm under her covers and freezing in her room, just the way that she liked it. She reached out to silence her alarm and was disappointed when the musk of body odor followed her movement. With one fatal sniff, her morning in bed was over.

Tossing the covers aside she allowed the chill of the room to sweep over her body. She slid her legs off the bed and found her soft cotton pajama pants laying bunched on the floor. She slipped them on admiring the cute but obscure anime character on them.

A shower was in order and then breakfast, after that she suspected there would be more research to follow. Raz grabbed a shirt and threw it on, and took her towel from the hook next to the door. This definitely was not like living in the life of luxury, but she had her own room, and she was safe. It was more than she had growing up.

Raz walked to the bathroom and gladly found it unoccupied. She started the shower and waited for it to warm up before undressing and stepping in. From there it became ritual. Wash the body with soap to cleanse, then using oils for the hair to purify (and smell good).

Stepping out of the shower, she dried quickly. She applied oils to close her body off, preventing all foreign bodies from entering. After she used the oils, she dressed and headed back towards her room. Breakfast was only a few moments away, and the thought of that made her smile.

The smile faded when she got back to the door. There was a note folded and taped to her door. It was the first time she had found a note taped to her door, and as is the custom in her life, she took all new things with ninety-seven percent loathing and three percent curiosity.

Raz walked into her bedroom and placed the wet towel back on the hook and unfolded the letter that was left for her. She was not surprised to find unfamiliar handwriting on the note.

Raz,

I looked around the house and found that you were missing a few items that will come in handy tonight. Please go to your magic shop and purchase the following items for a compound we need to make this afternoon.

- Sulfur, pure rock form, we will grind with pestle and mortar
- Shaved rattlesnake skin
- 6 – 8 dried maggots
- 6 dried adult botflies
- 6 dried black widows
- 2 fangs from a black mamba (rattlesnake will work in a pinch)
- 3 dried scorpions
- Leaves and stems of Rhubarb, tomato plants, dried Wolfsbane
- Anvil Dust (or iron shavings in a pinch)
- Sea Salt, not that iodized stuff in the pantry
- Bone Shavings

Remember to have gloves for us both, we don't want this on our skin once done. See you at 4 to mix!

~ Michael

She read the list over a few times. An uneasy feeling grew every time she finished. There were some heavy-duty black magic ingredients on this list, and she was not sure what Michael had in mind. Of course, she could say the same thing if he asked for unicorn farts, magic wands, a monkey's paw or any other number of things. Apart from small talk, she did not know the man.

Remembering that there was a guest, she sighed to herself. Company meant not wearing pajamas to breakfast, it meant a bra, a shirt with no holes and real pants. She dressed quickly taking time to look over the list again.

She already knew that she would have to make several trips to get everything on this list. In her community, witches were certainly curious. They were always asking what you were working on, and with this list of ingredients, she didn't want to answer too many questions.

First, breakfast and coffee. She tucked the note in her back pocket and left her room in search of caffeine and nutrition. Passing by the dining room, she saw that Josh was already busy flipping through old manuscripts that Michael brought with him. In his outstretched hand was a coffee mug still steaming with heat.

"For you sleepyhead." Josh did not even look up from his reading, whatever it was it held him in rapture. She took the cup gladly and sat next to him at the table.

"What's got your attention?" She took a sip of the coffee offered her and smiled as its warmth washed down her throat. Glancing at the book he was reading she could tell that it was a handwritten journal of some kind.

"One of the many journals Michael has written. He has had some fascinating thoughts over the years, that he either was too busy to follow up on or forgot about." Sliding a piece of plain paper into the book as a homemade bookmark, he closed it and looked at her. There were about fifteen stuck in that book alone.

"These old school exorcists are a different kind of hardcore. To the point of brutality sometimes." Josh sighed, closed his eyes, and pinched his nose with his thumb and forefinger. He did that when he was chasing an idea down the rabbit hole. He sighed loudly and little too dramatic for it not to have been planned.

"Are you headed out today? I think I have something that might work for us but need to get to a few places to get what I need to construct it." Josh asked.

"I am headed out and can drop you off. I've got a lot of stops so I don't know when I can pick you up." She leaned in her chair, looking into the kitchen. She could smell the remnants of breakfast coming across the house.

Nodding towards the kitchen, she glanced sideways at Josh "What did I miss in there this morning?" As if on cue, Gus walked from the kitchen with a plate in his hand. He smiled at his sister, in the annoying yet loving way only a brother can smile at his sister.

"Eggs and French toast. Preacher made coffee, and from the smell of it, he did it before the sun came up. I made a fresh pot." He shrugged "Neither of them are here, I don't know where they went, they didn't leave a note. Both cars and keys are here though."

Raz took the plate gratefully; after all, you cannot oversleep and expect a warm breakfast. Not in a house filled with what feels like family. She took breakfast and began eating.

"If you can drop me in downtown Woodstock I can pick up a few things and wait for you to pick me up at St. Michaels afterward." She could tell by how excited Josh was that he would wait as long as she needed and would only complain if he felt he could not tinker with his idea tonight.

"That's like three miles away, are you sure you want to walk that far?" She knew the answer before she asked. She and Josh were probably the two most active people in the house, followed by Gus and Preacher a very distant fourth.

Josh shrugged, as she knew he would. "Three miles isn't bad. Let me change real quick, and I will be ready." He stood and left, heading to his room to change.

Gus slid into a chair across from Raz, a cup of coffee still steaming. "What do you think of Michael?" Never one to beat around the bush Gus asked what was on his mind.

"I haven't really thought about it. I'm surprised he is here, I didn't think Preacher liked him that much." She paused to eat another bite of French toast. Her brother missed his calling; he should have been a chef.

"But he brought us a lot of new books." She pulled her note out of her back pocket and handed it over to Gus. "He also gave me a shopping list."

Gus raised his eyebrow slightly as he opened it. "Anything good?" There was a doubt in his voice; Raz wondered what she did to provoke it. Gus was always intuitive, she wondered if it was her wording, posture, a facial tick that she didn't know she had.

"Nothing" Raz handed the list to Gus and raised her eyebrows waiting for a response.

Gus let out a low whistle as he read the page over. "You're the witch, but this looks like nasty stuff. Do you know what he has in mind?"

Raz shook her head. "No, but I have a date with the internet to figure it out. I figure I am going to have to stop at four or five places to get what we need and avoid questions that I don't know how to answer."

Gus nodded. "When you find out what it is for let me know? You've got me curious." He handed the note back across the table to her, which she took and tucked into her back pocket.

"Of course. So, what are your big plans for the day?" Raz finished off her French toast while Gus answered.

"I'm going to continue research on the Holy Relics. If Michael truly possesses the Chains of St. Peter then in theory, we only need to find one more to be bigger and meaner than anything Hell can throw at us. Sounds worthwhile."

It did sound worthwhile, but Raz was resolute in staying skeptical. Josh came out of the hallway dressed in his usual attire, black slacks, and black button-up shirt. He was one white collar away from looking like a priest. If imitation was the highest form of flattery, then Preacher should be very flattered.

Raz slid out of her chair, grabbed her keys and her purse, and they were out the door and on their way to run their errands.

17.

Gus found himself alone for the first time in a long time. It wasn't that he was an introvert, quite the contrary, but when you lived with your boss, sister and someone you quickly started to think of like a little brother, you begin to wish for quiet moments.

Especially when your boss was an exorcist. Correction, The Exorcist. With the dishes wiped down and his coffee refilled, he looked over the mess that used to be the dining room table. He sighed to himself looking over the chaos and jumble of old texts and books.

He remembered the first time he saw Preacher. Preacher was so confident that Preacher almost seemed aloof. Gus and Raz were so scared for their mother's soul that he almost seemed disrespectful. He was beyond confident to the point of cocky.

It was only a few years ago, but it felt like a whole lifetime since Preacher was talking to his Aunt about the condition of his mom and how he and the Church could make it better. The understanding was that the Church would allow the exorcism, but the family had to remain quiet. The family would praise Jesus for the recovery and never mention an exorcism.

Gus wasn't sure if Preacher was working within the Church at the time of saving his mother, and he never asked. But at nineteen Gus made a promise to Preacher as he left his house.

Gus remembered his mother hugging him for the first time in months, his sister too. Everyone was crying, holding on tight. He disengaged from the embrace as he heard the exorcist leaving the room and walking down the hall.

"Father?" His words echoed through the hallway, and at that moment he wondered if the house had ever been that quiet. He wasn't sure he was heard until the priest stopped walking and cocked his head to the side to show he was listening.

"Thank you, Father. If I can ever if my family can ever repay this….." the priest's hand went up to silence him, and he fell silent.

"It is Gods will that we met. Gods will that your mother is free. There is no payment, other than to God." Preacher didn't look back, he just left the family to be whole together for the first time since what seemed like forever.

Time passed, days turned to weeks, then weeks to months. Over a year went by, and Gus watched his sister grow up and look for answers as best she could. He watched as she found her peace in Wicca. He did what he was comfortable with and found his solace in research and facts.

He never found what he was looking for. He never found a way to become a priest without leaving his family. Also, he didn't want to have to damn his sister (thou shall not suffer a witch to live). He thought, read, and struggled to find his place.

Then one day there was a knock at the door. Preacher was standing there. He was disheveled, with tears brimming his eyes. He was a broken form of the man that he once was. Preacher was hunched at the shoulders where he once stood proud. He looked at Gus but refused to meet his eyes.

"I need help. If you remember me, you remember who I am and what I have done, please remember your promise." Somehow Preacher's voice sounded small. It was scary for Gus to think back on.

That's all that needed to be said. Gus walked down the hall and began packing his bag when Raz walked into the room. A brief talk, she was packing her bag as well.

Gus pulled himself out of the memory and sat behind a pile of rolled parchments. At first, he was excited about these old tombs of knowledge. That faded almost immediately as they turned out to be very fragile. The ink was faded, and they refused to stay unrolled. The awe of working with old scrolls was quickly replaced with the frustrations that they brought.

He took the one that he was working on last night and slowly unrolled it. Fortunately, the penmanship of this one was excellent, and he was not going blind because of bad handwriting. The text was very dull though and seemed to describe in painstaking detail the diet requirements of some long dead Cardinal Baudet, who was an adjutant of Pope Clement V.

Rolling the scroll carefully back up he placed it to the side and took another one from the pile. Once unrolled and placed in front of him he looked at the parchment and the chicken scratch handwriting that covered it. It made his eyes want to cross. Unfortunately, there was no date to give him reference for when it was written. He was staring at something that could have been written at any point in history.

Gus sighed. Whatever language it was in, it wasn't English. He looked over the document to see if there was a translation in the margins or at the bottom, but he didn't have any luck. Slowly he rolled the scroll and placed it to the side to be translated later.

Scroll after scroll, the pile started to dwindle slowly. Collections to be translated, piles that he didn't think essential and a pile to follow up on. He was going to need a way to put these in order and find out all he could.

Leaning back, he pinched the bridge of his nose and let out a sigh. The table was in worse shape than when he sat down to begin with. He would need to organize it better. He let his mind wander over the best way to get things straightened out when he heard voices coming from the basement.

The voices were muffled, and he couldn't understand what was being said, but he recognized Preacher's tone. He assumed that the other was Michael. It was good they were back because he didn't know where to put these scrolls that he didn't think would be of help.

He stood from his chair, stretched his sore back muscles and headed down to the basement. He crept down the stairs quietly. He used to love sneaking around the house as a kid. He stepped lightly on his instep as he saw in ninja movies. With every step down the words becoming clearer.

"You should take this more seriously Brandon. You need to learn quickly, do not disrespect your gifts or these teachings." He could hear Michael clearly. He took the few steps left and opened the door.

As soon as he entered the garage, he noticed it was cold. It wasn't chilly, it was icy. Preacher and Michael were facing one other holding two bottles of whiskey each. They looked like two old wild west gunslingers ready to take a shot at each other. Each one wearing a sneer, their bodies tense as if they were waiting for a fist fight to start between them.

Gus cleared his throat to get their attention. Slowly Preacher and Michael tore their eyes from one another and looked over at Gus. Michael now wore a blank, emotionless expression. It was a mask crafted after years of working within the Church. Preacher, on the other hand, wasn't trying to hide his agitation.

"Sorry if our arguing disturbed you and your studies, is there something that you need Gus?" Michaels tone was flat, and from what Gus could tell, normal. There was something just a bit off about the sound, but he couldn't place his finger on it. It had been there since Michael first spoke, so he let it go.

"There are some scrolls that I don't think I need to go through just yet. I wanted to know where to place them to keep them safe." Gus felt like he did when he was a child and walked in on mom and dad fighting, he knew that he didn't do anything wrong, but it was still awkward. He was waiting for an explosion of anger to come at him.

There was no explosion of anger. Not even a sign to show frustration or annoyance. Michael just simply smiled. "Of course, let's look at what we have set aside to see if there was anything you missed that might be of importance." Simple as that, Michael headed towards the stairs. He was still double-fisting bottles of whiskey but looked eager to help. He didn't even glance at Preacher as he left.

Preacher didn't take his eyes off the old man as he moved, his scowl still in place. It wasn't until Michael was on the stairs and out of sight that Preacher relaxed.

"Everything alright with you two?" Gus asked. He wasn't sure what he expected as a response, but all he received was a curt nod. He figured that would be all he received in the way of an answer, so he let it go at that.

Gus retreated back upstairs and found Michael standing next to a trunk that he had not seen before. Michael was looking over the piles of scrolls running a hand over them. It was the touch of a man looking over a beautiful collection that he was proud of. He plucked one off the table and turned it over in his hands looking at it from different angles but not opening it.

Without looking back, Michael asked "Which pile did this come from? Is this one that seems to be unimportant?" Michael placed it back into the pile that he retrieved it from, and glanced over at Gus.

Gus shook his head, "No that is a pile that needs translation, I don't know the language."

Michael nodded approvingly. "That is good. Something easily dismissed because it's not immediately understood can be a fallacy. This scroll describes the journey of a young man after he came of age and left his father's house. The only item he was to inherit upon leaving was his great, great, grandfathers hammer. Boring to read really, until you see the name at the end, Lehabim, son of Mizraim, son of Ham, who in turn was the son of Noah."

Letting it sink it for a moment Michael was silent. "When you follow the lineage of Lehabim, his family settled into the area of Ancient Libya. Little is known about them other than their nomadic nature, warrior lifestyle, and affinity for hammers."

Michael looked back at Gus with a sad smile, like he was remembering something meaningful and personal to him. "Which of these piles do you think less important than the others?"

Gus shrugged a little like an embarrassed child. "When you put it that way, I am not sure I think any are less important. Maybe I just don't currently have the right context."

Michael nodded like the lesson was learned and reached down to open the trunk by his knee. "That is good because there are some more." Reaching down he opened the truck to reveal rolls and rolls of parchments, and volume upon volume of books. "I did tell you that I do not pack lightly." Michael smiled and walked back towards the stairs to head back down.

"You may want to give him a few more minutes Michael. Let him cool off."

Michael paused and glanced back at Gus. "He is only upset because he knows that I am right and he needs to stop acting like such a child. He will get over it." And with that, he turned and headed back down the stairs.

Gus looked at the volumes of literature that sat on the table and inside the trunk. He wondered briefly how long it took to mass this volume of texts and if Michael was the one to amass them all.

First, though, he needed to get this house into order. When Raz and Josh got back, they would probably go right into working. Everyone would want to eat, and that meant a clean dining room table.

Carefully he placed the scrolls into the trunk and moved the books out of the way for the place settings. As he came around the table making a full circle of wiping it clean and getting things out of the way he bumped into the trunk. If he hit it, then others would too, so that meant it needed to move.

He bent at the knees (always lift from the knees), and he grabbed the handles on the trunk and lifted. But it barely moved. It was heavier than he thought. Holy crap, how did Michael move this in here on his own?

He sighed. He would get Josh or Preacher to help when they were free. Turning his mind to dinner, he walked to the kitchen. It seemed like a good night for chicken parmesan over angel hair pasta.

Father Michael spoke English well enough, but there was something about his dialect that made him think that there was more Italian blood in him than just living there for years. He thought it would be nice to bring him back to the old world while he was visiting. Add some oven roasted Brussel sprouts, and maybe a baked parmesan cauliflower. The dish came together in his mind like an artist visualizing a painting before it is finished. That was tonight's meal. He would have liked to have red wine with it, but they were out of red wine. Whiskey would have to suffice.

18.

Preacher was annoyed. Annoyed didn't really seem actually cover the emotions that he was feeling, but he couldn't think of another word other than annoyed. Michael went from the berating-overbearing-no-fun-having clergy that Preacher remembered, to a benevolent, caring, teacher that he always wanted. He did it in a blink of an eye, and he did it for Gus.

He wasn't sure if he was more annoyed that Michael could do that or if, as usual, Michael was right about his behavior. He was acting childish. Well at least acting like a rebellious teenager. He really should start thinking about the task before him. But the task was so vague. Go find a Demon then get the information from a Demon, then don't get eaten by the Demon. Like calling Demon four-one-one.

The fact that this Demon has somehow walked the Earth this long, and has never been discovered by the Church, made no sense. There was a theory that the Joined could extend the lifespan, but this was too close to immortality for comfort.

He walked to his woodworking bench and found a mason jar full of screws and sawdust. He dumped the contents, hastily blew out the dust and poured himself half a jar of whiskey. Usually, he wanted his whiskey chilled, but right now he didn't care.

He drank half his glass in one swallow, taking comfort in the warm burning sensation that came down his throat. Thinking about the endgame he wasn't sure what he had to gain. He would save the women that he loved from being possessed by a Demon, but after that, there wasn't a lot to look forward to. Even if she could forgive him, he would never forgive himself.

With some effort, he shook himself out of the train of thought. There would be time to have a pity party once the Demon was out of her. He heard light footsteps coming down the stairs, Michael was coming back. Preacher poured more whiskey in the jar.

"You should start packing for tonight. This is going to be something that you have not faced before. Iron Chains. Holy Water, Salt. I have Raz picking up some items to make you something special."

"You're still not going with me, are you? It's a shitty pattern you have here, give me a little knowledge, a little training and then off ya go, leaving me on my own." Preacher took a sip from the jar. "I shouldn't be surprised though should I."

Preacher walked passed Michael and through the door that separated the garage from the basement. Four smaller rooms branched off the hallway, two workrooms with benches and tables, a bathroom, and a workroom that Josh was sleeping and working in.

Preacher walked into the first room. The first bench sat covered in small bags of rock salt, empty shotgun shells, primers, black powder and a press for manufacturing the rounds at the house. A five-gallon bucket sat underneath the bench half-full of water, three crucifixes resting in the bottom of it. It was like a slow churn for holy water.

Knives and throwing stars were hanging on one of the walls, with iron chains hanging below them at different lengths. A small shelf in the corner housed a medium sized nine-millimeter pistol and several hundred rounds of ammunition.

Preacher took his leather bag still packed from his last hunt and sat it on the table. He was careful not to knock over the container of communion wafers on the table. He removed the shotgun, cracked the short barrel, and unloaded the spent ammunition. Michael raised an eyebrow at the room as he took in his surroundings.

"This seems more violent than I remember teaching you." Michael walked over to the wall of knives and chains. "Unless of course, this is a strange sex room. If that is the case, then we need to have a confession."

Preacher let the joke go without giving Michael the satisfaction of laughter. Somewhere deep inside though he chuckled to himself. Silently he plucked the cleaning kit from a shelf in the corner, sat on a stool, and set himself to cleaning the weapon.

Michael busied himself with inspecting the room, silently walking from item to item looking at each. "You have quite an arsenal here. What do you imagine you will need for tonight?"

"My usual kit. Gutenberg Bible, olive oil, wafers, cross, holy water, iron chain, and rope. If it gets crazy, I'll have iron knuckles, the shotgun, and my wits. This isn't my first rodeo."

"Rope? With chains, guns and...... your wits, why are you bringing the rope?"

"Charlie Bronson's always got a rope." Preacher smirked "If it's good enough for him, its good enough for me. Plus it's reusable and will soak up holy water and olive oil. Duct tape can be used for binding a body in a pinch, but that is usually more difficult than just trying a knot."

Michael let out a low, slow sigh, a sign of his disappointment in his pupil. "What about the pistol?"

"You know as well as I do that the pistol is for self-defense. I usually won't bring it. I shot the first Joined that I came across and it didn't even phase it. I had to resort to reloading the bullets with iron or filling the hollow points with holy water sealed with wax before it had any effect.

Michael nodded slowly, his eyes closed almost as if he were centering himself. "I pray that soon you will be able to free all of those that should be freed, even those that are Joined."

Preacher let the words rattle in his brain like a pinball bouncing around the machine. Ideas bounced off one barrier to meet another lever to propel it further. Why would Michael say that? Preacher wondered if that was a clue he should take the pistol tonight or if Michael was just playing the pious priest, hoping for peace and tranquility?

He took a glance over at Michael and saw that he had his eyes closed and his head slanted at an odd angle towards the door out of the room. It was only a split second that Preacher was looking at Michael before he seemed to be drawn back into the world. "Raz and Josh will be returning soon. I will leave you to this cleaning and packing, I don't think I'll be of much use to you."

Michael stepped out of the room and headed back towards the garage leaving Preacher to his work. It wouldn't be long before he would need to assist Raz in combining the ingredients that he requested of her.

He walked into the garage and plucked a mason jar off the shelf. There was one errand to run before they returned though. It would be rude to send Raz on an errand and not fulfill his part of the obligation.

He slipped into the shadows and allowed the emptiness of nothingness to roll over him. He emerged from the shade of an oak tree, miles from the house he was just standing in. The wind blew lightly causing the leaves to rustle above him.

Tombstones of various heights and design lay in neat, tight rows surrounding him. It was a good day for a funeral. Glancing down the hill, he could see the services were coming to an end and began a slow, somber walk towards the grave.

He read in the obituaries that Lloyd Webster passed away peacefully in his sleep surrounded by his family after a long, fierce battle with cancer. Lloyd was a good man, who served God faithfully even after being drafted and sent to Vietnam. Faithful to his Country, Corps, and wife, he lived a long life full of hard work and good deeds.

Of course, none of that mattered for his purpose. He needed graveyard dirt from a freshly dug grave. This was the only service being held in the area that he could find, well, the first one that he saw. This man's virtue and good deeds in life were utterly irrelevant in this decision. Part of him would like to believe that Lloyd would like to contribute to the good fight one more time, so maybe that is why he quit looking for other funerals.

The pastor was leading the widow away with her children closely in tow when he slowed his walk. Friends and family slowly made their way back to their cars leaving him alone near the grave with the funeral home attendants and cemetery workers waiting to fill the grave. Waiting for a respectful moment (which also ensured that none of the guests would return) he walked to the gravesite.

The funeral home workers were busying themselves with gathering up the photos and the chairs while the cemetery workers waited patiently. Michael approached slowly and waved at them to get their attention.

"Good afternoon gentleman." Michael smiled pleasantly as each muttered their greetings to the old man walking through the cemetery. "If I could trouble you, Lloyd was a longtime friend, I wonder if you could spare me a moment alone with him."

Michael did his best to look the part of a pitiful and sad friend. The workers apparently either bought the story or didn't care because they all gave a nod and respectfully walked away. Michael took a knee near the grave and took the jar out of his coat pocket. He scooped the dirt into the jar, filling it to the brim.

Making the sign of the cross he stood and without a word, he began making his way back to the shade of the oak tree across the graveyard. The breeze was gentle as it brushed across the exposed skin on his arms. It was a good day for a funeral. One-day, Hashmal would leave him, and he would be placed in the ground to rest. He hoped that when that day occurred, it would be a day like this.

He made his way to shadows of the oak tree. Michael had always believed that he should be buried in the catacombs in Rome. However, looking around at the serenity here in this place, and feeling the sun on his skin, he began having second thoughts.

Maybe Georgia would be a good place to die after all.

Sighing deeply, he shook the emotions off and stepped back into the shadows of the tree. Sliding through nothing as if he were nothing, he slipped back to the garage in silence. Taking in the surroundings, he heard Preacher in his armory working and could sense Gus upstairs working on the texts. Being alone Michael shed a single tear for himself and allowed it to roll down his cheek.

Wiping the tear from his cheek, he straightened up and centered himself. There would be time enough to grieve for his own demise later. As if on an emotional cue, one of the garage doors opened. Raz and Josh stood outside waiting for the door to open. Raz carried several bags, all of different colors and sizes. Josh on the other hand only had two tiny bags. The two were halfway into the garage before they noticed him standing there.

Raz let out a startled yip and then calmed herself as she looked at the old man. Josh, however, was lost in thought and headed straight for his room to work.

"I went to five places to get all these things and had to make up two young cousins that have a creepy fascination with poisonous creatures just to make sure that no one asked too many questions. You ready to tell me what this is all for?"

Michael didn't seem to notice any anger in her voice, but there was an edge of annoyance. He nodded slightly and smiled a paternal smile "Of course. Let's get to work." He let her lead the way into the basement past the armory.

Raz's workroom was much different than Preachers armory. There were pictures of different Japanese Anime characters on the walls. Each wall had four shelves running the length of them. The right wall carried jars of herbs and other solid substances packed so tightly that they almost touched. On the back wall, there were live plants, UV lamps to help them grow, and jars of liquids filled to various degrees.

The left wall seemed like a collection of random objects, rocks, glass, and other objects that may come in handy when spell crafting. Several books lined the bottom shelf, most of which Michael recognized on sight.

Raz dumped the bags on the table that sat in the middle of the room. She reached in one and produced two sets of rubber gloves that came up to the elbow. She took a set and held it out to Michael. "I am ready when you are."

Michael took the gloves and smiled his teachers smile. "First things first," he paused and nodded to the books on the shelf. "I will make, and you should take notes. You never know when this could come in handy."

Raz smiled as she went to pick up her personal spell book to annotate this in.

19.

Josh was standing over his bench looking at the components scattered before him. Springs of various sizes, plastic cases, and 200-pound test fishing line were organized haphazardly in only a way that would make sense to him.

He finished winding the fishing line around a spindle, set the spring and closed the casing. He slowly affixed lead weights to the end to give it weight. He lifted it off the table and pulled on the string making sure that he hadn't used too much weight. Too much weight and it wouldn't retract. He pulled out some of the test line and let it go. The line snapped in so quickly that the case broke apart in his hands and pieces of his device flew across the room.

He allowed the puzzle to roll through his mind as he picked up the pieces. Once everything was gathered, and on the table, he determined that the case was the problem, not the spring mechanism. Having that much strength on the retraction would allow the device to function correctly.

A knock on the door frame drew Josh's attention from the project in front of him. Gus was standing in the doorway looking at the items on the table. "What are you working on now?" Stepping into the room Gus walked over to the table looking over the springs and cases.

"Retractable crucifix. Got the idea from the retractable badge holders, pull out to scan card, then let go and it returns. I thought that it could have applications for emergency restraints, might be able to add a release button so it could fly across the room and wrap up an arm or something." Josh shrugged. "But the first attempt did nothing but make a mess, so we'll see."

Gus grinned. "I like the thought. Kind of like a garrote, but for Demons."

Josh cocked his head to the side, common for when he was troubleshooting a problem. "That would be possible if I could get an iron alloy that might work. The problem would be how stiff the wire is."

"What about piano wire? That's what all the criminals in the movies use right?"

Josh nodded slowly. "Piano wire might work, but they stopped using iron wire in pianos in the mid eighteen hundreds. It's all carbon fiber wire now. You would get the same effect from the fishing line, neither will soak and retain holy water, maybe some holy oil but that would cause the wire to rust."

"How do you know anything about piano wire?" Gus asked.

Josh grinned. "I played piano since I was little. I've always been musically inclined. I could name every piece of the piano and give you a whole lecture on its history. I remember things easily if I read something twice, I usually don't forget it." He sighed and looked at Gus. "I really could have been a good musician if I would have stayed off drugs. The pressure of being good musically and wanting everyone to like me was too much though. So, I did what I thought I had to do. That's how the Demon found its way in. I was weak, and it exploited the weakness."

Gus nodded needlessly and rested a hand on Josh's shoulder. "You are no longer weak. You are helping us take the fight to the enemy and doing an excellent job of it." Gus smiled and gave Josh's shoulder a squeeze like a big brother would to a younger one. "Dinner is in 30 minutes. I'll need your help moving a trunk that Michael brought with him before dinner. Can you come up in a few minutes to help me move it?"

Josh nodded absently while staring at the table in front of him. He was apparently moving his mind back to the problem in front of him. "Wait, who moved it to the dining room? Couldn't they move it back?"

Gus moved over and shut the door to Josh's room. He walked back over and lowered his voice to almost a whisper. "Michael moved it in somehow. I tried to move it, and it will not budge. Let's just move it out of the way and the rest we can figure out tomorrow."

Josh nodded. "I will pay more attention, and we will figure it out." He paused for a second "What do you know of Preacher and Michael? I have not heard any stories. I've never thought to ask of Preacher's past, it felt like an intrusion."

Gus paused for a moment. "He has always played those cards close to his chest. Preacher doesn't talk a lot about how things were before he left the Church, other than they didn't work for him. There hasn't been a conversation about what happened after he left. Not with any detail anyway."

Gus smiled and put his hand back on Josh's shoulder "Preacher saved my mother, and he saved you. As strong as he is in the mission we partake in, he is just as weak somewhere else. When he wants to talk about that weakness, we will be there for him. We practice faith during these exorcisms. Its faith in God and in Preacher to guide us through. The joining of the Church and Witches has not taken place in over eight hundred years. There is no real record of what happened when it did. It is the curse of being on the wrong side of history."

Josh allowed the words to sink through for a few moments. "I am frightened that when he needs me, I won't be enough."

Gus chuckled in a comforting way, somehow he was able to convey through laughter that no judgment was passed. "We both do, but the only way to make sure that we are is to do the best we can. You are doing great, and you should be more confident. Keep tinkering. It will count when it matters. But more pressingly come help me move this chest."

They shared a chuckle as Gus walked out of the room. Josh watched as Gus went across the hall to Michael and Raz in her workshop.

Raz had a book in front of her, and even from a distance, he could see the page was full of her bright penmanship. Leave it to Raz to take notes in the most vivid colors of the rainbow. Michael was wearing yellow dish gloves that stood out brightly against his black long sleeve shirt. He was grinding something in a dish with a mortar. Whatever else he was, Michael was old school. Gus gave them the dinner count down.

Upstairs standing in front of the trunk with its lid open Josh just stared down. The chest was full of books and scrolls. "He moved this by himself? Are you sure that Preacher didn't help?"

Gus nodded. "Preacher was in the garage with me." Gus closed the lid, and the two bent down and took hold of the trunk. Together they lifted straining to get the chest out of the dining room and into the living room.

Grinning slightly, Gus looked over at Josh, "Told you it was heavy."

Josh nodded. The aroma of dinner was coming from the kitchen, and it smelled terrific. "When am I going to be able to eat whatever is making that smell?"

"Soon, can you help me set the table? Raz and Michael are making something that requires industrial gloves, they don't get to touch the plates."

Josh nodded and went down the hall to wash up. Once done there he set to work setting the table. Not making place settings correctly, instead, Josh was putting a plate in front of a chair and then putting silverware on top. Josh knew the proper order of etiquette, but no one here seemed to care, so he did not bother with it anymore.

Raz's laughter bubbled up from the steps shortly before footsteps could be heard coming up them. The two entered into the dining room and saw Josh setting the table. They seemed almost like two teenagers caught sharing a secret.

Raz stifled her laughter and headed down the hallway towards the restroom. Michael grinned to Josh and walked into the kitchen where Gus was placing dinner into serving dishes. He could hear Michael and Josh exchanging words about the meal back and forth, though he couldn't make out the words.

Maybe the brother and sister were being polite to the old man. There was something inside of him though that made him question that thought. Both Gus and Raz had expressed their concerns about Michael, yet after being in his presence for only a little while, their apprehensions seemed to just evaporate.

Gus brought in a large plate in one hand with enough chicken parmesan to serve the house and neighbors. In the other hand was a large platter of pasta that was glistening light off of the oils it was coated in.

As he set them down on the table, he looked at Josh and then back at the table. "Glasses? Some of us would like to drink something that doesn't come straight out of a bottle. There is a pitcher of water in the fridge also. Grab that as well please."

Josh went to the kitchen to get the items that were requested. It was an unusual request really because generally by this time everyone was drinking something and usually carried their own glasses to the table.

He returned clumsily with the pitcher of water and four water glasses. Preacher would bring his own whiskey glass. As a former addict, he saw troubling signs in Preacher and his drinking. He also knew that Preacher was not ready to have that confrontation yet. Doing so would only drive him further down the rabbit hole, and if that happened, Preacher could be lost to everyone.

Josh heard the basement door open and the familiar thud of Preachers coming up the stairs. Josh took his place at the foot of the table, and Michael sat next to him. He was a little surprised that Michael didn't sit at the head of the table honestly.

Gus smiled at Raz when she returned from washing up and waved her into the kitchen. She followed him in, and they came back with salad bowls and an antipasto of caprese. Gus was feeling his Italian flair this evening apparently.

Raz and Gus sat at the table in their usual places across from each other. Usually, they wouldn't wait for everyone, they would just dig in. But with the company present, it only seemed right.

Preacher came up with his "go-bag." The leather bag that he carried on all exorcisms was in his left hand and an empty mason jar in his right hand.

Solemnly Preacher sat the bag down in the living room before going to the kitchen and filling his mason jar with ice. Retrieving a bottle of whiskey from the kitchen, he joined them at the table. Looking at the food in front of him Preacher smiled.

"If I would have known this is how we would eat Gus, I would have brought company home a long time ago." The comment drew laughter from everyone except Gus who thought (rightfully so) that his cooking was always excellent, and Michael, who didn't know any better.

Preacher reached and took hold of the pasta plate when Michael began to cough an obnoxiously fake cough. He didn't stop until all eyes were on him. "I assume we pray and give thanks here." Michael stretched out his hands to Gus and Josh. Then gave the rest of the table the "old innocent Priest" look that he had down to a science.

20.

After the prayer, smiles seemed to find every face except Preachers. Food and compliments went across the table with the ease of a summer breeze. Michael seemed to avoid looking too far in Preacher's, direction and that was fine by him.

One drink for Preacher led to another, and to another. Preacher seemed distracted playing with his food rather than eating it. For Preacher, the feeling was like being lost in a small crowd. Something he already felt more comfortable with than he should. Especially when he was sitting at his own dining room table.

"So Michael, after so many years within the Church what does it feel like to be retired and not have to live within all those stuffy rules?" Raz giggled as she asked the question, she always liked to mess with the clergy a little.

"I think I like it very much." Michael paused to ponder his words "I enjoy being free from the rules and politics that go on inside the Church. You wouldn't believe the ego of some of these humble priests."

Preacher scoffed and looked at Michael. "I remember your ego, and it wasn't exactly small."

"Perhaps not, but it was small enough to accept my place and the wisdom of those that came before me. I learned many lessons over the years and had the privilege of passing on my knowledge to others."

Preacher finally took a bite of food, and it was heavenly. Having Gus in the house was indeed a blessing. "You passed on some good lessons and some difficult lessons. But at the end of the day, all of them were the same. It's Gods Will, or its part of Gods plan, or the Lord works in mysterious ways. There was never anything concrete to cling to, nothing to rationalize, and the older I get, the less sense it makes."

Michael chuckled. "Your statement reminds me of a story. You see there was this man on a religious pilgrimage walking across Europe. Halfway through his journey, he found that his gold had run out, and innkeepers wouldn't give him charity."

The pilgrim found a cave that overlooked an orchard and a field where sheep grazed, and there he stayed for a few days. One day he saw the boy who tended to the sheep was asleep in the field and someone had stolen all the sheep. When the Lord that employed the boy found that all the sheep had been taken he had the boy put to death.

When our pilgrim heard this, he threw up his hands to God, cried out about the injustice, and dared God to come forth and explain himself. God, of course, did not appear to explain himself. Instead, an Angel appeared before him and said that God had sent him and he will be joining him on his pilgrimage.

The two journeyed to the next city several miles away and reached the town as the sun was setting. They arrived weary and tired but met a Knight who brought them to his home and shared food and wine. The Knight had only an infant son, and he was the pride of his life, and he spoiled the infant as only the wealthy could. The Knights wife died in childbirth, so the child was all he had.

The pilgrim and the Angel were shown to their room for the night and laid down to sleep. The pilgrim woke in the middle of the night to see the Angel leaving the bedchambers. Curious, he followed the Angel into the infant's room where he witnessed the Angel smothering the baby in his crib.

The Pilgrim wanted to confront the Angel but was afraid to do so. He was only a man, and this was an Angel of the Lord. Who was he to reprimand the Angel?

Early the next morning the two left the city and went towards the next town. It took all day, and when they arrived, a nobleman met the two and offered to house them for the night. The nobleman was rich. The house held all the comforts one could desire. It was large and warm, decorated in the finest of things.

Preacher tasted the baked cauliflower and thought it needed more salt. "Gus, could you pass the salt?" Gus acted like he wasn't even spoken too, he was listening to Michael's story.

The nobleman had a golden chalice that was his most prized possession. He drank from it more frequently as the night grew longer. He spoke of its beauty, the smoothness of its texture, and above all else, its value.

The next morning as everyone slept the two departed the house of the nobleman. On the way out, the Angel stole the golden chalice. The Pilgrim saw the Angel take the chalice and thought to himself that surely this was like no other Angel in Heaven. Still concerned of the sins but relieved that it wasn't murder, the Pilgrim moved on in his journey and headed for the next city.

It wasn't long before they found themselves at the edge of a cliff. There they stood pondering which way to go. To the north was a bridge only an hour away. To the south, it would take days to get to a bridge. After a while, a hermit came upon them, and the Angel asked most politely which direction the nearest bridge was. The hermit pointed in the direction of North and treated the two politely.

As the hermit began to pass on his way the Angel grabbed him and flung him into the river below and to his death. The Pilgrim thought that indeed he was traveling with an agent of the devil and shouldn't proceed any farther with this companion.

"Gus, could you pass the salt please?" Preacher raised his voice more this time to try to make himself heard, but no one even looked in his direction.

But the pilgrim was only mortal and knew that he could not dare subject this being to his wrath. He suffered in silence as they made their way to the closest bridge and to the next city. That night they slept in the wilderness, creating a small fire to keep any predators at bay.

They reached the next town during midday and went house to house asking for solace and a place to sleep. The pilgrim had no coin to offer and was refused time and time again. It wasn't until night that they came upon a home where they were greeted most ungraciously, almost hostile. But finally, they were afforded a place to sleep in stables with livestock.

That night they ate the scraps from the families table that was a combination of broth and slop. They slept in the stables on hay that smelled of horse piss with no pillows or blankets. Many hours before sunrise they were awakened by the man of the house when he was preparing the horses for his day.

The Angel came from the stall and offered the stolen golden and jeweled goblet to the man as payment for housing and feeding them. The token was most gratefully accepted, and the two were dismissed from the property.

"Gus, please pass the damn salt!" Preacher's voice was loud. He was starting to become angry that no one was paying any attention to his request for salt.

Once they were clear of the home, the Pilgrim turned to the Angel and denounced him. You are an agent of the devil! He exclaimed I refuse to walk with you any longer! But the Angel smiled a gentle smile and asked him why he felt this way.

You smothered a baby in its crib, stole from a man that let us into his home, threw a helpful man off a cliff and gave the only person that refused to help us a fortune in the form of a goblet that you stole. In every way you could have flourished in evil, you have. Also at every chance, you have turned away from justice and the righteousness of God.

The Angel looked at the Pilgrim with a stone face. The boy looking over the sheep was put to death for losing the sheep. God did not intervene because the boy was a rapist and a murderer and should have been put to death because of those crimes. God allowed him to be killed because of those sins he had not repented for.

The child that I smothered in its crib died innocently. His father, before the child was born, was a devote Christian, pious and generous. After his son was born he spoiled the child, and left those in need that he once helped in poverty. He placed the needs of his child before all, including God.

I stole the chalice from one who prospered from God's Grace and then placed the value of his possessions above God. Before he had the chalice, he was amongst the most pious men in the world. The man turned to drink once the chalice was his, instead of turning to God. I took the idol and soon he will stop drinking and return to God.

The hermit that I drown was indeed a good Christian. However, he was going to a city of sin and inequity. Soon he would have found himself in a house of flesh and gambling. He would turn to un-repented sin before death, and he would have gone to hell.

The one that housed us in his barn when there was room in his house to give. It bothers you that I gave him a chalice when he gave us nothing. This man's heart was black with sin, and he will burn in hellfire for the end of time. What should it matter if I gave him gold? His children will see their fathers' evil and not partake in it, but they will look at the rewards of the cup and bring blessings to those around them because of it.

I am an Angel of the Lord God, and I know his will. You are human and should not presume to know what lies before you or after you. You can only see what you know in the present. Live your life in service, and question not the Will of God.

The Angel dissolved into the air leaving the pilgrim to ponder his words and works of God.

"Would someone pass the fucking salt?" Preacher slammed his hands on the table and stood up. His outburst jarred the group's attention from Michael. Gus and Raz looked at Preacher with a mix of horror and astonishment. Josh made the sign of the cross and slid his chair back away from the table.

There was a flash of light that came from behind Preacher as he stood. It cast a long dark shadow on the wall behind him. Clearly visible in the shadow were Preacher's head, arms, torso, and a pair of wings that stretched from his body, reaching the corners of the room. Preacher's eyes were a churning blend of the same Golden hue that Hashmal presented, only black tendrils were visible coming from his irises. Each color seemed to be vying for control as they swirled and smoldered in Preacher's eyes.

Michael took a salt shaker from in front of Josh and slid it down the table towards Preacher. The table started to shake as Preacher watched the shaker slide towards him, causing the plates to rattle and water to spill from glasses that were almost full.

Preacher grasped the salt shaker in his hand and forcibly inhaled. Everyone could tell that he was trying to calm himself down and gain control of his emotions and the situation. Preacher forced himself back into his chair, grabbed the bottle of whiskey near him, and began to chug.

He forced his eyes closed and let the familiar burn in his throat center him. Setting the bottle on the table, he let the warmth of the whiskey fill his stomach, and felt it start to spread to the other parts of his body.

"Sorry." Preacher seemed to be struggling to catch his breath slightly. "It seems like I am going through Angel puberty at the moment. I just need a minute to cool off I think." Preacher took a few more deep breaths. "Michael can answer any of your questions. Please send all of them to him."

There was a stunned silence in the room as everyone looked at Preacher then to Michael. No one wanted to be the first to ask anything, but everyone wanted to ask something. Suddenly there was a cacophony of sound as everyone started asking something at the same time.

21.

The light had faded, and the shadow dispersed leaving the room a little dimmer somehow. Questions flew over each other rapidly, and louder each time one was ignored. Michael did his best to keep his calm but even he was taken by surprise. He raised his hands to slow the questions and gain control of the situation.

"One person at a time. I can't understand anything when all of you are shouting." Michael kept his voice even and allowed his old tone of authority to come through. This wasn't the first time that he found himself in a room of terrified children. These weren't children though, they were young adults. They had faced Demons before and defeated them. This time it was their mentor unfurling his Celestial presence over the walls because he wanted some salt.

Raz slid her chair back and pointed at Preacher. "What the fuck was that?"

Michael looked at Raz "First, watch your language." Michael raised an eyebrow asserting his authority over the table. "Secondly, given the circumstances and the request for salt, I would say that was rude and slightly selfish. Especially since I was telling a story." Michael shrugged as he looked around. No one seemed to think his joke was funny, except Hashmal who was laughing inside his mind.

"The question that you really want to be answered is 'Why did that just happen?'. That is a more complicated question. Preacher's mother was joined at his birth. It is unclear why, but he was born Nephilim. His Celestial side lay dormant for years almost as if it were locked away inside him."

"His abilities helped but were passive. Now they are becoming more active, and it will take us all some time to get used to it. It's a good thing. The power of the Nephilim has been absent from the earth since the time of the flood. It will be refreshing to have a heavy hitter on our side for once."

The three looked from Michael to Preacher who seemed very busy closing his eyes as tight as he could and massaging the bridge of his nose with his thumb and forefinger.

Without taking his eyes from Preacher Josh spoke to Michael "You could have told us."

Michael considered it for a moment before answering. "Yes. However, he asked that I not disclose his condition until he told you. It was his information to share." Michael shrugged "The sanctity of confession and the relationship between priest and confessor is still privileged."

"You are retired. Sanctity of confession should not apply." Gus made a matter of fact statement as naturally as he would have told someone his shoes were untied.

Michael furrowed his eyebrows in frustration. He could see that this team would dissolve if confidence in Preacher were shaken. So Michael did what he thought was best, he assumed the mantel of leader and mentor.

"And you know nothing of which you speak. You have not been to any college, much less seminary. Do not speak about the things you don't know. You have no more right to question me than a child has the right to talk back to their kindergarten teacher. I am here to help, and for me to help there will be times when you need to keep your mouth shut and your little opinions to yourself."

Michael stood suddenly, and the chair slid back to the wall. "Father Brandon needs three things right now. Leadership, support, and research. All of you have done a satisfactory job in your roles so far, and this is not the time to falter."

"Now, please clear the table and get back into your work. Father B.... Preacher and I will be departing soon. There are things to complete and work to be done."

Josh looked over at Preacher who was leaning back in his chair still massaging the bridge of his nose and taking long deep breaths. "He doesn't look like he is going anywhere, to be honest." Again, Gus stating facts that were as clear as the nose on his face.

"He will have to get over it. There isn't a choice, and there isn't much time." Michael motioned to the plates to get them moving and thinking about something other than what they just witnessed.

"What is the big hurry? I think we all need a minute to figure this out." Josh sounded assertive for the first time since coming to the team.

"Since Raz is the only magical practitioner on this team I will allow her to answer. Raz as a witch what is the most effective time to work your spellcraft?"

"It would depend on what you are trying to do. Certain spells are cast at different times of the year and under certain star alignments for better results. But that's only for a few highly powerful rituals from what I have gathered."

Michael nodded his approval, "Old magic requires adherence to much stricter rules. The more powerful the magic, the stricter the rules. Tonight there is a lunar eclipse, and there is little doubt that Baba Doek will not sit idly by and let it pass without furthering her goals."

Gus started to clear the table avoiding eye contact with Michael. "Is 'End of the world as we know it' magic possible during a lunar eclipse? I would hate to waste my last night on Earth looking over books and scrolls."

Michael consulted with Hashmal silently, to the room it looked like he was merely thinking. "It's doubtful. The darkness doesn't last long enough for heavy magick like that to be cast and take effect. But anything is possible."

The answer seemed to satisfy Gus, he nodded and took the first load of plates into the kitchen.

Raz stood and stormed out of the room. The house was silent except for the sound of her heavy footfalls and slamming of her door. Josh gathered up the rest of the plates, leaving the glasses for later. On his way out, he stopped near Preacher and placed his hand on his shoulder. After a reassuring squeeze, he left the room and disappeared into the kitchen.

Holding in a groan Preacher reached for the whiskey. "Well, that could have gone better." Preacher took a drink of the whiskey. "Not to sound like a broken record, but what the hell was that?"

"That was an attention grabber from the divine side of yourself. Throughout history, it has been something used to prove to humans that you can speak with divinity and the authority of God."

Preacher sighed. "Okay. Why am I tired now? I feel like I just ran a marathon."

"A Joined being will use the soul's power to accomplish divine or nefarious acts. Similarly, you will as well. Think of it like a new muscle that you need to work out and exercise. It will get better, and you will recover quicker."

Preacher sighed on the inside. He was starting to recognize the Michael-Hashamal switches. He wasn't sure if it was a comfort or an annoyance at this point. He nodded his understanding though. He didn't feel like having an argument at the moment.

He could feel some of his strength ebbing back into his system. It was good to know that Hashmal wasn't full of complete crap.

"Was what you said true? The world won't end tonight?" Preacher slid his chair back from the table. "I should get dressed for tonight's 'festivities.'" Preacher glanced at his bag taking a mental inventory of his items. Michel nodded, and Preacher headed down the hallway towards his bedroom.

As Preacher came closer to his room, he felt like he needed to check on Raz. He couldn't explain why, but Preacher passed his room and took the door handle to Raz's room and turned the handle.

It was locked. That was not unexpected, but it was unusual for the house. He knocked lightly on the door. Not sure what to expect, he waited silently in the hall. Several seconds passed, and Preacher almost retreated into his room to change when the door opened a crack.

He could only see half of her face. One bloodshot eye and one damp cheek told him enough of the story to understand.

"We should have talked about this sooner. I'm sorry that everyone had to find out this way." She nodded from behind the door. "We'll talk when I get back okay?" Preacher let himself sound as sorry as he felt. Raz nodded again then softly closed the door. Preacher sighed to himself. "Okay then, good talk." He said it more to the door than to himself.

He stepped into his room and closed the door. He quickly undressed and began dressing in his vestment. For Preacher, there was a comfort in preparing for an exorcism that his former colleagues had found unnerving. At least he always knew what kind of fight he was going into. Preacher guessed that there would be more things to unnerve his former colleagues if they discovered he was Nephilim.

Leaving the silence of the bedroom, he found Michael waiting for him in the hallway, also dressed in his vestment. "I didn't think that you were coming with me. Was there a change of heart?"

Michael shook his head. "No, I will be taking you to the location, but there are other things for me to do this evening."

Preacher nodded and went to find his bag of tricks. It was next to his chair in the dining room where he had left it. Gus was sitting at his usual place with a trunk of scrolls sitting next to him.

"I should have told you, and I am sorry that I didn't. I am still trying to wrap my own head around it, and I didn't know how to bring it up." Preacher paused waiting for Gus to look at him.

After what seemed like an eternity, Gus looked up to Preacher and made eye contact with him. "I can understand the dilemma and the hard choices you had to make." There was a pause, and Gus broke eye contact. "That doesn't mean that I condone it. When I agreed to come help, and Raz joined me, I thought it was understood that there wouldn't be any secrets. For me to continue to help you, I need to believe that Raz and I will be safer with you than on our own."

Preacher stayed in the dining room to consider his words. He was about to respond when Michael walked into the room. He looked between Preacher and Gus quickly. "Is there something that I can help with? We really should be on our way."

Gus looked at Michael and responded in the span of a heartbeat "We are talking about the trust of a family. Something you know nothing about. I have not been to any college, much less seminary, but I know more about family than you do. Please do not ask about the things you don't know, I don't have the time to tell you about it."

"Ouch, three points for a senior citizen burn awarded to Gus." Preacher started making his way from the dining room to the garage. When he noticed that Michael was not moving, he grabbed him by the back of the collar and started dragging him with him, "Let it go, old man, the youth must occasionally out think the elderly. We have other things to do tonight than cause the fall of my house remember?"

The footsteps started, and Michael followed without thinking. He was almost down the stairs to the garage when he remembered that yes, there were more important things too.

Once alone in the basement, Michael was able to take a second to think about what had just transpired in the dining room. "This is truly your house, isn't it? Not Gods house that you dwell in, but yours. Your house, your rules. Your way or the highway, right?"

"That's not right. In this house, we are a team. No one is better than the other, no one voice is louder than the others. All of our lives have been touched by evil, and we deal with it the best we can."

Michael nodded, not making eye contact. "I may have spoken out of turn upstairs then. I will apologize to everyone tomorrow and smooth things over."

Preacher grunted. "Let's worry about apologizes when we get back." He held out his free hand to Michael. "Right now I need to go kick the ass of some Super-Demon, and I need you to take me where he his."

Michael nodded. He took Preachers' hand and stepped into the nearest shadow. They disappeared from the garage leaving no trace that they were ever there.

On the other side of the garage door, Gus was listening to the conversation. After a few seconds of silence coming from the other side of the garage, he opened the door and walked in. There were no garage doors open and no outside security lights on. There was no indication that the pair shouldn't be in the garage.

Opening his cell phone, he looked at his most recent call history and selected an old familiar name that he knew he could trust, Bobby. Pressing the send button, he waited for an answer.

"Y'ello." Came the familiar greeting. The slight country twang of Bobby's voice was always comforting.

"Bobby, its Gus, ya have a second?" Straight to the point, no time for small talk.

"Sure, but I don't have anything you asked about the other night. Well, nothing concrete anyways if that's what you're calling about."

"No, sir. Something new. Ever hear of Nephilim?"

There was a silence on the other end of the phone, Gus assumed that it was Bobby thinking about an answer. After a second there was some static, Bobby was always reliable for a bad connection when something was important.

"Son, I am not an encyclopedia for the unexplained. What do you need to know?" Bobby's annoyance came through loud and clear through the static and lousy reception.

"I need to know what they are. They were mentioned once in the Bible, but that's my only reference. I need to know if they can be killed and how." Gus tried to sound normal like it was a run of the mill question.

"Give me a day or two, I'll look through the old books and call you back."

The line went dead like normal. Bobby wasn't one for goodbyes or lingering conversations on the phone. Gus had never met Bobby in person, but it seemed to be how he lived his life, and that was okay by Gus.

Returning upstairs to the scrolls he had access to, he made a mental note to track any reference to the Nephilim himself as well. The information would be the key to him navigating through the minefield that he was in. Knowledge would be his guide.

22.

His vision swam as they came out from the Darkness. The two were standing on the side of an old road that had been neglected for quite some time. The pavement was cracked and littered with potholes. There were no streetlights anywhere in sight.

Across the street from where they were standing was a large four or five-story brick building sitting on the top of a hill. It was dusk, and the sun was setting behind the building making it look like something out of a painting.

The wrought iron fence at the edge of the property stood tall. What was left of its black paint glinted in the fading sunlight. On top of the fence stood decorative spikes that were visibly sharp and detracted from the peaceful scenery.

Two brick pillars rose twelve feet into the air acting as a support for a closed iron gate. A simple bronze plaque rested on one of the cornerstones reading 'Rinehart's Asylum for the Relief of Persons Deprived of Their Use of their Reason. Established 1886 in the Commonwealth of Kentucky.'

Preacher inhaled slowly a long controlled breath. It was cold, much colder than a few seconds ago. He reread the sign just to make sure his mind wasn't playing tricks on him.

"Didn't feel like mentioning that this was going to be at a run-down old asylum did ya. We really need to work on your communication skills when it comes to important information."

Michael shrugged. "First, this place only looks run down. Bolfry has filled it full of patients. Secondly, I don't see how it would matter. Would it be better if you were to find the Demon in a rundown dingy motel room, or in the back of a strip club? Where you confront, the Demon isn't important. Even if it is in an abandoned asylum for the criminally insane."

"Michael, if you are giving me a choice, I will take the strip club any day of the week. Is he going to be going out later?" Preacher asked hopefully.

"No. It was a test, and before you ask, you failed." Michael nodded at the facility. "Inside you will find answers, but Bolfry will show you what he wants to be seen. He is a Trickster, lies are where he profits."

Preacher nodded and started for the gate. Michael reached out and grasped Preacher's arm, stopping him in his tracks. "Raz and I made something special for you today, just in case." Michael reached into his pocket and pulled out a small round glass vial filled with a dark grey powder.

"I like to think of it as goofer dust on steroids. Break glass in case of an emergency item, try not to get any on you." Michael grinned.

Preacher took the glass vial and took a close look at it. A small round glass container had a cork stopper at the top. The contents were an ashy gray sand mixture that shimmered when Preacher shook it in the light.

He tucked it into one of his pockets. "Do I want to ask more?" Preacher already knew the answer to the question. Preacher turned his head to Michael to say thanks, but he was already gone.

Preacher looked at the distance between him and the front door. He smiled to himself, it was shorter than the distance between his home and the liquor store, so he closed his eyes and stepped into the closest shadow.

He stepped on to the doorstep of Rinehart's. The double oak doors painted red stood before Preacher solid and foreboding. Preacher reached out to the right door to test the door, and it clicked, pushing slightly he opened the door with no resistance. The building was old, and there were no security cameras to been seen.

Pushing the door open completely Preacher walked into the reception room. Using his bag of tricks Preacher hit the door and closed the door behind him. The waiting room that he found himself in had a plush oriental carpet and two high back leather chairs to sit on. The receptionist desk was topped with marble, lending an air of authority to the counter and those that stood behind it. There was a faint smell in the air. One second it was there, the next it was gone. Like spoiled milk off in a corner somewhere.

There was no one behind the counter to present authority, just the sterile smell of a hospital to welcome him. Only one set of double doors were in the waiting room leading to the rest of the hospital, and they stood wide open, an invitation for Preacher to walk through.

The place was immaculate, considering it was abandoned. Preacher looked down the hall half expecting to see some orderly or nurse running this way or that. Taking care of their nightly duties or checking on the patients. There was no one there. No noises of people walking down long halls or squeaky wheels on linoleum like other hospitals Preacher had been in before.

As Preacher stepped through the doorway, he saw movement out of the corner of his eye. A rat or maybe a cockroach skittered along the baseboard of the waiting room, but when he looked at for the movement, there was nothing there.

Stepping through the double doors Preacher found himself in the center of a long hallway. Cinder block walls stretched to his left and right, painted a blinding white that reflected the light from the ceiling lights in the hall.

Preacher looked left down the long hallway. To his right, a light flickered in the corner of his eye. Preacher looked, and everything was different. Down the hall Preacher saw a rat, diving in and out of piles of trash that had collected along the floor. The smell of urine, both animal and human, assaulted his nose with a sudden onslaught.

Preacher's eyes watered from the smell. He blinked away the tears only to see that clean white hallway again. The aroma was gone as if it never existed. Preacher wasn't sure what kind of mental assault he was under, but he could sense the presence of evil.

From what Preacher could tell the hospital was empty. No sound came from the line of doors down either side of the hallway. He wasn't sure what he expected coming into an asylum, but he thought that there would be some noise. Either the scream of the insane, the squeak of rats, or the sounds of critters running the hallways, something. The silence was consuming, he couldn't even hear the hum of the lights in the ceiling.

Preacher turned to the right and walked to the nearest door. It was either steel or iron, he couldn't tell. He knew by the size of the hinges that it was heavy and definitely meant to keep something strong inside. The door took a key to unlock that Preacher didn't have, but there were two other openings that he could access. The first was at head height, and it slid right to left as a standard observation window would work. The second was a door that would lift from the bottom and raise upwards probably to allow food trays to slide into the room. There was a lock on the lower door that prevented Preacher from opening it, not that it would have been his first choice anyway.

Apprehensively Preacher took the handle of the observation window, which was just merely a knob welded onto the sliding metal plate. He slid the plate to the side exposing a crisscross metal mesh and peered inside.

The room was unlit except for the light coming in from a window high in the wall. Bars were ominously placed on the window to prevent escape. The walls were padded in an attempt to keep the occupant from injuring themselves. In the center of the room was a single bed and occupant. Light spilled in from the hallway bathing the occupant in its light.

She was bound hand and foot with restraints. A thin hospital gown covered her body, but even covered Preacher could tell she was little more than skin and bone. Her hands and feet contorted at odd and impossible angles struggling against the restraints.

Her head shot up and looked at Preacher through the observation window. Her face showed apparent signs of Demonic Possession. Her eyes had sunk deep into her skull. Sores had formed on her face and split, oozing puss. Deep cracks had formed on her lips, splitting them, and the streams of dried blood had trickled down her chin and throat.

Her head shook violently, and her mouth moved like she was shouting. Preacher couldn't hear anything from the room at all. She screamed in silence, and the restraints moved without making a sound. Preacher pushed back from the observation window and closed it. He stepped back and observed the door, looking for the wards that would seal this room so effectively.

The only thing that he saw was a white painted metal door. He made a mental note to talk to Hashmal about these wards, but for now, there was something wrong. Preacher closed his eyes and focused. Taking a few deep breaths, he cleared his mind of any pre-conceived notions of what an Asylum should look like. When he opened his eyes again, the perfectly white painted hallway was no longer there.

The cinderblock walls were dirty, a mix of yellow and brown. Trash and debris cluttered the hallway edges. The nicely white painted metal doors were rusty with age. The only thing that was new on them were the locks. Wards were written on all the door frames. They looked like they were a mixture of Greek, Roman, Latin, and Hellion in language.

A scream of pain and torture came from behind Preacher echoing off the hallway. Preacher spun around, but the sterling white hallway was back. Preacher turned and looked behind him again, and the bright light and clean hall didn't waiver.

Preacher headed in the direction of the screaming. After all, when you are looking for monsters, you always went towards the scream. His footfalls landed silently on the tiled floor as he came back to the center of the hallway. A wide staircase led to the upper levels of the hospital. In Preacher's experience, you only went upstairs to find the monster if it was confined in the bedroom of a family home.

A few steps further down the hallway Preacher came across a door marked 'Maintenance.' The door swung open without a sound revealing a poorly lit room behind it. Cinder block walls in this room showed their age. Most of the paint was chipped away revealing water stains on the wall. Stepping in Preacher found himself in less of a room, and more of a hallway. Pipes ran along the wall, air conditioning ducts ran above his head.

A faint mildew smell was present in the hall, which was a comforting smell after the false smell of the sterile hospital. Preacher was starting to understand that it was all an illusion. Some grand illusion for anyone that entered that this was exactly as they expected it to be. The front door didn't need to be locked because the illusions were the actual locks.

As he looked down the hallway the light faded and turned to a dark blackness. It was something like a bad dream. He could tell there was a light beyond the darkness, but for some reason, he couldn't see through the darkness to see it. He knew this was just another illusion, but he didn't have time to try to fight it. It was easier and faster to just go through it.

Walking down the hall was like driving through fog. He could only see inches in front of him and the darkness never lifted. He made his way cautiously through the hallway until he found himself at the top of a staircase. "Here we go." Preacher muttered to himself, then took the first step down the concrete stairs that were before him.

Each step down was like taking a step closer to Hell. The moist air became thick, and the heat rose with each step towards the basement. Preacher was no more than four steps down, and the air felt like a hot, humid day in Florida during summer, before a hurricane.

The closer Preacher was to the basement floor the more clearly he could hear. There was screaming coming from the basement level. The screaming voice was layered making Preacher think the scream wasn't coming from an average person. It sounded like how a Demon screams during an exorcism.

The stairs ended in a large room with cement floors and sparse lighting. Aged wooden work benches lined the wall in front of Preacher carrying ancient torture tools from pliers to spikes. In the corner rested an old rusted open helmet inspired by the Iron Maiden.

Preacher spun around to observe the rest of the basement behind him. His eyes settled on the only movement in the room. A man in the obvious states of possession was bound to a chair. Leather straps wrapped around his head, torso, arms, and legs. These straps had similar wards on them as the rooms above did.

This would not have been such a horrific sight, but the chair was covered in small iron spikes, and the demon-possessed man was nude. Preacher was not sure how long he had been hovering over the spikes in a sitting position, but it would be impossible to move without the spikes piercing and causing agony to the Demon.

A man was sitting on a stool with his back to Preacher. He had on a white doctor's coat and a pair of black slacks. He was rocking back and forth facing the Demon. He was muttering so quietly it was hard to hear what he was saying, but Preacher could tell that it was repetitive. "…the right question. Ask me the right question. Ask me the right question. Ask me the right question…"

23.

Preacher sat down his bag of goodies silently. He pulled out his iron knuckles and slipped them on his right hand. He removed a vial of holy water with his left and opened the top.

Observing the room, the unknown Demon was on a torture device, sitting next to him had to be Bolfry. He sat on his stool next to a large black metal pot of some kind. On the wall behind the two was a shelf with several books. The bookends were large stallions painted red.

Hanging next to the bookshelf was a German Dress Uniform from World War II, with the SS emblem displayed on the collar. Resting on the top of the uniform was the hat. The symbolism was not lost on Preacher. According to the text left by King Solomon, Bolfry was to appear on a great red horse, dressed in the guise of a Soldier. Even if the uniform was over seventy years old, the Nazi SS uniform managed to bring forth disgust, fear, and rage in decent people.

The Demon in the chair grunted in pain, "What do you want me to ask? I will ask, just tell me what you want me to ask!"

Bolfry rocked back and forth faster now. "I cannot tell you what to ask, or I will not see it. You can only ask once. ASK THE RIGHT QUESTION!" Bolfry reached into the pot and removed a writhing creature that squirmed and thrashed. He placed it on the Demon, and suddenly there were blue discharges of electricity.

'Was that an electric eel?' Preacher thought to himself. There was splashing coming from the black pot. It looked like there were several eels.

Preacher grinned as he improvised a plan. There was a good chance that the idea would work. Now all he needed was for a Demon to do precisely what he wanted when he wanted.

Snowball's chance in Hell anyone?

Preacher had never observed anything like this. His nightmares were not even this dark. Hashmal had failed to describe what he was going to find. Damn it, why couldn't this be in a strip club. Preacher made another mental note to hit Hashmal in the face when this was finished.

Preacher stood swiftly and took a few quick steps forward. The movement got the bound demons attention. The bloodshot eyes of the Demon made contact with Preacher, and for a few seconds, he paused his struggles, content for a moment. The Demon seemed almost happy to see the man in Priest garb step into the room.

"I know the right question. If I ask will you be happy enough to let me go?" the Demon asked Bolfry, who was still rocking forward and backward on his stool. Bolfry nodded to the Demon. The Demon shifted his weight, in agony, and nodded to Preacher. "Who is he?"

Belfry's rocking back and forth stopped abruptly as he heard the question.

"NO! That is not the right question!" Bolfry began rocking back forth again. "He is the one known as Preacher." Bolfry paused. "And he is early." Bolfry nodded his head, and an unseen force pushed the Demon possessed man onto the chairs' spikes. The flesh of the possessed sizzled like a steak on a hot grill.

From the length of the spikes on the chair, Preacher did not think the Demon would die quickly. It was a terrible death, even for a Demon. Bolfry turned his head and looked at Preacher, "It's quite tricky you know, always trying to know everything all the time."

Bolfry stood and turned to face Preacher and let out a low sigh "You see, it's all in the questions that are asked. Ask the right questions and you will get the answer you want, ask the right question wrongly and you get the answer you want to hear. A subtle but distinct difference. So ask your questions Preacher and be on your way. Other matters demand my attention." Bolfry walked over to the Demon sitting in the Judas Chair, the life was going out of the body slowly.

"You assume I am here to ask you questions. I could be here to send you and your food supply back to the pit."

Bolfry sucked in the air over his teeth making a hissing sound. "You are not. I have seen this, and I know how it unfolds. You will leave and I not be in the Pit." Bolfry placed his hand on the arm of the dying Demon, a soft glow started from under his fingers, and gold spread over his arm. After a few seconds, the arm of the demon from elbow to fingers had transformed into gold.

"I didn't know I was coming here until today. How could you have foreseen it? You are not omniscient." Preacher stated

"That is not the right question!" Bolfry closed his eyes for a second, just longer than a normal blink. "I know because I was asked, and as such, I have seen it."

"If you can see the future why did you say I was early? Shouldn't you always be right?" As a rule, Preacher didn't do banter. But he needed to know what he was dealing with.

"That is not the RIGHT question!" Again, Bolfry's eyes closed and fluttered, just longer than a blink. "I see the most probable outcome at the time I am asked. You humans and your free will can cause ripples and sometimes even change the outcome that I have originally seen."

"Who asked you if I was coming?" Preacher was intrigued that he would be a topic of conversation with Bolfry

Bolfry's head cocked to the side, and he twitched "That is NOT the right question!" His eyes closed, fluttered and reopened just longer than a blink. "No one. You asked the question wrongly. Now ask what you came to ask."

"What does Baba Doek have planned?" Bolfry grinned and tilted his chin to his chest. He closed his eyes, they fluttered, and he opened them again.

"She wants to break Tartarus of course. She wants her body back. She wants us all to have our bodies back." Boflry's grin turned to a smile. "Imagine how delicious they would all be. Their bodies tender, meat so soft from lying still for so long."

Bolfry let a giggle escape his lips. "They would be so tasty. Weak like chickens, to make nuggets out of." Bolfry's tongue darted over his lips.

Preacher snapped his fingers loudly several times to get Bolfrys attention back on him. "How do I stop Baba Doek from breaking Tartarus and freeing all these bodies?"

"That is not the RIGHT QUESTION!" Same routine, eyes close, flutter and then open. Just longer than a blink. "You'll have to kill her."

Preacher immediately felt enraged. There had to be other ideas to stop Baba Doek that had not been explored. "How will I find Baba Doek to stop her?"

"That is NOT THE RIGHT QUESTION!" Bolfry ran his fingers through his hair, pulling it back from his face as he screamed at Preacher. His eyes rolled upwards into the back of his head and fluttered then returned. Just a little longer than a blink. "You will follow the omens. You will hear thunder overhead when there are no clouds in the sky. An unkindness will proceed a murder, and these shall point the way. You will know you are close when you find the bewitched, and inside the city when all the church bells ring off schedule."

Of course, Bolfry made no sense to Preacher, but he memorized every word of it. Preacher stepped forward to Bolfry and looked into the barrel next to him. Electric eels swam over each other. Occasional bolts of electricity could be seen between them.

"You could have answered me more accurately. Understand that in this room I command with the voice of Christ our Lord. Your Lord and Redeemer. You will submit to the will of Christ! Praise Christ and all he has done for us!" Preacher had reigned the power of the holy just as he did for all exorcisms.

Bolfry smirked "Praise Christ? Oh, Praise God too, please. You may as well praise Moses's staff, or Noah's hammer or either of their cocks. You might get a more pleasant answer than talking to God."

Preacher smiled. "Bolfry, is tonight the night you go back to Hell?" Preacher when into automatic mode. One-One thousand. Preacher tossed the Holy Water in his left hand at Bolfry then dropped the container. Bolfry's eyes closed before the water made contact. One-thousand two. Preacher swung as hard as possible with iron knuckles. Bolfry's eyes fluttered as the first drops of Holy Water hit his face and began to steam.

The iron knuckles did not make contact with Bolfry. There was nothing there, only an empty space where the Demon once stood.

From behind him, he heard Bolfry grunt. "No."

Preacher panicked. He reached in the dark tub and grabbed an electric eel. He was in about to throw it at Bolfry when the electricity hit him, and he fell to his knees. The eel fell harmlessly at Bolfry's feet.

Preacher was on all fours struggling to catch his breath. He naturally assumed he would be killed. He felt Bolfry straddle him. The legs of Bolfry were supernaturally strong, hugging him around the ribs.

"I do not go to Hell tonight Preacher. I do not go to Hell again. Not now, not ever. But Preacher you should know this. Remember this no matter what. When your aim is low, you need to pull harder." Bolfry stepped away from Preacher allowing him to move.

Preacher scrambled forward on his hands and knees, turning himself to the room to see Bolfry was gone and the room was empty. Except for the dead Demon. Preacher felt a release of energy when Bolfry disappeared. From above he heard creaking and scraping as doors were being opened. Preacher realized that Bolfry left the building and the wards lost all of their power.

All the Demons were free and knew he was there. Preacher scrambled to his bag and grabbed it. He could hear the horde in the hall above him. The maintenance door was smashed open, and they were coming down the darkened hallway. Preacher reached into his pocket and pulled out the glass vial that Michael gave him.

Inhuman growling and screaming were becoming louder, and finally, Preacher could see the first of the hoard at the top of the stairs. Then another appeared, and then a third. Preacher threw the glass at the Demons thinking back to Michael's advice. In case of emergency, break the glass.

The vial hit the first Demon on the chest and fell to the ground smashing. Black dust flew into the air covering the top of the stairs, specks landing on the bare arms and feet of the Demons at the top of the stairs.

Where the dust landed on the exposed skin, embers began to glow. Red-ish orange welts began to rise on their skin. The Demons reacted quickly growling and scratching the welts, falling backward from the powder.

Preacher gathered his bag and stepped into a shadow, it was time to head home.

24.

Baba Doek admired her handy work. The parchment that the Slovakian emissary presented to her lay before her flat on the ground. At its center, a copper bowl rested to receive the offering. Sitting to her right were the offerings of barley, wheat, and sage. Of course, that was the light stuff, there can be no question that the dark spell needed blood to be cast.

She only had to wait for the moon to begin to darken and begin her incantation. All of her senses were on high alert. She could hear the shallow breaths of Castor and Pollux behind her. They were there to ensure that no one would prevent or interrupt the ceremony. Based on her meeting with Bolfry there should be no interruptions, but one could never be too cautious.

She looked to the sky allowing a little satisfaction to sink into her. Everything was going according to her plan. With force of will, she centered herself. It took more effort than she would have liked.

Wars were lost because of ego. Celestial battles were lost because one party fell into a monologue more often than anyone cared to admit. Flatter a superior enemy until they talk themselves into your trap.

The first part of the moon began falling into shadow. Stretching out her right arm she motioned Ramil to come forward. In the distance, there was a flash of red eyes, and she heard Ramil start walking to her. He lead the lamb to slaughter on a rope leash.

With her left hand, Baba Doek pointed to the distance on her left and heard the incantations begin from the group gathered there. Led by one of her favorite Tricksters, the group of witches began summoning fog into the cemetery they had gathered in.

Incense, barley, wheat, and sage went into the bowl. Baba Doek didn't bother with matches, she simply summoned her power and called the fire forth in the bowl. Flames of blue and yellow leap to life. They took the offering gladly and produced little smoke. Ramil handed her the rope to the lamb that she accepted without looking.

Half of the moon had disappeared. A slight feeling of panic set in. Baba Doek yanked the rope and brought the lamb over the copper bowl. The blonde-haired woman had a gag in her mouth, and her wrists were bound. Baba Doek looked over the body for the final time. Her body was tight with youth, she was nude and would make a good sacrifice.

Baba Doek pulled the woman until her neck hovered over the bowl. Baba Doek cut her throat with her naturally sharp nails. Blood spattered into the bowl red and hot, steaming in the cool night air. It was a skill to catch the blood in the bowl and not spill it everywhere.

Once the bowl was almost full, she skillfully lifted the head and casually tossed the little lamb to the side. The incantation provided by the Slovakian Demons had been committed to memory with ease. She began the spell just as the light faded from the moon.

The eclipse had begun. Continuing her spellcraft Baba Doek carefully took the bowl and started pouring the thick liquid onto the parchment like a paint. From left to right the parchment soaked in every drop and did not allow any to spill to the ground at all.

The blood was black in the darkness. It shimmered and rippled with the spell being cast. Baba Doek allowed her mind to focus on the item that she desired. It was ancient, here on Earth long before the time of Christ. It was an arm bone of a long-dead Nephilim, found randomly in a field and turned into a tool. First, it was used as a trowel, the farmer that found it handled it well. But this bone is different. It is made from the forbidden breeding of human and Angel and over time its influence could be seen.

As it enhanced his deepest insecurities, he became more mean spirited, violent and jealous. One day he began arguing with a merchant at the market about the price and quality of his goods. In a fit of rage, he grabbed the trowel off his cart and killed the merchant.

Throughout history, the trowel went from owner to owner exploiting any weakness it could. Artisans changed it over the years, so it was no longer a trowel, but it was always a much beloved almost idolized item to the owner.

She felt the item calling to her since she took possession of this vessel. Its siren song beautiful and faint, and unfortunately hard to track. She pushed the desire for this bone into the parchment and watched the blood roll and change, currents lifting to show patterns.

Baba Doek's vision became blurry as she as assaulted by images. A street followed by a sign, followed by a building. She focused on the details as they flashed before her. In the building, down a hall, through a door.

It was waiting for her inside of a box, sitting quietly on a shelf, calling to her. The once subtle siren song was like an explosion of sound now calling to her. It was so clear she wondered how it was ever obscured in the first place.

The visions ceased as rapidly as they came to her. She was back in her vessel, staring at the blood-soaked parchment. The light of the moon broke through the eclipse, and she was back where she started. The parchment began to crack, breaking and dissolving into the dirt and disappearing into the ground as if there were nothing there.

She stood gracefully and looked at her soiled black yoga pants and shoes. She loathed these clothes. Peasants in the middle ages wore more clothing than this. It was the last time that she sent Castor to pick up clothes. While he did technically meet her criteria of inconspicuous and disposable, it was utterly undignified for a King of Hell to be running around in glorified spandex.

She looked at Castor. He was staring out at the darkness waiting for an enemy to emerge. His desire to engage and destroy her enemies without thought of consequence to himself was admirable. "Castor?" she called it just loud enough for him to hear her.

He turned and looked at her feet submissive. It was instinct for him after all those years in Hell. His submissiveness pleased her in the same way a dog's owner is gratified when the dog sits on command.

"Clean the body of this lamb and take her to my sanctum. The host will be inhabited before daybreak and have more meaning than you ever did."

Castor nodded. "Yes, Mistress."

"Does it please you, Castor? Knowing that you are going to bring one greater than you into this world?"

"Only if it pleases you, Mistress. I am yours." Castor stood stoically as a good Solider stood. If there was any emotion behind the mask, he wore it did not show.

Baba Doek nodded "Then go. Pollux! Gather everything needed for a summoning spell and have those witches bring forth one of mine to fill this vessel." Baba Doek nodded to the group of witches gathered nearby.

Pollux turned to her voice. Like Castor, he did not look above her ankles. "It will be done."

"Ramil, let's go gather my prize." Baba Doek touched Ramils shoulder, an act that was out of character. "It is so close Ramil. I couldn't have imagined how close it was." Baba Doek was pleased, and she let it show. The absurd idea of starting Armageddon was almost laughable. Hellion politics was too fragile and split. There were not enough leaders in the Pit with too many followers. While on Earth there were too many leaders and not enough followers.

She could fix this problem. Soon they would all unite under one. He would lead to the fall of Heaven and the equality of the Earth.

Ramil nodded and stepped back slightly breaking their contact. "Yes, Mistress. I shall follow your lead."

Composing herself, Baba Doek walked forward and entered a shadow. Ramil followed the ripples to a parking lot just a couple dozen miles away.

Before them stood Gwinnett Police Department. It had to be the headquarters building, and it was closed after business hours. The single-story brick building with large glass windows that were mostly dark on the inside. Baba Doek looked at the outside of the building, frustrated that she could not shadow step into the evidence room directly. Looking closely at the construction of the outside of the building, she could not see any wards that would prevent her entry.

"Why can we not step inside?" Baba Doek asked.

Ramil took a step forward. "Let me look." He took a step forward and disappeared. Baba Doek could hear him on the roof of the building. He was on the left side of the roof, then on the far right side.

She saw him emerge from a shadow and then he disappeared again. After a moment she felt him emerge from a shadow beside her. "The building has been recently blessed. The doors and windows have been sanctified with Holy Water."

"Do you think it was done on purpose? Or is this simply a coincidence?"

"Most likely coincidence. If it were done on purpose, it would have been done after the janitorial crew left for the evening. With your leave, I shall break the ward."

Baba Doek nodded, and Ramil stepped into the shadows disappearing. A few moments passed, and there was a scream from inside the building. Following the first, there were several more. The cleaning staff ran from the building, followed out by hundreds of wet rats. The rats smelled of the sewer and as they scurried over the door frame their wet feet first contaminated the Holy Water left by the blessing, then finally destroyed it.

Baba Doek felt the barrier fall in front of her. She envisioned the room that her spell revealed to her and she stepped into a shadow. She exited in darkness. The room filled with steel shelves, filled with cardboard boxes. Closing her eyes, she listened for the sirens song. It was louder than she had ever heard. It screamed in her mind, louder than ever. It was the sweetest thing she had ever heard.

Step by step she came closer to the item she most desired. She went to the end of the row, and she moved in the direction the song sung to her. Instinctively she knew when she came to the right aisle.

Baba Doek moved down it instinctively like a dog to a dog whistle. Calling to her it came from a simple box that looked like all the others. The only thing distinguishing this box from the next was a single marking. 'A. Rodriguez, 17M-7.7. Murder, 6 counts.'

Pulling the box off the shelf and onto the floor Baba Doek spilled the contents out. Wallet, keys, change, lip-gloss, purse. All evidence in a crime, all evidence that Baba Doek could not care less about.

The last item in the box, contained in a plastic evidence bag was what she was looking for. Even through the plastic bag, the bone gleamed white. She finally had it. One item acquired, one-step closer.

Unable to resist Baba Doek ripped open the evidence bag and held the brush in her hand.

25.

Baba Doek's eyes fluttered and closed. Images pressed in her mind, a history of lives the brush has influenced came rushing to her. A significantly powerful memory came forward, and Baba Doek found herself staring out of the eyes of someone other than herself.

It was thirty-nine years after the death of Christ and his followers were spawning like roaches. The festival today displayed the execution of thirty-nine Followers of Christ as a demonstration for those who refused to worship the recently named Roman God Caligula. Outside of the palace, the festival was a big energy-filled event. She was sure that Mars would be pleased.

Baba Doek looked through the eyes of Agrippa the Younger as the sun was fading over the horizon leaving the sky in hues of pink and purple. The event hosted tonight would be even more of a spectacle. A masquerade ball was being held inside the palace as an honor to Jupiter, where a sacrifice double the amount of this afternoon would take place. During the executions, her love would demand dancing under the blood, and as a God himself, he would lick the blood away, cleansing the souls of those he cleaned.

She ran the brush through her hair, stroke after stroke. The ivory handle of the brush was so smooth it could have been bone and was a comfort in her hand. She looked to the balcony that allowed the light into the room, and there stood her brother, her emperor, her lover. Before he was crowned Emperor, he was known as Gaius Julius Caesar. Now all in the empire hailed him Caligula, Emperor of all of Rome. He was the father of her child Nero.

She stood, and her movement caught Caligula's attention. She smiled as only a lover can and patted the seat that she just left. He walked over to the chair and removed his golden oak leaf crown, setting it on the amour in front of him. He unlatched the ruby encrusted golden pin and allowed his toga to fall to his waist.

Caligula had more hair on his shoulders, back and chest than he did his head. Agrippina was the only one he allowed to see him nude unless he had a mask on. He let her begin brushing his hair on his head, which he kept cropped short in the traditional Roman style.

It did not take long before Agrippina had finished making the hair on his head feel silky and clean. She pushed him forward and started brushing the hair on his neck and shoulders. Her emperor was a hairy man, and while she found it evidence of his manhood, he found it embarrassing.

There was a knock at the door, and Caligula sat up and quickly affixed his pin and tunic to cover as much of his body as possible. Baba Doek watched through the eyes of the stranger as he stood. He walked back to the balcony looking over the courtyard. Agrippina opened the door to the chambers to see who was there. Before she could make an attempt to dissuade the man from entering he barged into the room.

"Have you gone mad?" Cassius Chaerrea walked straight towards the Emperor. "You cannot be planning to replace the heads of the Gods with yours!"

Caligula turned his cold glance to the intruder. "Is this how you would talk to your God? If my brother Jupiter were standing beside me would you still have the same tone?" Cassius took a step, and Caligula continued, "I did not think so." He stepped forward and grabbed Cassius by the hair and pulled him to the balcony.

Caligula was stronger than his physic showed. Cassius found himself looking over a crowd of drunken Romans, celebrating the carnage that had just taken place and anticipating the carnage to follow. Music from the street rose to his ears, street performers were doing their best to keep the crowd jubilant and in a festive mood, while merchants sold their wines and meads at outrageous prices.

Cassius felt the rip in the back of his tunic, and then felt the sharp point of steel at his back. "I am Caligula, God of all you see before you, and of all, you feel behind you. Do not scream because I would like to prefer to have you alive."

Then Agrippa watched as Caligula bent Cassius over at the waist on the balcony and took him. Caligula knew he was equal to the Gods and he did not have a problem acting like it. When Casious's natural bodily lubricant expired, Caligula made cuts with the dagger on Cassius' back and used his blood as a lubricant. Baba Doek could feel Agrippa's excitement as she watched, growing wet between her legs.

When Caligula climaxed, he stepped back and observed all the blood on his toga. Indeed it would have to be changed. As he turned, he almost tripped because Nero was standing so close behind him.

The toddler made and held eye contact with Caligula, something that was never permitted. No one should look at God in the eyes. The sentence for making eye contact was death. Baba Doek watched as only Agrippina's pleading convinced Caligula that he not need to kill Nero.

Agrippina did what she had to do in the days following to protect her son Nero. She was married to another man, and everyone believed her son was her husbands. She was brushing her hair with the ivory-handled hairbrush when the guards came for her and her son to exile them.

The brush instructed Agrippina to leave Nero in the company of her family in case she was found by the Royal Guards and murdered. Fortunately, Jupiter (whom Caligula once called a brother), was protecting her and she was alive when Caligula was killed by members of his own Senate and Praetorian Guard. Rumor had it, although it was never confirmed, Cassius Chaerrea caused the fatal wound. It was a slice across the throat, which he used fornicated with to gain his masculinity back.

Baba Doek listened as the bone handled hairbrush influenced Agrippina, and she found her way back into the arena of Roman politics. Using guile and deception to secure her sons future, she married Nero to the new emperor's daughter.

She taught her son that there should be no mercy in his life for his enemies. She blamed the fall of her former lover on tolerance, even the kindness that he showed Nero. She eradicated all of it in him.

Baba Doek watched as Agrippa brushed her son's hair with the bone-handled brush. She knew that it would speak to him as it did to her. It would only take time to do so. It didn't take long, she knew he was being guided when Nero killed his brother, securing his ascension to the throne.

With nothing to stand in their way, Mother and Son ruled the Empire for years. The years were marked with excess to exceed his real father, Caligula.

Nero acted under the direction of his mother hunting the Followers of Christ in their secret places of worship. Once captured they would be tortured for the names of other Christians and then murdered in the most heinous of ways. One of Nero's favorites was to bath them in blood, cover them with the skins of animals and sick his starving wild dogs on them.

The brush made Agrippina grow paranoid. She knew her son plotted her death. He had her exiled, but without the influence of the hairbrush, he soon recalled her. So she did what any spiteful mother would do. She went to the cities dungeons and emptied them of all the Christians. The last one out of the cell she knew as Peter. To her he was an annoyance, spreading the teachings of a long dead martyr. But she thrust the hairbrush into his hands before he fled the prison.

Confused, but eager for freedom he took it and fled to the streets. He did not hold it long before it passed to others and it touched them. Through their eyes Baba Doek watched the Apostle Peter die at the order of Nero by inverted crucifixion and then the burning of Rome.

Baba Doek's vision blurred as the brush brought her through time. She ignored much of what she saw allowing it to blur through her, only gleening random images that she may want to explore later. She saw a Pope's ring, a Queen's crown, and then blackness as it was stored untouched for years.

Then there was light and loud sounds of explosions, cries of pain. The smell of blood and gunpowder and fear filled her senses as several blurs of time whipped past her. Suddenly there was a calm that filled her. It turned into anticipation for things to come, but that has already passed. It was the anticipation of reliving a well-loved memory.

It was a typical day when the artifact came into the Grese household. It was brought inside in a small leather bag that Alfred used to carry his lunch to and from work. It was during dinner that it first touched Irma's mind.

She was thirteen and beginning her transition to womanhood. The change left her feeling physically and emotionally awkward, and as such, she was often ridiculed by her peers. But the mean girls were not her peers, not according to the League of German Girls. As the Hitler youth for girls, it taught her about all the evils the Jew's had inflicted on her people.

The brush sang to her during dinner. Sitting at the table with her father, two brothers, and two sisters, she was disengaged. She could barely peel her eyes from her Fathers lunch sack. After dinner, her family followed their normal routine. The children had their homework inspected and were quizzed by their father on the benefits of the Nazi party.

Instead of falling into a sound sleep on this night though, Irma heard the call of the brush. After her sisters had fallen into a sound sleep, she felt the pull so strongly she slipped from her bed and gathered a candle and match. Once she was out of her room, she struck the match and lit the candle.

Quite as a mouse, she crept down the stairs to her father's bag. She knew that she would receive a beating by going in her father bag, but the urge to get into the bag was so overpowering that she opened it without concern and found a wrapped package with a card attached to it.

There was an envelope that was addressed to a Miriam Kleinhienz. Irma knew that this card was not for her, her brothers or sisters or her mother. She threw it on the floor with disregard of the consequences. The item that was inside was hers, she felt it talking to her and knew it was so.

Opening the package she saw the hairbrush for the first time. It was so beautiful that she couldn't help herself. She started brushing her hair. Stroke after stroke it became silky, stroke after stroke she became more attractive. Stroke by stroke she felt more affirmed that the League of German Girls was for her and the Jewish girls that bullied her knew less than nothing. Every time the brush went through her hair she became more convinced, she would be able to make those girls suffer.

Irma was so lost in thought she didn't see her mother come into the room, or open and read the letter addressed to Miriam. She remembered her mother shaking her by the shoulders asking where she found this hairbrush, and she remembered pointing at her father's bag. It was already morning, she was made to put the brush down and make breakfast.

Routine attempted to take hold this morning except Irma felt compelled to keep this new brush. She hid it in her school bag. She knew her mother would not allow her to keep it and would use the brush to prove her father's infidelity. Baba Doek watched as Irma took the acid cleaning solution from under the sink and poured some into her mother's morning milk when no one was watching.

For Irma's family and the community, it was a tragic day when later that afternoon Berta Grese was found dead of an apparent suicide. As more questions were asked about the death the more it divided the family. When Irma left her house at fourteen, no one asked questions.

Baba Doek observed as Irma quickly found her stride with the Nazi party. Soon she found herself in control of the females of Auschwitz concentration camp. Singlehandedly she would dictate those to be sent to the gas chambers. It was easy at first, merely picking the Jewish girls that didn't lose their initial beauty and appearance. Unfortunately, as those beautiful people were killed, she had to become more particular. The first ones she killed she was able to have skinned for personal memoirs. She had lamp shades, blankets, and sandals made from the skin of those killed. Her favorite item made of skin was a riding crop that she carried with her at all times.

One of the gifts that the hairbrush gave her was sexual freedom that she never questioned. It was a freedom that she never thought to feel given the upbringing she had. If it was to her advantage, she felt nothing morally wrong about letting someone have their way with her. Over time though she often found herself having her way with them.

Baba Doek was amazed as Irma sent hundreds to their death in the gas chamber every week with impunity. She would look for the weak or sickly first, as any good Nazi would do. Then she would look for males that did not sexually arouse her. Any Jewish female that was able to keep her beauty after a month would be beaten. Irma would use her riding crop on the prisoners face, and breasts often causing scars, infection and sometimes death.

She became known as the Hyena of Auschwitz before she was transferred to Belen, where she became known as the Bitch of Belen. The brush flourished through Irma until the Allies captured the camp she was in control of. At the age of twenty-two, Irma was the youngest person hung for war crimes in "modern" history.

Irma's last words? "Mach Schnell" Make it fast.

The relic fell to history again. It sat in several museums, behind glass partitions never touched. Finally, it was part of a lot that went up for auction and was sold to someone who did not understand what they had.

The brush sat through the silence of history and movement until it met Annabella. Annabella was devoted Catholic, a faithful wife, and mother of five. All the neighbors knew her to be pleasant and always helpful.

Her husband found the brush at an estate sale and thought it would be a perfect gift for his wife. She seemed depressed since she found out that she was pregnant again with their sixth child. He felt that she would like it, but he couldn't afford it, so when no one was looking, he slipped it in his pocket and saw himself out.

The bone finally found itself in companionship with a vulnerable person for the first time in seventy years. Baba Doek watched as Annabella depression quickened the influence the brush had on her. Baba Doek experienced the depression compounded by anger frustration and helplessness.

Annabella looked at her body and saw a now fat stomach covered in stretch marks where a once taunt stomach was. Baba Doek shared the loathing Annabella had for her body. Over time the voice of the brush was able to show Annabella that it was her children's fault she looked the way she did. It was their growth in her belly that caused her to look this way. She had five children in ten years; the fault was her husband's inability to pull out in time to keep her from getting pregnant.

The fault was her mothers, who never taught her how to be a mother. She saw her hair was no longer shiny and healthy; it was because her children took too much of her time for her to take care of herself.

Her husband didn't make much money, and they were stuck living in a trailer. All seven people living in this cramped little trailer because he couldn't get a job that paid more than minimum wage. Baba Doek listened as the brush told Annabella how to retake control. She would lose the weight once she had time to concentrate on herself, once she became single and free of these needy ungrateful children.

Annabella started with her husband. He was sleeping on his back snoring loudly again. He knew that his snoring kept her awake. He was selfish still, the brush told her. She slipped from the bed and went to the kitchen. She only had one good knife in the kitchen, and she took it back to the bedroom.

The knife went into her husband's throat smoothly reminding her of cutting through warm butter. She thrust it three times, pumping into his throat just like he pumped into her. There was little struggle, mostly gurgling and bloody froth escaping his lips. The look of surprise in his eyes made Annabella feel truly alive. Baba Doek felt the spray of blood as it splashed across Annabella's face.

Her oldest child died just as quickly and silently. The screaming began with her second child and continued until she silenced them all. The tasks became more brutal and messy as the children tried to run away.

When the police arrived, they found Annabella sitting on the front porch of her trailer. She was still dressed in her pajamas covered in blood. She was gazing off into the distance brushing the blood from her hair stroke after stroke. She didn't speak or resist when she was arrested, it was as if she was in a trance.

Charged with six counts of murder among other things, the brush was tucked away until Baba Doek found it. Baba Doek smiled as the memories played in her head and as they faded she found herself back in the evidence room.

She turned to the closest shadow and stepped through, she needed to see Josiah. He had some deals to collect on.

26.

It was dark when Preacher stepped back into his bedroom. He put his bag on the floor and sat on the edge of his bed cradling his head between his hands. The nightmare asylum that he left shook him to his core, yet it also comforted him. It reaffirmed the foundation of his belief that Demons are spawns of evil and as such, they must be eradicated from the face of the Earth.

In the silence of his room, he couldn't ignore his own questions about his soul. His belief that he was saved by Jesus Christ's death on the cross and subsequent resurrection was in question. Would salvation be extended to a Nephilim? Would continuing his good works cement his salvation? He wasn't sure if that was something that Hashmal could answer. He also wasn't sure that he would believe an answer that came from him.

Preacher stood and undressed. Picking up his rosary Preacher knelt by the side of the bed as he used to do as a child in school. Starting with the first large bead, he began the prayer, "Our Father who art in Heaven…" he lost himself in the words of the prayers seeking guidance and comfort.

He lost track of time and eventually ran out of beads to pray on. He had no more clarity than he had when he began. He was frustrated and found himself exhausted. He crawled into bed and fell immediately to sleep.

His dream started with a dark and oppressive feeling. He was standing in a bathroom, but it wasn't his. The black and white tiles he saw at his feet were vaguely familiar. He was shirtless with his hands on either side of the pedestal sink, the cold feel of porcelain ran along his fingers and into his palms.

Staring down at the sink he recognized it in some abstract way. It could have been the rust stains encircling the drain, or the chip in the paint just under the hot water knob, he wasn't sure. He recognized that the sink was in the bathroom at the old Italian monastery where he learned his craft. He also realized that the sink was closer to him than it should be and his hands were his child's hands, young and smooth without age.

Startled he looked into the mirror and saw his adult image staring back at him. There were differences in his appearance though, his muscles were more defined like he worked out six hours a day and didn't drink. He face was set with an angry scowl, staring at his younger self. The mirrored face flared its nostrils and snarled, baring sharp pointed inhuman looking teeth.

Preacher backed away from the mirror, frightened by what he saw. The courage that he took with him into every battle with evil was gone. Preacher backed up until he something stopped him. It felt like a wall, where there should have been bathroom stalls. He wanted it to be a wall, but he felt fabric where the stone should have been and warmth where there should be coldness.

Taking a step forward he spun around to find another grownup image of him standing there. But this version did not look angry. On the contrary, he seemed very comforting and benevolent. Dressed in his usual cassock, this version of himself knelt before him.

"Do not be afraid, just remain aware of what you can become. A sink turned on behind, and he spun again. Standing at the sink was Botis in his full Demonic regalia washing his hands.

He looked at Preacher over his shoulder, "Do not lie to yourself, you are better than that. It's already in you, and it will grow stronger than you can imagine." Botis turned off the water and reached for a paper towel to wipe his hands. A toilet flushed from behind Preacher, and he turned towards the sound.

Bolfry bustled out of the stall zipping his zipper and muttering to himself. He glances around the bathroom with a confused but amused look on his face. He glanced from Preacher to the older Preacher, to the Preacher in the mirror and to Botis.

Bolfry mostly stifled a giggle then sucked in some air through his teeth. "Well isn't this just a motley crew of unfortunate creatures. Why am I here? Ask the right questions!"

"You and your questions. You should go back to the Pit and recharge that brain Bolfry, you give the rest of us a bad name." Botis spit out Bolfry's name like it left a bad taste in his mouth.

Bolfry flicked his wrist and Botis flew backward past where the wall should be and into darkness. Bolfry straightened himself and Preacher saw him for the first time not acting like a crazed maniac. His gaze fell on the young Preacher, intelligent eyes glared at him through the glasses on his face.

"You can ask me more questions if you want. Botis appears strong and fearsome but we both know if I returned to the Pit I would be running the place and he would have to lick my hoofs. His king is weak and does not hold the support that I would hold if I were there."

There was a thud in the mirror, and the angry Preacher was staring at Bolfry. "How do I get out of here? LET ME OUT OF HERE!"

Bolfry glanced at the mirrored image of Preacher and cocked his head to the side like a dog would when it was confused. "That's not the right question. You are already out of there." Bolfry pointed at the young Peacher, "You are already in there."

Young Preacher immediately looked at the mirror, but it was an empty space. It wasn't a mirror anymore, it was a frame with a black mass inside it. The Darkness filled the mirror, rippling and moving. Almost like it was alive.

"And so are you." Bolfry addressed the older benevolent Preacher. Young Preacher spun his head and saw the older comforting image of him was gone. When Preacher looked back at Bolfry, he was his adult self. He could tell because Bolfry was no longer taller and not quite as terrifying as a moment ago.

Footsteps echoed out of the darkness behind him. They were heavy steps, those of a warrior coming to battle. Bolfry looked over Preacher's shoulder into the Darkness that he had cast Botis. His eyes belied a fear of whatever was coming out the Darkness.

"How do I save M.C. from Baba Doek?" Preacher had seen the eyes of predators when they discovered they were prey. Bolfry was going to flee, not fight, and this was the question that he should have asked when he had the Demon cornered earlier tonight.

"You need to understand that she may not be able to be saved. You should prepare yourself if you need to destroy her." Bolfry continued to look beyond Preacher into the Darkness.

"That's not the right answer." Preacher found himself parroting the words he heard Bolfry used so often.

"Perhaps not what you wanted to hear. But that doesn't mean that it isn't the right answer." Bolfry stepped backward, retracing his steps into the bathroom stall and closed the door.

The footsteps from the Darkness grew louder. Preacher could feel evil radiating from the Darkness almost like the waves when he stepped into the ocean. Apprehension tugged at his mind, creating terrors that he could not see. He felt the weight of someone watching even though there was no one to be seen. Just the sound of footsteps coming close becoming louder with each step.

Preacher turned to face the darkness, his right hand felt light absent the weight of the iron knuckles. His left wrist itched slightly without his rosary wrapped around it. Physical reminders of how naked he really was.

Not knowing what else to do Preacher closed his eyes and began praying. It was the same prayer, Our Father, which he recommended to everyone that needed help. Most clergy, including himself, were raised on the belief that this was the strongest prayer taught.

Halfway through the prayer, the footsteps stopped. Preacher continued his prayer all the way through, only an amateur would quit halfway through a prayer. He opened his eyes to the Darkness but saw nothing coming through.

Then the laughter came from one side of the Darkness, then behind him, then back to the Darkness. It was M.C.'s laughter, but it was warped. It was as different as it was familiar. It bounced off the walls, into his ears and broke his heart. Tears filled his eyes, she was his sin.

Her integration was his fault at the core. If she were not his lover, she would never have been there. His guilt felt like an iron weight around his neck, and he fell to his knees. Her footsteps brought her out of the Darkness into the room.

She was wearing a red velvet halter top with a high neck, black leather pants, and high heels. Her hair was long and free-flowing with dangling earrings and a necklace made of teeth. The same chain that was present when she gave herself to the enemy and became Baba Doek. He dropped his gaze to the floor, numb seeing her in front of him.

She stepped forward and knelt in front of him. "You couldn't destroy me could you Doek?" She ran her index finger from his throat to the tip of his chin and lifted his gaze to meet her face. "Could you face a world without me in it Doek?" She laughed a full and hardy laugh as the first tear ran down Preacher's cheek.

"I'm the guilt that keeps you going, the fuel in your tank. But you have no idea if you can do your job when it comes to sending me back to Hell do you?" She leaned in close and kissed the tears off his cheeks. "Don't cry Doek. You are the only one I wish I had never met. That has to mean something, after all without you I wouldn't have become Joined."

The sob escaped him before he knew it was coming. He leaned back away from M.C. because it wasn't really her, not the M.C. that he remembered. He felt helpless at that moment. He could feel waves of evil washing over him, but he saw the love of his life.

"Without me in the world Doek, what is there to love? What is there to fight for if you have to destroy me?" She knelt in front of him and leaned backward, sitting on her heels. "Face it Doek, I am the Yin to your Yang, the Zig to your Zag. We are intertwined, and this is a long road that you don't want to walk down. It's not too late to walk away Doek. Live your life away from evil. Find a good woman, live a good and honest life. Have some kids and grow old, grey, fat and happy."

There was music in her voice as she tempted him. It was a lullaby that all children had a desire to hear. It said you were going to be okay, you were not in danger. Somewhere inside Preacher's mind danger was ringing like a smoke detector. Once Preacher heard the sound he grabbed on to it and followed it back to the source of the noise.

Once he gave into the sound his right hand shot forward and grabbed Baba Doek by the throat. Preacher stood up to his full height and lifted Baba Doek off the ground. She was surprised and struggled, kicking and trying to scream. Surprised at his own strength Preacher looked to his arm, only to find himself staring into the refection of the mirror.

In the refection was an angry looking Preacher, his nostrils flaring and a manic smile on his face. As Baba Doek struggled for breath, as M.C. was dying in his grasp, the mirrored Preachers mouthed two silent words to himself.

Two words that caused Preacher to wake up from his nightmare.

"Thank You."

27.

Shortly after Preacher fell into a slumber, Josh was waking from his. His idea for a spring-loaded crucifix was still rattling around in his head. He knew that he was close to getting it to work, but he wasn't sure that the function would be quite like he wanted.

He opened a more substantial, sturdier casing than he was working with the night before. He put in a bigger spring and wound the string tight again. He closed the housing and affixed a crucifix to the bit of wire protruding.

He aimed it towards the wall and pressed the release. The crucifix flew outwards and smacked the wall with a thud, shortly followed by the remainder of the string in the device. One problem solved, another question presented.

This problem could wait until after some coffee and so he headed upstairs to the kitchen. As he left his room he noticed Gus standing in what he thought of as the armory. Gus had a jar on the table that was filled with a black fog like substance.

"Is that from the Demon the other night?" he asked Gus.

Gus simply nodded and tapped the jar again, looking for a response. "It hasn't dissipated and doesn't seem to respond to external stimulus."

Josh snickered. "You mean tapping on the glass doesn't do anything. Gotcha."

Gus straightened and looked at Josh. "I am going to take this to storage, if you want to go with me."

Josh nodded. "Let me grab some coffee and clean myself up real quick and I'll go with you." His gaze fell back to the jar, "Why are we keeping it?"

Gus shrugged nonchalantly. "We will take items that could cause harm to others and store them from time to time. Dolls, mirrors, paintings or cursed items that we think may allow for a recurrence of activity after we leave." Gus bent over the jar again and tapped it with his fingernail. "Besides, from what I can tell, this is the essence of a demonic spirit, we might be able to discover something important with it."

Josh nodded and headed upstairs. He was glad to see a fresh pot on the counter, the smell of a dark roast filled the kitchen. The only jobs he had been on with the team had been exorcisms, they left him with books to read when they went to investigations and cleansings. Since he had come on board the focus has been almost entirely on unjoining the Demons that had managed to complete the possession process. He knew that the majority of the income that Preacher made came from house cleansing, and completing exorcisms that the church refused to do based on evidence, storing items was new.

There was a working website where people could send emails, and if it was something that the team felt they should look into they did. He heard Gus coming up the stairs and met him in the dining room.

"Any recent jobs that we need to look into?" Genuine curiosity filled his voice. Josh thought a bit of normalcy would help lower the tension in the house. Since Michael came to the house and Preachers revelation things were so tense that you could feel the strain in the air like an electrical charge.

Gus nodded. "We got an email last night. The family claimed that there were objects that were moving around the house unexplained, knocking on walls and footsteps are being heard in rooms that are not occupied."

"Does it sound Demonic?" Josh knew that before possession Demons went through several processes while they weakened their prey. The first step was usually things like this, called infestation. At this stage, it can be easily mistaken for a mischievous spirit. It's not until the second stage, the oppression that it can truly be identified as Demonic.

Gus simply shrugged. "No attacks or physical manifestations. The family doesn't feel threatened or like they are in any danger. But they want it checked and if necessary cleansed. They are about an hour away, told them I would check the calendar and call them back if we could fit them in the schedule."

Josh nodded and started to head down to the basement to clean up.

**

Gus looked over the table that was covered in scrolls and notes from each member of the team, except Preacher.

Gus sighed and allowed his frustration to roll through him. When he agreed to help Preacher, he did not, could not, have anticipated this swing of events. He struggled with reconciling the Bibles teachings and knowing his sister practiced witchcraft. Now he had to add this Nephilim business into it all.

The word of God was vague, to say the least about the Nephilim. More precisely there was only one line in the Bible that even talked about the subject. Gus was hoping that Bobby would have more information on the condition because from what he had learned in this line of work, ignorance the worst thing possible.

He could remember the first few calls he went on with Preacher. There was an adrenaline spike that occurred when he arrived on site. It was a reaction his body went through because he didn't know what kind of scary thing awaited on the inside of the house. Over time he found the spike was less high, but the danger was just as real.

Raz did not show up before they were ready to leave. Either she was out running, sleeping, or avoiding the group for the time being. None of those things surprised him. Gus went down to the workshop and wrapped the jar in a soft cloth, then placed it into a small plain wooden box.

The two drove in silence the short distance to the storage unit, which to the disappointment of Josh was a plain storage unit. Gus entered a code and drove into the facility.

"So, we have this place set with a trap or two, let me point them out before you get yourself shot." Gus said as he unlocked the door and pushed it up.

Josh was surprised at the size of it. Somehow it looked much bigger on the inside. Gus pointed to the rolling door, a large devil trap circle was painted on it. "There is another that is painted on the ceiling."

Gus stepped over low wires and ducked under higher wires and placed the box on the shelf of a shelving unit that was similar to the ones in the garage at home. The unit was full of Knick-knacks, pictures, plates, and several boxes.

Josh struggled at first to follow the wires to their destination. He followed one wire to a shotgun, but the others tucked into shelves and he couldn't see where they went. It was apparent that no one would break into this storage unit without pain.

"Preacher has been collecting these things for years. I don't even know what is in most of these. He's not all that big into labeling." Gus carefully made his way back out of the unit, and into the car.

On the drive back Josh was left wondering what was in all those boxes, and what they could learn about Demons from the jar they just placed inside the storage unit.

28.

The most significant problem with being a Demon isn't existing as a disembodied spirit that has to attach to a human host to really live in the world. It certainly was not the label of evil incarnate, Demons had undoubtedly earned that over the years. It is politics. One minute you are minding your own business and the next you are being told to cash in half of your first born child contracts that took almost a decade to make, for a more powerful Demon to make a deal of her own.

What makes matters worse is that no one really makes first-born children contracts anymore. They are tough to negotiate and enforce. They have their own set of special rules and loopholes that need to be tended to. Regardless Josiah found himself calling in three of the five he had made because of politics.

Adding insult to injury, he was carrying two infants in their car seats, while Ramil carried one and led a fourth human tribute with a dog collar around his neck towards Sanctuary. Baba Doek was wearing sensible attire, instead of her usual dresses and high heels led them towards Sanctuary.

Entering a Sanctuary is different for every Demon, and different for every Sanctuary. This Sanctuary was located in what was once the city of Ophir, Utah. Human population in Ophir was twenty-five. It was formerly a mining town, but once the coal ran out the town shriveled and died.

The power of the Sanctuary denied shadow stepping into it. So that left walking or driving and Baba Doek wanted to walk. They emerged from a shadow a mile from town and started walking. It was cold, and snow had freshly fallen in the area. They trudged toward Sanctuary, the only evidence they left behind them were the shuffling footsteps of the human they were dragging with them.

Politics in Demon society were complicated, to say the least. Sanctuaries were established to create neutral places for Demons to meet in safety. No one would have a home-field advantage when conducting business in Sanctuary. These places were governed by a set of rules called the Covenants, and the Covenants were enforced by some of the most ruthless that Demons and the Fallen had to offer, the Knights of Hell. The Knights were Satan's Royal Guard. Dedicated to the one that holds the throne and the safety and sanctity of these Sanctuaries. In general, the Knights were complete badasses.

Josiah had never been to one before. He kept his dealing in the business of taking souls and doing his regents bidding. The war for power in Hell has been going on since the disappearance of The Morning Star, with one King or another vying for control and holding it for only a short time if they even acquired it, to begin with.

Baba Doek was in mid-step when she crossed the invisible barrier to Sanctuary. It sent a shudder down her spine. Josiah tried to anticipate the feeling he would have when he passed the barrier. It was such an unexpected sensation like an invisible weight was placed on his shoulders. His strength waned slightly as the barrier dampened his powers.

Glancing back over his shoulder he noticed that all four of them were now leaving tracks in the fresh snow. His feet were much colder than a moment ago. As a Joined he felt temperature changes, but neither hot nor cold actually bothered him. Humidity was annoying but still tolerable. This cold, wet sensation on his feet was something he remembered as he searched his host's memories. This was too much like being human for his taste.

The four trudged on through the snow, finally approaching Bowman Gulch. As Baba Doek made it to the edge of the drop off she cast a spell. She spoke softly into the eternal night. Ripples wafted upward in the air while several demonic sigils and wardings burst into fire in the air. Squinting into the flame, Josiah saw a building that wasn't there before. It was a wooden structure that stretched several hundred feet in either direction. Several windows were set in the walls to allow the occupants a view of those arriving before they got there.

Baba Doek pushed open the wooden door that was in front of her with ease and walked inside. Ramil nodded to Josiah in an unsettled deferring. Somewhere in the recess of his mind Josiah made a note to mock him for it later.

Josiah walked in without missing a beat. "You're a star Ramil, thanks." Once he crossed the threshold, he heard several low conversations murmuring through the building. Within seconds all conversation volume died down, and Josiah felt all the eyes in the building on him and Baba Doek's entourage.

The inside of Sanctuary was dimly lit with a reddish glow that surrounded all the light sources. There were no electric lights, just balls of glowing magick. Otherwise, it seemed to have the feeling of an old dive bar that made Josiah feel more at home.

The inside was larger than the outside, another smart piece of spellwork. Booths were along the wall, and several tables filled the space on the floor. Josiah wanted to say out loud that it was bigger on the inside but didn't want to sound cliché or like a first-time visitor to Sanctuary.

Josiah followed Baba Doek to the empty bar with Ramil behind him. Baba Doek stopped at the bar, though she had the attention of whoever was behind the bar as soon as she walked into Sanctuary.

He was tall for any measure of tall, standing at over six and a half feet, but he was lean and gaunt, underweight for his height. He had fiery red hair and beard, which stood out on his pale white skin. Bright, intelligent blue eyes darted out from under the fire red eyebrows on his face.

He looked over the foursome and his brow furrowed in a mixture of annoyance and amusement. When he spoke, he had an accent that Josiah couldn't quite place. "I will welcome Damballa in your current incarnation. King of Hell and now a regent on Earth I hear, congratulations." He looked at the group, Damballa in the body of a twenty-something, Ramil in the body of someone who used too many steroids and wore a size too small shirt, and Josiah, still in his business suit.

"Baba Doek now. Joined and happy." Baba Doek had an ease to her voice. "Don't be a bother Red." Baba Doek looked over her shoulder to Josiah and Ramil. "I come bearing gifts and bribes, just as you like it." Baba Doek paused for a moment to let what she said to sink in. "Boys, this is Malphas, but he likes to be called Red. Red, these are my Boys."

Malphas nodded without taking his eyes off of Baba Doek. Red seemed to fit him though, his hair was over shoulder length long and fiery red, but his full mustache and beard had grey and white mixed in with it.

Red glanced at all of them before he settled back on Baba Doek. "What do you want?" He paused only a second before he continued. "I never trust a voodoo goddess, especially one that comes bearing gifts." Red nodded to the children being carried by Josiah and Ramil.

If his comment bothered Baba Doek, he couldn't tell because Baba Doek laughed at what was apparently a joke.

"No more souls allowed into kids dolls Damballa. We've had too many movies already!" another voice shouted from a booth that Josiah couldn't identify. Ramil turned to his side of the bar, the red eyes of his warrior flaring.

Baba Doek grabbed him by the shoulder. "Remember The Covenants Ramil. No violence in Sanctuary." Baba Doek then turned to face Red. "As artistic designs go, I have not done any movie work for a while. Hence the series turned to shit. You are right; however, I am here to pay you for an early release."

Red raised his index finger. Josiah could tell that Red was interested, especially with the infants in tow. He pointed over to an empty booth behind them. "Sit. I will join you shortly." He turned and walked away without another word.

The foursome slid into the booth, and Josiah found himself looking awkwardly between the children and Ramil.

A small grey figure caught his attention as it scurried across the floor and then disappeared, only to reappear on their table.

The creature looked like the bastard offspring of a gargoyle and a gremlin. It stood maybe two feet tall and was grey like a stone. It boasted bat-like ears protruding off its broadhead. The creature had yellow catlike eyes, pointed teeth, and a forked tongue hiding behind large lips.

It stood holding three paper cards in claw-tipped fingers. It offered one to Baba Doek, which she took. Then it offered cards to the two male Demons after she received hers. The creature spoke in a broken nervous English. "Red says, he says, first refreshments are, they are on the house. Tell me, tell Morty. Morty, that's me. And I'll make sure they are on the house."

Baba Doek barely looked at what the Imp handed her before answering. "Three of the Nineteen Twelve Spiritus Vitae. Make sure it is the French virgins, not the Italian virgins. Italian virgins were usually whores in nineteen-twelve." Morty the Imp nodded enthusiastically and scampered off to get the order.

Josiah took a closer look around Sanctuary and now noticed the Imps all over the bar. They were crawling around looking for glasses behind the bar or pouring drinks from taps. A pair could be seen sweeping the floor, one sweeping and one with a dustpan.

"There are many more creatures than I thought would be here." Ramil's voice was coming across with more of an Eastern European accent than Josiah was familiar with hearing. Baba Doek nodded, without looking.

"Most of these creatures are born of sin and attach themselves to a person to exist through that life. Once their attachment dies most of them cease to exist. Some will continue as agents of Hell to make sure accidents happen, and people meet their timely demise. Others will find themselves in a setting like this. Red will give them enough Spiritus Vitae to take orders and sweep the floors."

Ramil nodded, and Josiah found himself doing the same. Existing outside of your immediate nature made sense to most Demons even if they didn't want to admit it. He saw Red coming their way with four glasses filled to the brim with the bright blue, almost white color of the Spiritus Vitae that Baba Doek ordered.

Making the essence of the soul into a liquid libation was an art. It was more difficult than cooking, brewing beer, or casting a simple spell. Josiah had on several occasions attempted to make it on his own and failed every time. Seeing this brought to his table he thought he may revisit the idea.

Sliding into the booth and pushing Josiah to the side like he meant nothing, Red sat in front Baba Doek. "What do you want Baba? It is Baba Doek now right?" He paused for her to nod in acknowledgment. "You have made a spectacle with these infants. According to the rules of Sanctuary, they shall not leave alive. But you were already counting on that weren't you?"

Baba Doek reached over and took a glass of the Spiritus Vitae that Red brought to the table. She lifted it to her nose and inhaled. "This is from South Africa, it is good, but not what I asked for." She sat the glass in front of her. "I need someone released early from one of your spirit boxes. I need it done tonight, about seventy-five years early." Baba Doek nodded to the sleeping children at the table. "These are first born contracts, from me to you, as payment for the release."

There was a long pause while Red thought about the proposition. "You brought a warrior." Red nodded to Ramil. "And you are formidable, even in my Sanctuary. You also brought a dealer." Almost absentmindedly he nodded to Josiah. "To me, that means you weren't sure what you were in store for, and maybe, you think I forgot the last time you were here."

Baba Doek seemed to stare through Josiah she was staring at him so hard. He glanced at Red without turning his head. "Her tactic makes sense, the last person that defied her she killed without mercy. That was an emissary from Regent Balisk, and wow that was entertaining. But here no violence is allowed. It's always better to hedge your bets on too many skills in your group than not enough."

It was Baba Doek's hand slapping the table that made Josiah aware that he was talking way too much and snapped him from the spell of Reds words.

Baba Doek motioned with her hand that slapped the table toward the children. "Three first born contracts for you, as long as you release him." She took the glass in front her and drank it in one single gulp.

Ramil reached in to take a glass, but Baba Doek stopped him by grabbing his wrist. Josiah thought he heard bones snap, but he couldn't be sure. Just to be safe Josiah didn't reach to a glass.

Red looked at Baba Doek so he could measure her up. Josiah knew the fight or flight signals in his prey and tried to ascertain the same signs in Red. Unfortunately Red was a mask of calm and poise. While in his Sanctuary he did not have to fight or flee. He enforced the Covenants here, and here he was more powerful than the three of them combined.

Red looked at Baba Doek and nodded at the fourth human. "What's that for?"

Baba Doek grinned. "Vessel on the go. It's like take out."

Red nodded. "You brought three because you know his crimes are the most serious. He destroyed three of your kind before he was subdued. He was placed behind the highest wards to prevent escape and has lived for one hundred and seventy-five years in a spirit jar because I commanded it."

Baba Doek didn't move, not even a blink. When she spoke, it was with her commanding voice, just like she was at home in her own domain. "Release him. The price is more than fair."

Red stroked his long beard. "I'll take all three, and a favor to be named later. If you didn't want him so badly, you could have left two outside in the cold to die before I made up my mind."

Josiah's mind was spinning, it was an excellent initial counteroffer. If he was told what he would be walking into he would have suggested something similar as an initial offer, Red apparently was not stupid.

Josiah let his true self come out. "This is the best deal you will get. We came in for a true deal, no haggling no fine print. Three first born contracts for this jarred soul that is almost at his expiration date." Josiah took the glass in front of him and offered it to Red. "But no unnamed favors in the future. Do we have a deal or should we go home," Josiah glanced at Baba Doek "She commands more souls in Hell than you can imagine. If you defy her and she manages to come out on top, you could lose this Sanctuary. I imagine you will lose this Sanctuary because Baba Doek holds a Key to Hell." Josiah nodded to the tooth necklace around her neck.

Josiah fully extended his arm with the glass in it. "It appears that you have postured and bolstered enough for the time being. Take the deal, touch the glass and drink with me. In case you haven't noticed, everyone is waiting on this deal to get done."

Red took a moment to let his eyes dart around the bar. The silence in Sanctuary was thick. The eyes of everyone were looking at the table.

Red grinned and began to nod. He lifted his glass, not to Josiah but to Baba Doek. "Yes," His eyes never left Baba Doek. "We have ourselves a deal."

Baba Doek brought her glass to his, and they clinked. Each drank while Josiah was left holding his glass untouched. Josiah allowed himself a moment of pride. This is why she brought him, to navigate the deal, not just because of the contracts. He swallowed his own alone.

Red took two of the infants as he stood. He looked back over his shoulder at Baba Doek, nodding at the third. It was evident that she was too follow and make good on the deal.

Baba Doek slid from the booth and followed carrying the third child. She followed him through to what could have been a kitchen. Not surprisingly though it was a chamber of horrors for those of weak stomach.

Immediately to her left, where usually a stove or flattop would be was a Demon, hanging by a strange (but brilliant) design of chains and spikes, covering his wrist and throat. If he pulled himself up to relieve the pain on his neck the pain would be inflicted on his wrists. Self-inflicted, choose your own torture.

Red led them further through to the back. Imps scurried out of his way like pets scared of their master. He finally stepped into what could have been an office. Red walked in and placed the infants on the floor.

Baba Doek followed and placed the third child with the others. There was an eerie quiet in the room. The sounds of the Sanctuary were muted and distant. Josiah quickly glanced around the room and saw the wards around the door to keep the room cut off from the rest of Sanctuary.

There was a wall full of shelves to the far side of the room. Each shelf held jars of different shapes and sizes from end to end. Some were smooth porcelain, others were different colored glass, while others seemed to be carved from stone.

Red walked to the wall and began looking over it. "Why him? With three first born contracts, you could get just about anything you want." Red took a jar off the shelf and rolled it in his hands looking at the inscriptions on it. "As far as Demons go he isn't all that impressive."

Red handed the jar over to Baba Doek, who looked the jar over before looking back at Red. "I know, he wasn't much of a Trickster. His mind is brilliant though. He would move along the worlds magical lay lines and bring the souls of the dead to Judgement." Baba Doek shrugged. "I have all the items needed for a spell to change the world as we know it. If I am right, he knows the location that I need to cast it from."

Red slightly raised an eyebrow, and Baba Doek returned an exasperated look. "Not the Apocalypse. It was thwarted, or it failed at least fifteen times. My solution is more elegant. Everyone will like it more. I'm going to crack the wards, I'm going to get our bodies back."

Red nodded. "Okay then, I'll let you get to it." Red walked by Baba Doek and headed out of the office. Just before he stepped out of the office, he paused. "When Christ died and the Morning Star sealed heaven, we knew what we were doing. Sealing away Gods wrath for killing his only Son, we knew what we were doing then. Are you sure you're not going to undo it?"

Baba Doek looked Red in the eyes without blinking. "Could you imagine anything better?"

Red grunted and stepped out heading back to his Sanctuary. Baba Doek motioned for Ramil to bring the human into the room. Ramil drug the man in the room on the leash.

Wasting no time Baba Doek cracked the seal and opened the jar. Thick black putrid smoke left the opening and swirled around the ankles of those in the room. It ran across the feet and twirled around their legs. As it came across the humans' foot, it congealed like a fluid, then started to climb with thick sinewy like tendrils up the body.

As it rose, it seemed to melt and become smokier. Like someone stretching before a run, the spirit spread and retracted as it worked its way up the body. Finally, as it made its way to the head of the human and swirled like a vortex around it. The smoke entered the mouth, the ears, nostrils, and even leaked into the eyes.

The human dropped to his knees gasping. Briefly tearing at his collar and his throat to get free. After the smoke was gone the human looked puzzled, then his face went slack. Laughter came from the vessel that was deeper than it should have been as he took a look around the room for the first time in over one hundred years.

He looked Baba Doek up and down and stood up. "That time passed quickly." Looking around the room, his eyes fell on the infants, and he looked back at Baba Doek. "You got me out early? You must be in desperate need."

Baba Doek nodded. "I need for you to draw me a map." She allowed herself a rare smile "Welcome back Anubis. I hope you're still a good artist."

29.

Preacher was going over his sixth scroll of the morning. He reached out for his cup of coffee and took a sip. The coldness of the drink startled him. He hadn't realized that he had been reading for so long. He stood and stretched his stiff muscles. Begrudgingly he headed for a refill.

After dumping the old in the sink, he refilled his mug. He headed back to the dinner table, contemplating the scroll he was reading – a superbly boring manuscript on the high intelligence of the Celestials compared to human intellect.

A blinking light on the phone in what they affectionately called the office caught his attention. He walked over to the small table and picked up the cordless phone. It showed that there were seventeen messages. Preacher raised an eyebrow and checked the ringer on the phone and found that the volume was turned down to mute.

It was strange that it would be muted. The phone was the team's financial lifeline. Preacher pushed the voicemail button and began to listen. The first voicemail was more intense than normal.

The person holding the phone sounded scared. When Preacher listened carefully, he could hear why. Someone else was in the room mixing English, Latin and Hellion languages. By the fifth voicemail, he could hear the panic in the voice of the caller. With the help of some narration, he could hear dressers and nightstands being moved.

Ten voicemails into the backlog and they were all from the same caller. At the tenth voicemail a cacophony of noise could be heard on the other end of the phone. Glass breaking, objects moving, and an extremely panicked brother breathing into the phone. The sounds roused Preacher's adrenaline. He could almost smell the Demon through the phone.

By the last voicemail Preacher was convinced that this was something he needed to act upon. The first voicemail was left at one-thirteen am. The last one was left at just after six am. Preacher looked at his watch and saw it was only after seven in the morning.

Hanging up the phone, he listened to the silence of the house. He was torn between waking his team and going on his own. Preacher put the phone back on the cradle and shadow-stepped into his bedroom to change into his full cassock.

After changing his clothes, he stepped into the hallway and found the house still quiet. Briefly, he allowed his imagination to create the thought that he was living alone and all his allies had fled, just because the house was so quiet.

He almost allowed doubt to creep in, but then he remembered where he was going. Fighting the already damned allowed for zero doubt. Preacher straightened his posture and headed for the closest shadow.

Preacher came through the shadow with his face inches in front of a houses vinyl siding. There apparently was still a lot to learn about shadow stepping. He quickly stepped back to the walkway of the house that lead from the driveway to the front door.

He turned and headed towards the houses steps to the front door. It was a house that was designed in the split foyer style that was very popular in the early nineteen nineties. Preacher climbed the stairs to the home and rang the doorbell.

It was quiet outside the home which he didn't expect once he was there. The voicemail he received from the house just over an hour ago gave him the impression that he would be coming into something different. It was possible that he took down the wrong address, but he wrote it down and checked it twice before he left.

Preacher rang the doorbell and waited for an answer. Time passed, more time passed than he thought it should. After several seconds Preacher knocked on the door. He hit loudly enough to make sure he was heard but not loud enough to be rude. It was a delicate balance from his experience. Everyone knew about the 'cop knock,' and he tried to avoid it at all cost.

More time passed. Preachers calm began to break. He knew what he heard on the voicemail and knew there was someone here that needed his help, and with every second that passed that no one answered the door, his panic began to grow.

The next set of knocks came harder. They were the knocks of authority that gets the attention of anyone inside. Preacher listened carefully, but couldn't hear anything on the inside of the house.

"The house is vacant Preacher." The voice came from behind him, and he turned to face who was talking to him. He saw two people, one was dressed very well in a three-piece suit. The other was much the opposite. His hair cut in a mullet, wearing a sleeveless t-shirt from an eighties metal band.

"We called, over and over again." The businessman spoke "We wanted to talk to you. We needed your attention." As he spoke with Preacher, his eyes flashed with red signifying him as a warrior. "You're a hard man to talk you."

Preacher took a step down from the landing towards the two on the street. "You have my attention. I'm not sure that is something that you want though." Preacher chuckled as he walked down the remaining steps. He looked over at Synder, "This is what I call irony. Demons are calling an exorcist and inviting him over. You must be the brains of this operation obviously."

Snyder's eyes flashed green as the insult hit its mark. "The plan worked well enough to get you here. So far so good I'd say." He shrugged. "We called because the enemy of my enemy is my friend. It has been brought to our attention that you have a grudge against the one that calls herself Baba Doek. We want to help you stop her."

Preacher stepped on the ground and sat his bag down. He doubted that he could get to any of the items in the bag to effect an exorcism at the moment, so it made sense to keep his hands free.

"The first rule that we learn as exorcists is Demon's lie. You follow the father of lies, so it is in your nature to deceive, mislead and destroy. You can understand why I do not believe you." Preacher put his hands inside the pocket of his cassock and with one hand found his crucifix and with his other found his iron knuckles.

Neither of the Demons moved. Snyder continued, "Our Regent is known as Balisk. He did not think Baba Doek would be a true threat, so he sent us here with an emissary. We crafted a map to lead her to what she desired most in the world. Balisk thought it might be something to jump-start Armageddon, but since the Covenants were enacted, we thought it was something else. Baba Doek destroyed our emissary's vessel. We cannot return to our Regent without vengeance."

The warrior tapped his chest "I am Malik, and he is Snyder. We think we know what she wants to do, but not the where she will do it. We cannot stop this on our own. Otherwise, we would not be here. We are here to make a deal."

Preacher casually strolled forward towards the Demons. "I don't make deals with Demons. It goes against the teachings of Jesus Christ." Preacher paused walking a few more steps closer to the warrior. That was the threat here. He pulled his left hand out of his cassock pocket and pointed at Malik leaving his rosary in the pocket. He would only have one chance for an attack.

"You're a Demon though, and you know the scripture. It is the whole 'Know thy enemy thing' right?" Preacher was only a few steps out of striking distance before the warrior backed up a few paces.

"Our sources tell us that she found a cursed item. A mighty cursed item." The voice came from the Trickster. "She wants to use it to cast a spell to open Tartarus and get all of our bodies back. While some of us think it's a great idea, others, like our Regent think not. In Hell, there is a line being drawn between those who think she would succeed and those who don't."

Preacher nodded acting like he understood, but he didn't really. "A civil war in Hell doesn't sound so bad to me. Fight amongst yourself and leave this world and these people out of it. I am okay with that."

Snyder shook his head. "A war in Hell will spill onto your world like you can't imagine. If she breaks through Tartarus and we get out Celestial bodies back, the Earth you know will no longer exist. Choose between two bad options Preacher, but the choice is yours."

Preacher didn't have a response, so he nodded and stepped forward trying to get closer to the warrior. The warrior held up his hand. "I don't expect your answer today, but soon. We want to help thwart her plans as we can. When you have made up your mind just step outside and call out for us. We will get your message. If you want our help to stop her we will help, regardless we will work to destroy her."

"I don't make deals with demons. My reputation should have made that obvious." Every step Preacher took towards Malik resulted in Malik taking a step backward. He was not going to let Preacher close the gap, so Preacher turned his attention to the Trickster.

But again every step he took the Trickster backed away. Snyder raised his hand and wagged a finger "Tsk tsk Preacher. We aren't the hugging type." He took another step backward. Snyder muttered something under his breath and made an arching motion with his palm outward facing Preacher.

Preacher noticed a flicker of shadow in the corner of his eye, something was rushing towards him. It was large but low to the ground and coming at him fast. He turned to face a threat. But when he turned there was nothing there. He spun back to the Demons, but they were gone.

Preacher wasn't sure if they had made themselves unseen or had fled the area. He didn't think they knew he was a Nephilim and didn't want to give it away by shadow stepping back home. So he sat on the bottom step of the porch and used his cellphone to order a ride.

It took about twenty minutes for the car to arrive. The time was spent in silent contemplation. Preacher tried to center himself and come to an understanding of the situation. The motives these Demons had were foreign to him.

Knowing that Demons had some kind of structure was disturbing even if it was as fragile as these two made it sound. Preacher found himself at home faster than he would have liked. He tipped his driver and made his way up the stairs.

Coming into the house the smell of coffee and breakfast flooded his nose. He walked inside and went to the kitchen. He made himself a plate of hash browns, eggs and bacon. Walking into the dining room he heard whatever conversation that was going on cease.

His crew sat around the table but fell silent as he took a seat. Preacher looked at them in turn, one by one. "I asked for your help based on the works that I have done for your family members or for you personally. We have become a family within these walls and through our works. Please, don't let us break now when we need to be the strongest."

Raz's fork slipped from her hand and fell to her plate. "You had no idea at all? In all these years you didn't know that you were something different or special?"

Preacher shook his head. "I knew that I was a better exorcist, but I never knew why. I was raised to be one, and that's what I thought it was."

Everyone sat silent for a moment almost stilled by the words Preacher spoke. Gus straightened himself and looked at Preacher breaking the silence. "We are all here to help you, Preacher, as long as you are acting in the will of God. But you are not the Preacher we knew, you're different now." Gus looked down at the table, then his plate before he finished. "I don't know how to stop you if you turn evil."

Preacher sipped his coffee and nodded. "You know right from wrong and good from evil. I trust your judgment as my team, more than I trust my own at the moment." Preacher began the story where it should start when he lost M.C. It proceeded through Botis, Bolfry, and concluded in his meeting with the Demons that morning.

After Preacher finished, no one spoke. Finally, Josh spoke up "Are you looking for our permission to work with these Demons? Because that goes against everything, you taught us."

Preacher shook his head side to side. "I am looking for forgiveness. I am looking for understanding. Above all, I am looking for guidance from my friends because right now, I don't know what to do."

"I think the most important question here is 'why'." Gus's tone was stoic and analytical. "We know that Demons lie, but they wrapped their lies in truth. So assume this is political revenge and we ask why are they coming to you?"

"She's powerful. It's possible they don't have what it takes to deal with her on their own." It sounded like Preacher was thinking out loud rather than making conversation. He held a thousand-yard stare looking at the wall but not really seeing it.

"Or they could be trying to kill you. This could be a setup." Raz sounded concerned.

Preacher shook his head. "They already had me on my own today. They could have attacked today if they wanted. I don't think that's the case. We know who, what and why. We need to figure out the where and the when."

Preacher started to formulate a plan. "We have to assume this is a powerful spell. Raz, reach out to local covens and try to get an idea about the conditions that need to be met for something like this. Also, pull everything you can from the web about Tartarus."

"Gus, get Bobby on this to see what he can dig up and then we will start on these scrolls. Josh, keep tinkering on your latest and greatest. I think we will need something they haven't seen before if we are going to survive this and be successful."

"What about working with the Demons?" Again, Gus had a very flat and analytical tone to his voice.

"We will consider it as a last resort option. We need to know more before we make the decision." Preacher met Gus' gaze. "I'm against the idea, there is nothing good that can come of it. In this case, the enemy of my enemy is still my enemy. So let's find out what we can and then have this conversation again."

With that, the team broke off to make calls, read scrolls, and ticker with inventions. No one was excited about the situation but having tasks to accomplish brought some of their normalcy back to the house.

□

30.

They sat in Baba Doek's suite accessed by a hidden door off her throne room. She neglected to hold court again for another evening, trusting her minions to carry out her orders and collect their due tributes on her behalf.

Anubis sat in a chair across Baba Doek slipping slowly on a coffee. The world was different from when he last left it. It was taking time to get used to the changes. Baba Doek smiled a thin strained smile at him. "How long will it take to fulfill my request Anubis? I am patient only up to a point."

"It will take some time. You are asking for something exact and knowledge that is very old. It is not an easy task." Anubis took the last sip of his coffee and placed the cup on the table. "I remember after the fall, I would still travel the world collecting the souls of the deceased and I would weigh the sin in their heart to the weight of a feather. I would stand in their judgment as I was created to do. Since the death of Christ, I have not been able to follow my lines or weigh my souls."

Baba Doek nodded with understanding. "You will be able to collect your souls again and weigh their sin. First though, we need to set things back to how they use to be. How long before I can get my map?"

Anubis sighed. "It could take weeks, maybe longer. I've spent the last one hundred and seventy-five years trapped in darkness with myself. It takes its toll. At least in Hell, there were distractions, leaders, and politics. In that jar the only thing there was me, and the memory of the fall." Anubis tapped the coffee cup. "May I have more of this? It was excellent."

Baba Doek nodded. "I'll send for more. I will also send for pencil, paper, and maps." Baba Doek motioned around the room. "I will bring you whatever you need to get started."

Anubis nodded. "My thanks. I do have one more request. I would like to see the spell. Knowing what you want to accomplish is one thing, but seeing how you will accomplish it another, and it may help me give you the best location possible."

Baba Doek took her time in nodding. "Your concern is flattering and unnecessary. However, out of respect for your craft, I'll allow it." She paused for a moment thinking. "After your get started on the map."

Anubis smiled and nodded. He watched Baba Doek leave the room. He looked around the room for a moment, taking in all the ways the world had changed since being locked away in the Dybbuk box. The lights in the room were not candles as they were when he last walked the earth.

Since following Baba Doek through her shadow step, he has ceased to be amazed. Her lair lay beneath a gathering site where music was not played with instruments but played through boxes places along the walls. He disliked the music of this time. It sounded metallic and repetitive. It seemed less skillful than the music he was used to. The phonograph had only been around for a few years before he was put in the Dybbuk box, and perhaps because of that the music that he heard recorded was more refined.

After a few moments, one of Baba Doeks human minions entered the room. He was carrying a large stack of paper and a box of pencils. He sat them on a nearby table and looked at Anubis and nodded. "I'll be back soon with your coffee. My mistress asks that you get started on your maps."

Anubis nodded to the human and watched him walk out of the room. He stood and walked to the table to begin his task. The pages that were stacked on one another were thin and almost see through. There were different colored pencils in the box, which he thought appropriate.

Anubis pulled out a green pencil and looked down at the map in front of him. He looked over the map, and his eyes settled on a small city outside of Rome. It was never really a significant city, but it was once a Nexus, where several ley lines crossed. It was his favorite place to start when collecting souls. He would shoot out on a line, which ran in a hexagonal pattern back to the Nexus. Then off in another direction, on another line to collect another group of souls.

Each time he turned, he was on a different and new line that crossed the one he was on. Simple small geometric patterns could be drawn if he kept to them, or he could explore the world sliding from one line to the next.

Each line pattern felt different to him as he rode it. Some lines felt like sliding down a river of lavender. While others felt like running on a beach during high winds, with the sting of sand pinging on his face. Anubis felt himself finding the River of Lavender and drawing those lines.

He found himself going from Rome to Greece to Bucharest, to Budapest, Milan, and then back to Rome. Each city spawned new lines and adventures. But they were not the silky Lavender. He followed only the Lavender lines, farther east then north and west, moving south across the river. Losing himself in memory that paper dissolved into feelings and souls that he touched.

It was like riding a bike as the saying goes. As Anubis drew seconds melded into hours. The smell of hot fresh coffee filled his nose and turned stale as he couldn't pull himself from his work, reliving his own history. He remembered souls he had judged fairly and without remorse.

Finally, once all the lines were on paper, he came back to himself. The atrocious noise from the room above could still faintly be heard. He could smell fresh coffee in the room, and as he turned he saw Baba Doek sitting in the seat he had once occupied behind him.

She was dressed differently than when he saw her last, she was wearing a deep blue dress, with sapphire earrings and black heels that made her four inches taller than she was. A necklace of teeth hung from her neck, something Anubis recognized as a Key of Hell. He found the irony in Damballa attaining the teeth of the original thirteen voodoo priests in Africa.

She stood and walked toward him. Each movement was effortless as she came towards him. In her hands she carried a steaming hot cup of coffee, the aroma met his nose, and he knew it came of Egypt.

He accepted the cup as she looked at the drawing he made. "You have worked for ten hours, but I see only one line." Her tone was harsh. She was trying to scold him, to challenge him to work faster.

In response, he only nodded. "That is one of many lines I memorized. One line is drawn, only fifty-one more to draw. Some are longer and more complicated, some are short and go from one place to the next and end."

Anubis took a sip from his coffee and looked at Baba Doek, "I have started my work for you. Is your spell ready for me to look at?" He took another, deeper drink from the coffee.

Baba Doek nodded in the direction of the table that she had just come from. Sitting on the table was her grimoire. Anubis walked to the table and opened the spell book. He opened the book and began reading.

He realized that this was not one spell, but several spells being cast at the same time. Several spells being cast by one caster. While it was not unheard of, it was quite tricky. Anubis saw that each spell would take a massive amount of energy, too much for one caster, even with a Key of Hell around her neck.

"This is solid spell work, but the energy required is too much. Even for you Damballa" Anubis shook his head. "Even if you could harness that much energy, you would need to cast this spell in a place and moment of total darkness."

Anubis took another sip of his coffee. "This world seems to be lit in a way that it has never been lit before. A lunar eclipse will not be enough now because of this artificial light."

Baba Doek nodded in agreement. "I have stockpiled the fuel for this spell, so that is not a concern. As far as darkness, humans have given us something called the internet, which I will expose you to soon enough. This fountain of knowledge takes out most of the guesswork when it comes to Astronomy. You find the place, and I will determine the time."

Anubis nodded even though he did not understand this internet that she spoke of. "Even so, this spell will take almost an hour. No celestial occurrence will last that long. You would have moments at most, not an hour."

Baba Doek nodded again. "That would be true unless you were to have the voodoo Key of Hell and you were the origin of the Voodoo religion."

Anubis nodded. "I understand." He picked up his coffee and walked over and removed the first page that he drew on from the pile. He took out a different color of pencil and began looking at the drawing of the Earth. "This will take some time, remembering the way I use to travel." He looked at the coffee cup, then back to Baba Doek, "Please send more of what you sent before. I know this is Egyptian, but this is shit compared to what you offered before."

Baba Doek chuckled. "I will make sure we send you only the best, but there are hundreds of different coffee makers and so many different ways to make coffee since you have been gone. We will send what you like, but I will expose you to the different ways we have available to make it. As long as you keep working."

Anubis nodded. "My thanks Damballa."

"Call me Baba Doek. Also if you need anything else let me know. If you need a girl or a boy, something to occupy your time, don't hesitate to ask. But don't let it occupy a lot of your time."

Anubis nodded absently. He was already thinking about the next line he ran. It was gritty and golden like sand. He liked to start this line in Cairo. Then west, south, east, south again. He would ride this line from desperate for water to too much water and back again. He would cross oceans, only to not see rain again until he made another trip.

These were Golden lines. They were longer and in many cases harder lines. More unforgiving than most. Like other lines, they crossed continents and oceans. Most importantly they crossed other lines.

Remembering his past became more comfortable the longer he stayed in it. New lines meant new pages supplied to him. Over and over he drew the paths he used to travel. Sometimes it took hours, but most lines took days for him to draw.

To Anubis, it didn't matter how long it took. He spent his time in his own head, remembering the texture of the leyline he would travel. Regardless of Baba Doek's demands to draw his map quicker. She was not a patient being, but she would have to learn how to be one if she wanted the map to be right.

As each page was laid on top of one another the line crossing could be seen, nebulas began forming. As he finished more and more sections there became eleven Super Nebulas that had more lines running through them than the others. There were two that were in the oceans, Baba Doek discounted those quickly. Trying to spellcraft on the rolling sea did not strike her as a good idea.

That left nine on land. One in Australia, one in Asia, one in Europe, and two in North America. One was located in South America, two were in Africa, and the last one in the Middle East. Baba Doek walked to her computer and opened her search page. She searched quickly for the next solar eclipse and its projected path of totality.

She quickly checked three of the webpages that confirmed the accuracy of the data. It should not have surprised her. Actions and events in the Celestial world were often dipped in irony, and this would be no different. Baba Doek was headed to Savannah.

31.

Tensions slowly abated at Preacher's home as days turned to weeks without any more surprises. Michael returned after almost two weeks since he left Preacher outside of the asylum. Preacher's questions about Michael's whereabouts were met with vague answers about taking care of the possessed that were released when Preacher left the asylum.

For safety reasons, no one went on calls alone anymore. It was never a concern until Preacher went on his own and was cornered by a couple of Demons. After that, it became a hard fast rule.

Raz mostly mingled with the white magick Wiccans who couldn't determine the conditions required for Baba Doeks spell. She heard rumors of dark practitioners that could help her understand, but she was reluctant to communicate with them. If she was not stuck staring at a computer screen, she was out running.

As time passed, she started work on the garden. She planted the seeds and watched them grow in the countertop garden. As spring broke she planted them in the garden outside. Gardening, like magick, is a process. If the process is followed correctly, then you will get the desired result.

Josh completed his spring-loaded crucifix for the most part. He was working on its aim. Something to do with weight and aerodynamics that Preacher didn't pretend to understand but encouraged the project without another thought.

Gus buried himself in research. His belief that knowledge would help him defeat the supernatural became frenzied. Preacher encouraged his enthusiasm at first, eventually though, Gus's quest to know everything began to frustrate everyone. He needed to take a break.

"Let's go for a walk." Preacher's voice cut into Gus's concentration.

Gus looked up at Preacher then back down to the book he was reading. "Ok, let me just finish this part of the book."

Preacher closed the book on Gus. "Let's go now. Suns bright, weather is warm, let's get some air and then come back fresh on the books." Sighing Gus nodded, and they went out the door.

The weather was crisp under the cloudless blue sky. The day was young and there was a little chill in the air, and overall it was nice. The pair remained quiet as they walked down the street.

"What are we doing here Preacher? Besides wasting time." Gus asked

Preacher met his gaze. "We are taking a break. Stepping back to get a little perspective and taking a moment to remember who we are." Preacher started walking down the street slowly giving Gus time to catch up.

"We are wasting time. Every second not spent trying to figure out this problem is time wasted." Gus almost seemed frenzied as he spoke. His eyes were wider than normal, and his tone was more aggressive.

Preacher stopped and looked at him with patience, almost smugness. "Let's evaluate, what do we know?"

"Baba Doek wants to reclaim her body. When that happens, all Demons can reclaim their bodies and crawl back out and walk amongst us. In short, it's the end of the world as we know it and I can't find a way to prevent it."

Preacher started walking towards the end of the street again. "Perhaps we can't find anything because it hasn't been attempted before. If it has never been attempted, it's likely that there is no record of it that we would have access to. We will have to find a way on our own to prevent it."

We also know that there will be Omens. Bolfry was kind enough to give us that piece of information." Preacher's voice was calm and level. "Until the first one takes place, we are not in a rush, and we are not on the clock yet. Let's not get so ready for a war that we forget to enjoy this peace."

Gus nodded. "It has been weeks since we have gotten a call that even closely resembles Demonic activity. It's like they have all just stopped, it makes me nervous."

They reached the end of the street and started back towards the house when the first rumblings of thunder could be heard. It started off low, somewhere in the distance and was easily ignored. Very quickly though, the thunder increased in volume and intensity.

The two stopped walking and looked at the sky for the coming storm, but the sky was clear. Only one or two white puffy clouds could be seen in the sky. As the thunder rolled over their heads in waves, another sound became audible to them.

It began with a single call from a bird. A 'caw' was heard in the woods that lined the back yards of the houses on the street. The call wasn't so unusual. Birds could be heard in this area all the time, even in the colder months, so the two barely noticed it. It was the number of return calls that cause them to hold their breath.

The call was returned a hundred times over, then another hundred times after that. The noise soon became just as loud as the thunder. Suddenly and without warning, everything stopped. The silence was deafening after the thunder and the birds. The only thing that they could hear was the blood rushing through their bodies, with the beat of their pulses.

The shadows of the trees were too thick to see through, but the number of birds it would cause to make that much noise would have to be massive.

"Preacher?" Gus was searching the tree line as well.

"Yeah?" Preacher didn't take his eyes off the tree line, trying to glimpse in the shadows. It was something that he and Michael had been working on recently, like Nephilim night-vision, and he was getting pretty good at it.

"Do you think we should head back?" Gus sounded nervous, the tension was tight in the air.

Preacher nodded. Slowly realizing that he was not trying to look through shadows into the trees. The darkness he saw was moving. It was thousands of ravens sitting in the trees. There were so many that it looked like shadows.

"Yes, Gus. That is exactly what I think we should do." Trying not to take their eyes off the birds they awkwardly started walking toward the house. They had only made a few steps when the sound of flapping wings filled their ears and sections of the shadows lifted into the air. The blue sky turned black as the ravens took to the air and flew their way.

"It's time to run." Preacher said, but Gus didn't respond, he was already running towards the house. Preacher took off in a sprint following him. The birds flew faster than the two could run. They flew low to the ground the first ravens quickly overtook the pair brushing by their heads.

There is a distinct smell that birds have. It's a powdery dander and dust smell that is light in the nose. Usually, it would be a noticeable but not an obnoxious odor. The number of birds combined with the cacophony of wings fluttering and the ravens cawing was frightening. The smell only intensified the fear they were already feeling.

The sky darkened as the swarm overtook them. Wings beat them in the head and around the face. Preacher grabbed onto Gus shirt collar with one hand and his arm with the other. Stepping into the shadows created by the birds above them he brought them through the darkness and into the garage.

Gus spun around, tearing free from Preachers grasp. For a moment he looked bewildered and confused. "That was, I don't know what that was. I was cold. Is that always so cold?"

Preacher nodded. "You never get used to it. Sorry I didn't warn you." Preacher started to head upstairs. "Let's go upstairs and check outside and see what we are dealing with."

Gus nodded, and the two headed upstairs. They made it halfway up the stairs and heard Josh. "What the hell is this?"

The two walked up behind Josh to get a good view. The front yard was covered entirely by ravens. Every inch of grass and every tree limb was covered in big black birds.

Preacher let out a low whistle. "Alfred J. Hitchcock, eat your heart out."

Raz came out from her room, dressed in matching pajamas of a Japanese anime that she loved to watch. She looked down the hall and saw the three men looking out the window. Even though she was wearing headphones, the three men could hear her techno music thumping loudly. She walked through the hall and opened the front door.

Stepping outside of the house she was met by hundreds of eyes. Every set of eyes fixated on her. Some birds tilted their head to the side, others just stared at her. The eyes were black, a never ending shadow.

A flurry of orange blur darted into the body of ravens on the front lawn. Claws ripped at feathers, causing all the ravens to take off into the air to avoid the assault. As the yard cleared of the large black intruders, only an orange cat stood proudly in the yard looking back at Raz. Walking over to a feather left from one of the birds, the cat pawed at it almost playfully then looked back at Raz as if to say "Well, you weren't going to do anything about it." It stretched and sauntered into the shadow of the front porch to take a nap.

Raz stepped back inside the house and closed the door in front of her. "You saw that right? What was that?"

"Those were omens." Gus's tone was flat and showed no emotion. Stepping backward a step Gus looked at Preacher. "Looks like we are on the clock."

Preacher nodded. "Thunder on a cloudless sky was an omen. Being attacked by ravens, not so much." Preacher looked at Gus, "We are the clock, let's figure out where we need to go."

There was a moment of silence as no one moved. "Preacher, we have tried scrolls, proverbs, testimonies, the internet," Josh paused. "What are we missing? Do you think Michael knows anyone in the Church that could help?"

"I will ask him whenever he gets back, but a flock of birds that large is going to get reported. Planes and helicopters will have to be diverted; people are going to take photos. Let's track it and see where it goes."

It did not take long before the internet exploded with photos and videos of the strange migration. From videos and pictures, they found the birds went southeast towards the city of Atlanta. Some fell out of the migration pattern and stayed in the city, but the majority left, heading farther south.

The massive flock shut down Hartsfield-Jackson International Airport for hours as they moved into the area. The flock dispersed even more as they passed the airport, and by the time they reached Macon, it was such a small group that it was no longer trackable.

More hours went by, and the sunlight faded to darkness. Gus cooked a simple dinner of meatloaf and roasted potatoes.

After dinner, Raz left her internet searches and grabbed a bowl and filled it with milk. She took a small plate and added what remained of the meatloaf. She took both to the front porch and sat them down. She snapped her fingers a few times, "Here Kitty, kitty…"

Silently the cat came out from the front porch and made its way up the stairs. It looked at the milk then the meat and then back to Raz. The cat purred, then rubbed his head on her leg. The cat pushed hard on her thigh then moved in figure eight between her legs as if to say thanks before he started eating and drinking what Raz brought out for him. Sensing the cat was pleased, Raz went in for the night, allowing it to eat and drink in peace.

32.

Time has a funny way of passing. When it is normally passing no one notices, a second is just a second. When you are doing something you hate, time seems to drag by slowly. When you are doing something, you enjoy the time seems to fly by quickly.

Days crept by slowly, and stress rose in the house. Everyone knew that with every tick of the clock they were one more second closer to the end. Raz was sitting at her computer when an email from one of her friends came across. She would have ignored it, but it was marked urgent and subject line merely read INFO.

As she clicked the email open Preachers phone rang.

"Hey Bobby, tell me you have some good news. We are beating our heads against the wall here." Preacher sounded tired. They were all felt like they working hard and getting nowhere fast.

"Seeing lots of omens taking place between you and me. A few dairy farms on I-16 reported that all their milk spoiled overnight."

"They could have lost power, or not cleaned properly. Doesn't sound like a demonic omen to me." Preacher retorted.

"This was different, the milk was coming out of the cows spoiled. Also, heard on the news that we have several bakeries local here that was closed for the day because the baked goods wouldn't rise. One store? Could be bad yeast or an oven but this is like ten bakeries."

A thud on the wall drew Preacher's attention away from the phone call for a second. It sounded like a storm had come into the area, the windows had darkened, and the wind was blowing hard."

"Okay, Bobby. That sounds more targeted. Is anything else happening?" Another thud hit the wall of the house. Then another thud. Harder this time. Raz went to the window and opened the blinds.

The sky was black as the crows flew over and into the side of the house. It was similar to the ravens, only the birds were smaller, and there were more of them.

"Preacher, are you there?" Staring out the window Preacher was stunned into silence. "Preacher?"

"Yeah, I'm here Bobby. We have a flock of crows here, larger than the ravens. This is intense."

"Sounds like you got yourself a murder up there." Bobby chuckled, pleased with his pun.

"A what? No one is being murdered. We are all inside."

Bobby chuckled. "A flock of crows is called a murder. From the sounds of it, you have a mass murder going on up there."

"Not a good time to joke Bobby."

"Yeah, for you anyway. Which way are they flying?"

Preacher went to the window and looked at the direction the murder was moving in. The sky was black with birds. Glimpses of light and sky were visible through the fluttering wings giving on a strobe light effect.

"They look like they are headed south, just like the last one."

"Dollars to doughnuts they are headed this way. Folks think the eclipse is causing all these animal migration changes, but knowing what we know about Demons, I just don't buy it."

"I don't either. Thanks, Bobby, stay safe. I'll be in touch." Preacher hung up the phone and continued to stare out the window.

"Preacher, I got something for you." Raz stood next to Preacher at the window staring at the birds. "A friend reached out to some people she knows that practice darker magick than I do. They are having a séance to call on dark forces during the eclipse. This part of the country will be in the path of totality and all light will be blocked from the earth for a few minutes."

Preacher nodded, silently thinking to himself. "So we know the when. I think that I know the city where she will cast it. Raz, find out how long Savannah will be in the path of totality please."

Michael came upstairs from working with Josh and looked out the window. "Crows? Interesting." Michael walked through the living room and into the kitchen to pour himself a cup of coffee.

"Perhaps this is the murder that Bolfry was speaking of?" Michael called back to Preacher.

Preacher opened the internet browser on his smartphone and ran a quick search 'what is a flock of ravens called?'. The immediate result came back 'a group of ravens is called an unkindness or a conspiracy.'

Both sets of birds were going south. The milk and the bread around Savannah were also concerning. These were definitely omens Bolfry talked about. If he were going to save M.C., he would need to follow them.

"She will have less than three minutes to cast her spell, the sun will only be covered up for about two and a half minutes," Raz said from behind the computer monitor. "That doesn't seem like a whole lot of time to cast something so powerful that it could do what she wants."

Preacher nodded, "It certainly doesn't. For some reason, it doesn't make me feel any better."

"It shouldn't." Michael was standing across the room listening to the conversation. "Baba Doek holds a Key of Hell, one of the seven most evil items on the planet. She will harness its power to bring Hell closer to the Earth than it has ever been before."

"So what exactly does that mean?" Raz stood from behind her computer to look at Michael. "I thought Tartarus was a different place than Hell, how does bringing Hell closer to Earth do anything for her?"

Michael shrugged. "Time works differently in Heaven and Hell than it does here. Hours spent in Hell can feel like months or years. By using the Key and bringing Hell closer to the veil, she will be able to slow time here on Earth effectively. Not by very much, but by some measure."

"Savannah has a thinner veil for some reason, so she could have a lot more time than two and a half minutes." Preacher frowned. "Raz, please go downstairs and let Josh and Gus know what we think. Then get started packing bags. We are going to Savannah in the morning."

Preacher dialed Bobby back. "Hello?"

"We'll be down in the morning. Swing by the house and get it ready for us if you could. We'll need food and provisions. We have until the eclipse to find Baba Doek and get things set right."

"Won't be a problem Preacher. You asked me to keep an eye on the house, so, well I moved in. The place is going to be ready for you."

"Thanks, Bobby. Do me one more favor yea?"

"Sure, what do you need?"

"Get the hell out of my bedroom." Preacher hung up the phone without waiting for a reply. He sighed and looked around the room.

"Michael, what do you think we need to take?"

Michael walked back to the kitchen, poured Preacher a large glass of whiskey, and returned to the living room. "Of course you will bring your vestments, but more to the point, bring everything that you that can slow down, stop, destroy or vanquish the enemy. These are Joined Demons that may be beyond saving. We may need to destroy them, prepare yourself for that idea."

Preacher took a long drink from the glass. "I love her Michael, I can't even think about destroying her."

Michael placed a hand on Preacher's shoulder. "You love a memory of what was and grieve for a future that cannot be. This burden that you carry is not fair, but you are a grown man and know that life is not fair."

Preacher took another drink of his whiskey and nodded as Michael spoke. The words washed over him, awakening the pain he felt at her loss all over again.

"What I need to know Preacher, is when the moment comes to act to prevent this spell, you will act. If destroying her is necessary, you cannot hesitate. Your grief will be unbearable but the world will continue to spin, and eventually, your grief will dull."

Preacher nodded. "I know. I will do what I have to do. God help me."

Michael nodded. "Good, I will start taking things to the car. I will start with the books, you pack what you think you need."

Preacher finished the glass of whiskey and walked downstairs to his workshop. He grabbed the iron chains and put them in a duffle bag. He added his big old bible, the pistol, and some rope. He took down a set of throwing stars and a few knives and put them in a second duffle bag.

He took the bags and headed to his room. He put his vestments in the bag, reverently and respectfully. Afterward, he added some t-shirts, jeans, underwear. It oddly felt like he was packing for vacation. Maybe he would take a real vacation once this was over with.

Preacher grabbed a few other essentials and started taking things out to the car. With the team preparing, he left them for the evening retreating to his room for prayer. He heard them packing and moving around the house. Slowly noises faded and the house was asleep.

He prayed for guidance and for strength. Guidance so he could find a way to stop Baba Doek without killing her. He knew that he could Unjoin her if he had the chance. He prayed for strength in case he couldn't.

He lost himself in prayer. Eventually, he realized that his prayers turned to pleas and then begging. He emptied his soul to Heaven and felt unanswered, empty and tired. As quietly as he could, Preacher walked to the front door and opened it.

"Malik, Snyder, I spoke to God this evening, but he didn't answer. We are headed to Savannah in the morning that is where Baba Doek is. You said you would help, and since God has stayed silent, I'm asking. We'll see you tomorrow."

Preacher went back inside to contemplate his decision. Somewhere in his past, he remembered the lesson that a poor decision was better than no decision at all. He hoped that was the case.

33.

Baba Doek sat in her new chambers below the old city of Savannah. Her lieutenants were barking orders and carrying out her orders creating a new place for her to conduct business. Crates of Spiritus Vitae were being brought from her Atlanta storage to this new place.

She observed the activities around her as she stroked her hair absently with the hairbrush. Slowly, methodical stroke after stroke she watched as others worked. Each stroke drove her to more profound peace and confidence than she had before.

Deeper inside Baba Doek's mind, M.C. was in her nightgown preparing for bed. She was sitting in front of a mirror brushing her hair. Jim had brought a new brush home with him for her to use. It looked like an ivory handled brush; it was solid in her hands. Holding it, she felt more energetic and happy with herself than she had in years.

From behind her, she heard her name whispered. "M.C." It was a breath of air, just above silent. She turned toward the sound, but there was nothing there. She turned back to the mirror and raised the brush to her head, but her reflection did not move.

She waved her hand in front of the mirror, but again her reflection did not mirror her. Instead, it merely tilted its head "This is interesting. I certainly didn't expect to find you here." The voice was M.C.'s.

Her reflection continued "Of course I have never been held by a Demon before either. Only humans, always humans. I guess that's why I found you here." The reflection looked around in M.C.s room. "This is a beautifully crafted prison, but no matter how nice the cage, it is still a cage."

M.C. closed her eyes and placed her hands on her legs pressing hard. She was losing her mind. She thought about Dr. D and techniques for relaxing.

The voice in the face in the mirror began to laugh. "You don't understand, do you? How simplistically brilliant this is." Her reflection motioned around the room. "None of this is real. It's all in your head, well the Demons head that possesses your body."

M.C. looked around the room, but it was exactly as it always was. She looked back to the mirror, but her reflection was no longer there. It was standing behind her, next to the bedroom door.

It looked down at the laundry basket, then back at M.C. "Take this laundry basket, for instance, it is never full, but you have never emptied it have you."

M.C. didn't know what to say. She has emptied the laundry basket and done laundry. She thought back to just last week when she... did not remember doing laundry. She let her mind think back to the previous load of laundry she did. The house was different somehow; it smelled different like men's cologne, and it was decorated differently. She could hear the sound of jazz on the record player in the living room.

"Jim must have been doing it lately." M.C. replied instinctually. That was the only logical explanation that she had. Jim was surprisingly considerate when she thought about it.

"Jim? Is he your lover? Where is he?" The other M.C. walked out of the bedroom and down the hall to the living room. M.C. stood to follow. The reflection made no sounds as she went down the hallway. The house was silent, and M.C. could only hear her footsteps and the creaks of the floorboards under her feet. The other's steps were quiet.

Her reflection stopped in the living room and looked back at her. "This may not be a web you have weaved, but you are both the spider and the fly in it. You fail to recognize and fight the illusion, so you allow it to keep you trapped."

"I know your pain child." Her reflection continued. "I feel it rippling under this façade. I know that it is easier to not remember and wrap yourself in this blanket of illusion."

M.C. shook her head, "No, this is real. I am dreaming, and you are not real! You are just my subconscious playing tricks on me!"

Her reflection nodded. "I wish that were the case. Unfortunately, that is not true. You are possessed by a big bad voodoo daddy – well momma. She has very nasty plans for the two of us. If you choose to remain here and hide from your pain, then we will both be doomed."

M.C. looked at her reflection then looked about the living room. She saw the flowers, the record player the furniture. All the things in the world that she wanted that made her happy. "You have not proven anything. If you are not my subconscious then what are you?"

Her reflection nodded at the brush in M.C.s hand. "I am in your hand. I am not sure how I came to be, but I have been in existence for thousands of years. I have been passed from one owner to the next, helping them reach their fullest potential."

M.C. laughed. "You're a hairbrush? What kind of nonsense is this?"

Her reflection made a tsk sound and shook her head. "That's both inaccurate and insulting. I am a sentient consciousness that, much like you is trapped within its own construct. You, however, have the choice to fight it and be yourself again. I will forever be attached to the brush."

Her reflection gazed at her. "You are sure that Jim is a real person and this is a real place?" Impatiently her reflection pressed on before she could answer. "Then describe how it feels when Jim kisses you."

M.C. shrugged. "It makes me feel good. Special."

Her reflection shook its head. "Tell me the details. Are his lips wet or dry? Is his tongue thick or thin? Does he nibble your lip?"

M.C. started to answer but stopped. It was the details that she was having problems recalling. The more she sought for the details, the more embarrassed she became. The more she fought to see through the fog the harder it became.

"You're starting to understand." Her reflection closed the distance between them and touched M.C. on the forehead with her index finger. When they made contact a spark of electricity jumped between them.

Images flashed in M.C.'s mind. She was walking down a flight of stairs. Then she was kneeling in front of Preacher as he was bleeding from a wound in his side. She heard a voice saying that it could save him if she let it in.

She felt her head nod, anything to save him. Suddenly she felt like a passenger in her skin. She saw her hand touch the wound, felt the skin knit under her fingers. She tasted the coppery blood in her mouth as she sucked her fingers.

M.C. staggered back and slumped down on the couch. Understanding broke through, knowing that she was just a passenger on a ride. Her reflection took a seat in front of her on the coffee table.

"This thing that controls you is only frightened of failure. Fortunately, this Demon is prideful and does not consider you a threat."

M.C. looked at her with a thousand-yard stare. She took a deep breath and tried to focus. "How do you know what frightens her?"

Her reflection smiled at her "It's simple really, as I am talking to you I am talking with her. Her plan to destroy me and use my power to get her body back. Waiting for the last possible moment to leave your vessel, making sure she kills you in front of the Preacher."

M.C. started shaking. "That can't happen." She shook her head violently. "We cannot let that happen."

Her reflection nodded slowly. "Those were my thoughts exactly. Now, I have an idea that can work, but it will take both of us working together to be effective. Can you work with me?"

M.C. nodded slowly. Her reflection rose took M.C. by the hands. The reflection slowly pulled M.C. to her feet and led her back to the bedroom. As they came in the reflection led M.C. to the mirror and sat her on the stool.

Taking M.C.'s hand in her own, she reached out and touched the mirror. It rippled like the water of a still pond. Once the rippling stopped, she could see the inside of a cavern, where several people were walking in crate after crate and stacking them on the walls.

The objects in the mirror moved, and M.C. realized she was looking out the eyes of the demon who possessed her. "Is there sound?"

"The radio. There has always been sound. You have chosen to remain ignorant. When the time comes, resist. Do everything you can to take control of what is yours."

M.C. turned her body to face her reflection, but there was nothing there. She turned back to the mirror and saw her reflection brushing her hair, but M.C. wasn't touching hers. "How do I resist?"

Her reflection smiled and put her hands down into her lap assuming the same position as M.C. "I would start with walking out the front door."

M.C. smiled slightly, and her reflection smiled back. They made eye contact, and they were staring at each other for a long time before M.C. realized that she was staring at her reflection. She looked down to her hand that was holding the new hairbrush, but it was empty.

M.C. looked around the room frantically. Everything was as she always knew it to be. She wondered for a moment if this is what it was like to slide into insanity. Everything was too unbelievable. She took a deep breath and reached out to touch the mirror.

It rippled, visions of a cavern came into focus. People were talking, but there was no sound. Quickly M.C. ran to the living room to turn on the radio.

34.

If you have never been to Savannah, you are missing out. The old world feeling that you get is not only vintage, but it is authentic. The trees that are growing and the buildings that are built are such a mix of modern and historic that it can give any academic a migraine.

The Spanish moss that hangs from the trees in many iconic films is very real. During the drive to downtown, there was only sunshine. Once on the city streets, the light faded, turning the cityscape gray for the rest of the drive.

Briefly, the team was able to glean some of Preacher's past. This was the place that he used to call home. Preacher, Michael, and Josh were riding together in silence. Just the sound to thumps and bumps of the interstate broke the quietness of the car. Then the interstate abruptly ended, depositing them into downtown Savannah.

Similar to their Atlanta home they drove through the city without stopping. Josh watched the city as it passed by him with a feeling of wonder. As Josh watched the water while they were crossing over one of the bridges to the island he had a sense of coming home. He loved the water and seeing the islands around Savannah made him feel more at home than he felt in a long time.

Once they drove over the bridge though he felt less like a tourist and more like a resident. Familiar chain restaurants lined the roadways, and it seemed less romantic every mile they traveled.

They took only three turns coming into the island before they were in a driveway. The house was a two-story, painted white with blue shutters. Preacher opened the garage doors with the code boxes, and they pulled in and started unpacking the cars.

The door to the house opened, and a tall, portly man came into the garage. He had grey coming into his short cut light brown hair and beard, which somehow softened his brown eyes. Quietly he walked up behind Raz.

"Would you like a little help? You look like you overpacked." The familiar country twang seemed to fill the garage.

Raz's smile could be heard in her voice. "Bobby?!" She turned around to see Bobby for the first time and ran the few steps to give him a hug. "Of course you can help carry the bags! You carry all our baggage anyway!" She pulled away from the hug and looked him over from toe to brow. "You look exactly like you sound. That never happens!"

She grabbed a couple bags out of the car and smiled at Bobby. "Where am I staying?"

"Inside and up the stairs, I put signs on the rooms. You can't get lost. Just leave the heavy stuff to us men." Raz kissed him on the cheek and headed inside. "Wifi password is on the note on your door. Go ahead and get set up."

Raz went inside to find her new room and make it her own. The others made quick work of unpacking the vehicles before heading inside the home, leaving Preacher in the garage. He stood in the garage a familiar place, but it was like looking at it for the first time.

Preacher walked into the house carrying his duffle bags. He tried not to look around too much, he didn't want too many distractions. It failed miserably, he saw the dining room table where he used to do puzzles with M.C., the record player that played all the old songs. Everywhere he looked he saw her.

He went into the bedroom and placed his duffle bags on the bed. He opened the first one, took out his vestments, and put them in the closet. Hanging on the left-hand side of the closet were all of M.C.'s clothes.

"I left everything exactly like it was when you left. Except for washing the sheets and making the bed."

Bobby was standing in the doorway. "I can box it up if you want. If it hits home a little too hard ya know."

Preacher shook his head. "It's fine Bobby. I appreciate it though."

Bobby shrugged "I know this isn't a social call, so what is the plan?"

"We know that the eclipse is coming tomorrow, we need to find where Baba Doek is going to cast her spell. There aren't many places I can think of where she can do it. So I'm thinking that we can split up and take a look around the city, see if there is anything unusual."

"Makes sense, where do you want to look?" Bobby asked

"Let me get my maps from the car. Then we will gather everyone up and talk about the plan."

Heading back to the car Preacher noticed that Gus was already in the kitchen getting familiar with his new surroundings and tools. A pot of coffee was already brewing on the counter; the team seemed to be falling into a rhythm quickly, and that gave Preacher a little piece of mind.

A few moments later the team was gathered around the dining table looking at a city map. Raz was actually looking at the map on her phone tagging places that she and Gus would visit. "Check out Forsyth Park, then hit the squares heading north towards the river. Look for signs of the Demonic. Hex signs, sulfur residue anything that could point us in the right direction."

Preacher slid two pairs of glasses towards them. "These could help, Raz enchanted these with her spellwork to see the unseen." He then pushed two pairs to Bobby and Josh.

"Bobby, you and Josh head over to Bonaventure Cemetery and look for anything unusual." Preacher looked over at Bobby. "I know that it's a large creepy old graveyard, but it feels like it would be a good place to check. Look for some similar things, but it's a cemetery so make sure that you check the fresh graves and make sure they are legit burials. "

"Michael and I will take River Street and City Market. It will be a lot more crowded there, and things might be harder to spot. Plus, I don't trust Bobby to make it past the second bar before he starts drinking. Once you have checked your area come down to City Market and we will meet there." Preacher put his own glasses on.

With the plan in place, the group dispersed, each heading to the cars. Bobby and Josh took Bobby's car, a mid 90s sports car that used to be red that had turned pink in most places because of saltwater and sun exposure.

Preacher walked to his car as Raz and Gus entered theirs. Michael looked at Preacher with a raised eyebrow "We are driving?"

Preacher nodded. "I told the two Demons where we are headed. I am pretty sure that they don't know that I am Nephilim, and I don't want to give that away just yet. So we are driving, eating dinner and going to sleep just like a couple of normal guys in case they are watching."

"Getting help from a Demon doesn't sound smart Preacher. I wish you had not done that." There was a tone of disappointment in his voice.

Preacher groaned. "I know, but something Bolfry said I couldn't shake from my mind. He said it would take help from Demons to stop her."

Michael got in the car, "Consider the source Preacher, consider which side he is on."

Preacher started the car, and they backed out of the garage. "Consider that the Fallen Angel inside you is technically in the same boat as these Demons. I can only take your assurance that he is on our side. So, I have resolved to do this my way and take any assistance that I can."

Michael sat in silence brooding for the short ride into the city. They parked the car in the bottom level of a large parking deck and began their search there.

“What do you expect to find in this garage?” Michael had an annoyed tone to his voice. If he wanted to make sure Preacher knew he did not approve of the plan he was doing a good job.

“Probably nothing, there are better places for this to take place. But this is going to take a ton of energy, so she had to store the Spiritus Vitae and transport it somehow. If they were using van or trucks maybe they are here.” Preacher tried to sound as confident as he could, but even as the words came out of his mouth, he knew how desperate he looked.

With a look of resignation Preacher looked at Michael. “They would just shadow-step them from one place to another wouldn’t they?”

Michael nodded “I would. There are many places here that would be adequate for casting, however. We know that Demons are arrogant and if given a chance will throw their might in the face of God. A church would be an insulting place to cast this spell. I wouldn't discount them.”

Preacher started walking to the elevator that would take them up to the street. “If they could tolerate the pain of being on consecrated ground. Isn’t holy ground supposed to weaken them?”

“In normal circumstances yes, however, these are not normal circumstances, and this is not a normal Demon. It could be worth a shot.” They rode the elevator in silence as Preacher contemplated the idea.

The elevator stopped, and they walked out onto the street. The light was almost blinding after being in the underground garage. Blinking rapidly to clear his vision Preacher looked over City Market in the city he once called home.

“I think you just argued yourself out of checking the churches. These are unusual times so the logical deductions on where this will take place cannot be considered. She will be where the veil is most thin in this city.” The certainty was back in Preacher's voice.

Michael nodded. "Hashmal does not like it when you use logic to justify acting illogically. I follow your thought though, so where should we start?"

Preacher squinted in the sunlight and pointed east. "Let's head toward the end of City Market and go around each building. We'll start in a grid and work our way back through City Market and further west through the rest of Downtown."

"It's as good a plan as any I suppose." Michael started walking through the center of City Market headed in the direction that Preacher pointed to. I wasn't long before he stopped in front of an art store and pointed. "I think I found it."

Preacher scanned the exterior of the building for signs of wards, hex marks, a neon sign that said Demons here… anything. But there was nothing out of the ordinary. Preacher followed the pointing finger of Michael to an Andy Warhol style painting of The Dude in full technicolor, from one of the best movies of all times (in Preacher's opinion of course).

"Michael that is not a sign for Demons. It's POP culture." Preacher continued walking towards the end of City Market, the smell of fresh food mingling in the air with spilled and sour beer. Preacher realized how much he had missed the city after being away from it for so long.

They started their search as Preacher suggested quickly clearing the City Market portion of Downtown. There was only one interruption as Michael insisted that the Jazz-Country fusion band that was playing at one of the venues was certainly a Demonic Omen.

The two continued their path south then back west. Building after building, block after block. The more time that passed, the more frustrating the search became. They had been at the search for over two hours when Preacher turned a corner and saw Malik and Snyder standing in an alleyway as if they were waiting on him.

Snyder looked over Preacher's shoulder as Michael turned the corner. "You have poor taste in company Preacher." His voice was flat and unforgiving, filled with pure disdain.

"I would have to agree, but he wouldn't listen to what I asked him to stop talking with Demons." Michael spat on the ground.

"Enough." Preacher's voice was firm and decisive. "Have you found where Baba Doek will cast the spell? We have not had any luck finding wards or hex marks yet."

Malik shook his head. "Not yet, but the wards will give it away. As long as you are sure this is the right place. You are sure this is the right place yes?"

Preacher nodded. "The only omen that we are missing is the church bells ringing off time. We are a day away from the eclipse so it should be coming soon."

Malik raised himself to his full height to make himself scarier, which didn't take a lot. "Failure to stop this has consequences beyond your understanding. It seems like our last conversation was not worth the effort."

"Our previous conversation was understood." Preacher took a few steps forward towards the Demons. "I could exorcise at least one of you right now without breaking a sweat, while my poor in choice friend takes care of the other. Don't you want to stay on the same team Demon?"

Malik didn't step back, but he did break eye contact and look away. Snyder stepped forward, brandishing a long knife. The blade was black and shiny like obsidian, not steel. It glinted in the sun drawing attention to its sharp edges. Preacher was not sure where it came from, he wasn't holding it a second ago.

"You need to stop threatening us human. We are faster, stronger, smarter and we are eternal. Ending your existence right here would be simple." Snyder's voice was full of hate.

"Enough." Malik's voice cut through the tension between the two groups. Snyder uncurled his fingers from around the hilt, and the blade disappeared in a puff of shadow.

"We are going to work our way back following the river. Any advice on where to focus would be appreciated." Michael was biting back an aggressive tone in his voice.

"Most likely a place where great evil took place. Murders, rapes, perhaps torture." Malik closed his eyes and took a deep breath in through his nose as if he could smell the acts of evil in the air. "There are so many places in this city that are saturated in evil; it is hard to tell."

"Okay, continue the search meet me in City Market in a few hours." Preacher walked through the two of them on the way to the river. Michael caught up to him quickly.

"They are gone for now. I still do not understand why you would agree to work with them." It was Hashmal's tone, not Michael's.

"You are going to have to show me that knife trick. That could come in handy." Preacher replied.

"It is as much the knife as knowing how to summon it. The knife was forged in the fires of Hell. Deadly, even to the Celestial. If you can get your hands on one, then I can teach you."

"Good to know. I'll keep my eyes open for one." Preacher's phone chirped in his pocket.

"News from our friends?" Michaels tone was back, Hashmal apparently had enough conversation for now. That was fine with Preacher.

"Raz thinks she's onto something, wants to meet up and fill us in. Ill text Bobby and Josh and have them meet us." Preacher sent the text message and looked at Michael. "I think I have an idea on where to go. Once we eat, we will check it out." The two walked back to the bustling city area in silence.

35.

Bobby and Josh arrived just as the pizzas did. The team was sitting on the patio of the restaurant with a map of the city spread out before them. The waitress waved at Bobby and sauntered off after giving him a wink.

Raz was a ball of excitement waiting to tell everyone what she learned. "Okay, so the squares were a total bust and completely boring until we got to Chippewa Square. There was one of those Ghost Tours going through and explained that it was once a cemetery, but when the city turned it into a park, they only removed the headstones and not the bodies."

Raz placed a circle on Chippewa Square on the map. "So we followed the tour for a little while before we were noticed and asked to leave. But yours truly turned on the charm, and the tour guide agreed to meet after the tour to talk to us about the city."

"It turns out that three blocks closer to the river is a haunted brewery, so haunted that they cannot even finish renovations to the building. Turns out that this building was originally built as a hotel and a favorite spot for the captain and crews of slave ships that came from Africa. During the hotel's height, there were no less than two murders a week as captains and crew fought amongst themselves."

"As the slave trade moved to other ports and cities the hotel was turned into a hospital, there was an entire floor dedicated to yellow fever when it hit the city. It was a floor that you were brought to die in quarantine." Raz circled the brewery on the map.

"Further south we have the Hamilton-Turner Inn, which is said to be the most haunted hotel in the city. Common hauntings of ghosts and poltergeists nothing terrible. Actually a little disappointing, until I looked up the actual history of the house. It was built for Samuel Hamilton, who was Mayor of the city at one point, but more interestingly he was the Grand Master of the Knights Templar. There's no telling what kind of relics and artifacts could be there." Raz circled the hotel on the map.

The waitress came back to the table with two pitchers of beer and several plastic cups. "Bobby's standing order, two pitchers. Always, no questions asked. At least this time he has people to help him drink it down." She placed the beer on the table and gave Bobby's should a gentle squeeze before she walked off.

Bobby at least had the decency to look embarrassed before he started pouring cups for everyone.

"Alright, so over here," Raz pointed back at the map. "This restaurant, The Pirate House is named because it was a bar where ships crews would visit after entering the city. Locals who dared enter were often drugged and kidnapped. They would be taken through tunnels to the river, placed on a boat, and the boat would leave."

"These men would wake up hundreds of miles away at sea and given a choice to work at sea or walk the plank." She shrugged. "It is also rumored that these tunnels were used to offload slaves from the ships that brought them."

"Slaves would be stored in the cellar for days until they could be moved to an auction site. Conditions would be nasty, lack of water and food, disease and vermin, truly ghastly." Raz circled the restaurant on the map.

"Finally further up the street is a random empty lot. The original building was a small warehouse. Over time it changed hands time and time again, and no one really knows the story of it until the mid-eighties. An investment group bought it and tore down the original building. During the teardown, they found a cellar that no one knew about. They opened it up and found One Hundred and Forty-two bodies chained to the walls. Apparently, there was a tunnel that ran into this cellar that collapsed sealing the room off."

"There was never any cellar on any blueprint of the building, so it was assumed that no one that owned the building knew it was there." She drew a circle around the empty lot on the map. "Now I didn't see it at first, it took a while for me to understand what I was looking at." She took her pen and drew a line from the Inn to the brewery. Then from the brewery to the empty lot. She continued the line crossing over to the square, then brought the line from the square to The Pirate House. She finished by taking the line from The Pirate House back to the Inn.

The group sat looking at the map in a bit of silence. Raz took her pen and drew a circle around the five-pointed star that she had made, revealing a pentagram on the map. "This spell will occur somewhere inside this circle. It doesn't make sense for it not to."

Raz sat down and grabbed a slice of pizza, looking between Preacher, Michael, and Bobby. The three were staring at the map, Preacher leaned over to get a better look at the map.

"Would casting anywhere inside the circle have a boosting effect on a spell?" Preacher asked looking at Raz.

"Of course, the closer to the center you get the more power it would be able to draw from the five different points."

“I have a plan. Michael and I will confirm if I am right about the location. Josh, you and Gus head back to the house and get everything ready for tomorrow. Ensure that we are ready to go when we get back. Ensure the rock salt slugs are loaded, empty all the magazines and ensure they are loaded with the blessed iron rounds. Bless the water and fill all the vials that we have with it. Take confession and prepare the communion for tomorrow.”

“Bobby, you will need to take Raz shopping. The Wardrobe should have everything that you need, Bobby has the key to get into it.”

Raz cocked her head to the side “What do you need me to cast?”

Preacher smiled a rare smile, he finally felt like he had the upper hand.

“I’ll need you to cast a banishing spell. A large one and I’ll need you to do it in the middle of the circle.”

Raz scoffed “I don’t know how to do that. I don’t know if I can do it myself.”

“Google it then. That’s always the first answer you give me when I have questions.” Preacher snapped.

“It’s not the same as saving contacts in your phone! This is serious magick, and it scares the shit out of me. So don’t be an asshole to me when I have reservations about casting something that could very well just kill me instead of banishing the demons from an area!”

“Language young lady.” Michael still had a distaste for swearing.

Bobby handed Raz a beer, which she promptly chugged. He filled her glass again and gave it back. “Relax, he didn’t mean to offend. I don’t think he knew he was being rude.” Bobby cut his eyes at Preacher to silence whatever he was going to say.

“Let’s take a walk over to The Wardrobe and see what they have. You’ll love the shop whether we find anything or not.” Bobby stood up as Raz finished her second beer. Bobby led her off towards River Street.

"That was rude. You need to make sure you make up for that." Gus's big brother voice wasn't something Preacher was used to hearing. "She's doing her best. We are all doing our best. I'm surprised that no one else has lost it and yelled at you yet." With that Josh and Gus left to prepare for the next day reluctantly. Michael left a tip for the waitress, and the pair headed towards River Street.

The steps leading from Bay Street to River Street are steep. Very steep, local athletes use them for leg day in their work out routine. Preacher always felt nervous about taking them, but he really wanted to see if Michael could handle them. He was pretty sure that if the old man fell, Hashmal could fix him up by tomorrow.

The steps ended at a cobblestone pathway that lead to River Street. As beautiful as they are, the stones are uneven and slippery. A true testament to the age of the city that Sherman failed to burn to the ground.

Preacher took a few steps towards River Street then paused. He looked up to the buildings that boasted entrances on Bay Street, two levels above his head. Above him, a dueling piano bar boasted its entrance, a place where he and M.C. had spent many nights. It was where he took her on their first date as a matter of fact. When the dueling pianos were not available, it was the best place to hear jazz in the city. He was pretty sure that M.C. hated jazz at first, most people do. It surprised him when she asked to be taken back on their second date.

Preacher felt Michaels hand on his shoulder. The gentle squeeze brought him back to today.

"Where did you go?" This was the compassionate side of Michael that made Preacher feel nervous.

"I'm just remembering a better time. Come on, we aren't far." Instead of continuing towards River Street, Preacher turned to the right and went into an ally way. It was a steep incline, and the cobblestones made it more challenging to climb than it should.

They walked through the back ally of all the businesses on River St. They walked for just over a block before they found the wards. It was on a brick wall, and wouldn't be too noticeable to the naked eye. But when you were looking for it, you could see the difference in the brick and the archway that use to be there. The old metal hinges that once held a gate were still in the wall. Preacher saw the wards without the use of his glasses. They blazed in red, silver, white and black markings.

Preacher nodded to the wards. "Is that something you can get through?"

Michael shook his head. "I wouldn't know where to begin. Hellion wards are not something I am familiar with."

Preacher turned to Michael. "I wasn't talking to Michael. I was talking to Hashmal. Can you make sense of these wards and get through?"

There was a pause before Hashmal responded. "I could get us in, but it would take time, and unfortunately all element of surprise would be lost if I tried." Hashaml looked at the entrance of the slave tunnels. "It would be akin to smashing down a door with a sledgehammer and not picking a lock."

"Alright. Let's walk down to the other entrance to the tunnels that I know about. Maybe we will get lucky, and they won't know about it to put wards on it."

The two walked the few blocks briskly down to The Pirate House, only to see that the entrance there was also warded.

"I was hoping that we could get in here and attack on two fronts." Preacher stood on the sidewalk staring down at the wards.

"I suppose that it is a good thing we have two Demons then. One to open the front door, one to open the back. It does seem serendipitous." Hashmals tone was solemn. Perhaps he thought Preacher was going to tell him 'I told you so.' Under normal circumstances, Preacher would have. Instead, Preacher just started walking back to City Market.

Back in City Market Preacher was sipping on a whiskey in the heat of the afternoon. Michael sat next to him waiting on Malik and Snyder to arrive. The ice in the whiskey was melting quickly in the afternoon heat.

Preacher still wore his glasses. He still held a healthy distrust for Demons and their motivation. It was a part of him that he never wanted to go away either. He saw Malik standing as still as a statue at the corner of a building staring him.

Preacher finished off his whiskey with one final gulp and stood. Michael followed his lead. As they headed toward Malik, he turned the corner and walked down the alley. The two pairs met in the alleyway.

"We found Hellion wards at the entrances to the old slave tunnels. It makes sense that the spell would be cast down there. Those tunnels have to be saturated in evil." Preacher kept his voice level and steady.

"You are ready for the attack to begin then?" Malik's voice came across lined with a mixture of aggression and excitement.

"Calm down Cochise, we still have not received the last omen. If we attack and fail, they can simply cast the spell tomorrow without interference or move if they know of another place that will be in the path of totality. We need to wait until tomorrow just before the eclipse to make sure that this fight, no matter win or lose, is disruptive enough that we can stop the spell."

"Have you seen the wards? Can you get us through quietly?" Michael spoke quietly from behind Preacher.

"I have not seen them, but I am sure I will be able to get us in. What are you going to do while we wait like little lapdogs?" Snyders hateful tone had not gone away. Preacher accepted that it never would.

"I am going to pray. I am going to pray for success, for my team, and in particular for you Snyder. I hope that one day you find your way back to redemption." Preacher turned and headed back out the ally and towards the parking deck.

He heard Snyder spit as he walked away. “Save your breath Priest, you may need it to scream tomorrow.”

36.

It was dark before Michael and Preacher arrived back at the house. They came in to find the dining room table covered in the standard, and not so standard tools of the exorcist trade.

Two rows of holy water vials sat flanked by a row of goofer dust. A box of shotgun shells sat beside the shotgun, and three magazines sat loaded next to the pistol. The iron chain lay curled up and rested next to the old Gutenberg bible. Preacher's iron knuckles resting on the chain.

Olive oil from Garden of Gethsemane sat next to Preacher's pectoral cross. Another crucifix sat next to the oil that Preacher had not seen before. The crucifix was affixed to a round disk with a small button in the middle. It must have been Josh's latest version of his thrower.

Raz and Bobby had taken over the other half of the table, sorting powders and herbs into various jars. "Were you able to find everything that you need to cast the banishment spell?"

Bobby nodded "We did, we were able to find something more capable than the internet to provide information once I sweet talked the proprietor."

"What he means to say is that after he offended her by hitting on her, I swooped in and saved the day. We have what we need, but we also have a big problem. This spell is going to take five minutes to complete, and that's with Bobby helping. While I am casting it, this spell is going to drain the energy in the area and collect it. It's likely they will know I am casting it."

Preacher nodded in understanding. "Do you think they will be able to trace this drain back to the source?"

"I don't know what they are capable of. I was hoping you two might know more." She looked between Michael and Preacher.

"I believe it is doubtful that they will be able to follow anything back to Raz and Bobby, but they shouldn't be left unguarded either just in case." Michael sounded confident enough to put Raz and Bobby at ease a little.

"That's smart, we should have Gus and Josh there with them to keep an eye on them. We will clear the tunnels on our own." Preacher had the air of authority around him as he did before any exorcism.

"We thought you might say something like that, so I got you a present. Can't have you storming the big bad Demon with that old relic." Bobby nodded to the double-barreled shotgun. He walked into the living room and came back holding a much newer gun. It was a pump action shotgun, but it had a pistol grip and collapsible buttstock. Also because it was sawed off, it could easily be carried under a large coat.

"It holds five in the tube and one in the pipe. You'll have three times the ammo before you have to reload. Also, it carries five additional shells on the buttstock so you won't have to dig into the box right away." Bobby's voice was full of excitement. It was evident that he really liked this gun.

"Thanks, Bobby. I'll do my best to get this back to you."

Josh and Gus came into the room and stood around the dining room table. Josh looked over the table, "This is what we have, do you think it will be enough?"

"All of you have done well. These items will have to be enough to see us through." Preacher slid three vials of the goofer dust towards him leaving two in place. He then pulled one row of the holy water towards him carefully.

Preacher glanced at Gus and Josh. "You guys split up these vials of holy water and goofer dust. You will be positioned to defend Raz while she is casting her spell. We don't think you will need anything, but better safe than sorry. Bobby, take the pistol. It's easier to conceal in public."

Preacher sat the new shotgun near the vials he sat aside, he looked over and plucked the olive oil and lay it next to his bottles. The Gutenberg Bible would be too heavy and cumbersome, so would the chain. He left them sitting on the table untouched. He plucked his iron knuckles off the chain and sat them in his pile.

"Were you two able to take confession and prepare yourselves for tomorrow?" Preacher's eyes darted from Josh to Gus. Both nodded as they met his gaze. "Excellent. I am going to pray now. Michael, if you would meet me here at six in the morning to finalize our plans and get breakfast for everyone, I would be grateful."

"It would be my pleasure." If there was any irritation in Michael, his voice did not betray it.

Preacher walked into his bedroom and closed the door. He turned the shower on and let it warm up as he undressed. Stepping under the shower, he let the warm water run over his body. He tried to let go of the memory of M.C. as the water ran down his body. He knew that if he made it to her, the Demon would attack him on an emotional level first. He also knew that it had the upper hand.

He stepped out of the shower and dried off. He pulled a pair of shorts out of his dresser and slid them on along with an old thin tee shirt. He walked to the bed and knelt beside it. Resting his elbows on the mattress, he cradled his head in his hands and began praying.

He wasn't sure how long he stayed there praying for strength, courage, humility, and wisdom. His knees were sore when he stood though, so he knew a long time had passed. He opened his bedroom door, and the house was quiet and dark.

Quietly he slipped out his bedroom and walked into the living room. He walked to the mantel and picked up a box of matches. Bobby really kept things as he had left them. He struck the match and lit the candles that were on the mantel. He walked and lit others that flanked the record player. He opened the top of the player and picked up the third album from the stack next to it.

He slid the record into place, turned the knob and lowered the arm. M.C.'s favorite Sinatra album started playing at a low volume in the living room. Preacher slumped down on the couch and listened as he remembered the better days of his past.

As Ol' Blue Eyes record played on, Josh came in and sat down next to Preacher on the couch. "Nervous for tomorrow?" The question was innocent enough, but at the moment, Preacher found it to be profound.

"I am. I am not sure if I will be strong enough to complete the task. I am worried that when I see M.C. again, I will not be able to do what needs to be done." There was a touch of sadness in Preacher's voice.

"Is it hard for you to be back here?"

Preacher was silent for a moment. "It's not as hard as I thought it would be. It's cathartic being back here though."

"I like it here. It's special somehow." Josh glanced at Preacher's empty hands. "No drinking tonight? That's probably pretty smart."

Preacher chuckled and nodded. "I'll drink when this is all over." The record finished its set, and the repetitive thump of the needle came over the speakers lightly. "Try to get some sleep, tomorrow is going to be a long day."

Josh nodded and crept up the stairs and back to his room. Preacher turned the record player off and replaced the record. Looking over the living room lit by candlelight he could almost see her laying on the couch. With some effort, he tore himself from the memories, blew out the candles and went back to his bedroom in the dark.

A few hours passed, and Preacher dressed in his vestments. It was a few minutes before six when he emerged from his room and found Michael in the kitchen waiting for him.

"Where are we going to get breakfast? It must be good for us to be leaving at this hour." If there was any annoyance from Michael, Preacher couldn't detect it.

"A place called Goose Feathers. Best breakfast in the city in my opinion." Preacher led them to the car, and they got on the road. The first few moments they were on the street were in blissful silence.

"So why are we really driving out for breakfast. The invitation last night was awkward."

"I do have an ulterior motive for bringing you with me this morning. There is one more favor I need to ask before this begins. I need you to take your sledgehammer magic and beat on their backdoor."

"A distraction while you enter the front door. I can do that. That leaves you with the Demons and no one to watch your back though."

"I am okay with that, the salt rock from the Sea of Galilei tends to become a huge equalizer. Plus I have three vials of the goofer dust that you and Raz made back at the house. But that's not the favor. Once you break through the wards, or they come out of the tunnel, flee. Make your distraction and then get out of the circle."

Michael remained silent waiting on Preacher to continue.

"The reason that the team is staying out of tunnels is to keep them safe. I am not sure that this banishing spell is going to work, but that is secondary to keeping them safe. Even with Hashmal riding with you, I would prefer you to stay safe and get out of the area."

"I will take that under advisement. Let's make sure we get far enough into the plan that I have the option to flee. If things don't go according to plan, I may have no choice but to come in and make a stand with you."

Preacher parked the car close to City Market and shut it off. "The plan will work well enough, I have confidence in it." He got out of the car and waited for Michael. They walked to a restaurant tucked into a small side street next to City Market and saw a line had formed.

It took some time for the restaurant to open and the pair waited in silence. It didn't take long; however once the place opened for them to place an order and get their food. They were back on the road quickly, the smell of breakfast and coffee filling the car. Preacher thought to himself that this would make for a great last day on Earth if the worst were to happen.

Everyone was awake when they returned, and they were happy to see breakfast arrive. After everyone had their coffee, the conversation became light and fluid. Preacher listened to the sound of happiness in a home that brought nothing but sadness to him in the last few years.

Today would be a good day to die.

37.

Raz and Bobby were in place early, with Gus and Josh watching over them. They wanted to be in the area well in advance to get familiar with not only the location but with the people in the square. They made sure they had enough space to lay down a blanket and wait for the square to fill.

Across town Preacher and Michael stood near the warded entrance to the slave tunnels. They were looking at the wards swirling across the brick exterior. Preacher checked his watch. “It’s almost time. Let’s see this through.”

Michael nodded at Preacher and extended his hand. Preacher took and shook it. “Good luck Father Brandon.” The handshake was firm, and there seemed to be a finality in it that bothered Preacher.

“You best be on your way Preacher. You’re not one to keep Demons waiting.” Michael spun Preacher around and gave a gentle push that sent him walking down the familiar cobblestone street.

Preacher wanted to stay to be reassured that this wouldn’t be the end but Michael was right, there wasn’t time. Preacher began walking towards his rendezvous with Malik and Snyder, the shotgun gently taping his thigh under his coat.

The pair were waiting for him as he approached. Snyder was glaring at Preacher with a snarl on his face. “You came alone? You are more foolish than I thought.”

Preacher smirked. “You haven’t seen anything yet.”

“Where is the rest of your team Preacher, we were expecting more than just you.” Malik's voice was level, but a tone of irritation lay just beneath the surface.

“My team is engaged in other efforts to assist us.” Preacher nodded to the wards. “It is time to get started.”

Snyder looked at Malik, who gave a short nod. Snyder walked to the wards and placed his hand on the wall and began muttering under his breath too low for Preacher to hear.

**

Just a few blocks away Hashmal knelt before the wards. He placed his hand on the ground a few inches before the swirling patterns. He drew from his celestial connection with the world and focused the power and energy collecting it and allowing it to fold in on itself.

With little effort, he pushed to power to the wards. He felt it slide out of hands and it slammed into the wards. The swirling patterns slowed, and Hashmal started collecting more energy. He gathered more power than before and expelled it to the wards. It slammed harder, and the swirls stopped completely.

Small fractures in the line work of wards began to form. Hashmal started collecting more energy again. More power rolled tighter, compressed more tightly this time. He released the energy into the wards pushing with all his effort.

The small fractures ripped into tears and cracks. The energy holding the wards together used these cracks to escape and explode outward.

Hashmal stood and wiped the sweat from his forehead. He grinned to himself. "That should get their attention."

**

The Demon came running into the chambers at full sprint his arms flailing out of control. He was a local, used for menial tasks like moving crates and guarding the door. Ramil had not bothered to learn his name. He came skidding to a halt and made a hasty bow. "My Lord, the eastwards have been broken."

"Broken how?" Ramil's eyes shot down the tunnel looking for signs of anyone following.

"Crudely My Lord, pure energy blasts." Ramil looked at the other two local Demons in the chamber. He wished that he could have persuaded Baba Doek to bring more Demons that he was familiar with.

"It must be Preacher and his pet witch. How many are left guarding the east entrance?" Ramils eyes darted to Baba Doek. Flanked by Castor and Pollux, she stood watching an hourglass. Sand ticked through grain by grain. Charmed to drop its last grain of sand at the moment the eclipse would begin.

"Three My Lord." The Demon stammered.

"Go back, take those two with you." Ramil nodded to the other two locals in the chamber. "Leave the tunnels only as a last resort. We only need to protect this spell."

The Demon fled back down the tunnel taking the other two with him.

"Do we have a problem Ramil?" Baba Doek sounded menacing most times, but there was an edge to her voice that made the hair on the back of Ramils neck stand up.

"Preacher most likely. The locals have been sent to deal with it." Ramil sounded confident because he was. Preacher always came after single Demons with a team behind him. There were ten Demons in these tunnels, it was unfathomable that a group of humans could actually disrupt this spell.

"You believe that to be enough?" Baba Doek didn't sound confident in Ramil's decision, but she didn't press it any further, and Ramil wisely didn't either.

**

The mortar between the bricks began to separate. Snyder removed his hand from the wall, and they watched as the tunnel opened silently before them. The bricks slowly turned opaque and seemed to lose its solid form.

Preacher reached inside his pocket and took out a vial of holy water. He stepped through the brick and paused allowing his eyes to adjust to the low light of the tunnels. Red glowing orbs hovered every few feet casting the shaft in an eerie red dim light.

The three stepped in, and the bricks closed up behind them. A lack of an immediate attack made Preacher's confidence grow. Michaels' distraction must have worked.

Preacher brushed back the coat he was wearing and raised the shotgun as he started down the tunnel. Malik reached out and pushed the barrel of the gun down. He held up a finger to his lips. "Too loud. Let us thin the herd before you begin blasting away."

Silently the two Demons took the lead and headed into the tunnel before him. Each was holding a blackened blade in their hands.

Further, inside the tunnel the air grew stale and humid. Water formed on the walls of the tunnel as it would in a bathroom during a hot shower.

The two turned the corner and slowed. Without a word between them, they rushed forward. Muffled sounds of a struggle started, and when Preacher turned the corner, they were quietly laying two bodies on the floor.

Preacher knelt beside the body that Malik laid down. The throat was sliced from ear to ear. Black blood flowed from the wound bubbling as air escaped through the wound. Preacher touched the wrist to get a pulse, but it was gone. The Demons own black blade remained clutched in its hand as the skin began to turn brittle and ashy. Preacher pried the knife from its grasp and slid it into his pocket.

The bodies of the dead Demons crumpled in on themselves, turning into blackish ash. Malik looked over to Preacher with a grin on his face. "Ashes to ashes as they say." Quietly he began walking forward and soon the lights started to get brighter.

**

Hashmal stood outside the ruined wards waiting for the Demons to come out. He knew that they could not ignore the destruction of the wards and he had to assume that an attack was coming.

His anticipation made it feel like he had been standing outside for hours. He checked his watch. It had been less than two minutes. He knew that Preacher would not be happy if he stepped through those wards, but it would be even worse should the spell be successful.

He drew upon his powers and stepped into the tunnel. The four demons on the other side of the tunnel were caught off guard. They were probably expecting an attack to come immediately after the wards broke. Hashmal reached out with his power and compressed the air around his body into a tight sphere. Violently he forced it into the tunnel at high pressure.

Four demons nearest him were lifted upward and cast back, away from the entrance of the tunnel. Two hit the walls of the tunnels, skulls crushing against the force the attack. One flew backward into the darkness landing hard with a snap of bone and a groan of pain. The fourth was sent into the ceiling with such force that when she fell her neck was twisted at an odd angle and vertebrae protruded from the side of her neck.

The injuries would probably have been fatal to a mortal, but these Demons would heal in time. It would give Preacher time to attempt to unjoin them should his efforts today prove successful against Baba Doek.

Hashmal's eyes glowed a bright golden color as he stood staring at the other two demons in the tunnel. They fled away from him running for their lives, and he gave chase.

**

Malik, Snyder, and Preacher came to the entrance of the cavern. Preacher looked inside and saw Baba Doek standing behind a table. The table was cluttered with items that he didn't bother to pay much attention to other than an hourglass, slowly letting sand trickle from top to bottom.

Behind her stood two individuals. One held a baseball bat with spikes driven through it, and the other had a long chain. There were large crates stacked near the wall next to them. Sweat glistened on their foreheads, which was odd because neither Malik, Snyder nor Baba Doek were sweating. Preacher found it curious.

Movement on the other side of the chamber caught Preachers' eye. A second Demon stood near another tunnel opening. He was tall, with long black hair and pale skin. Two different Demons ran out the tunnel near the other unknown Demon.

"It's the Fallen, somehow they found us." The tall demon took a few steps forward and threw his arms into the air like a V. Dust started to fall from the ceiling of the tunnel as it began to shake.

Michael came running into view, and the Demon threw his hands downward. Preacher locked eyes with Michael just as the ceiling gave way. The first of the blocks falling hit Michael on the head causing him to fall to a knee. Then everything fell, and Michael was swallowed in a shower of stone and dust.

"MICHAEL!" Before Preacher realized he was the one shouting, everyone in the chamber turned in their direction. Preacher lost himself in shock, he threw vial after vial of holy water at the Demons across the room while charging to close the distance.

Preacher threw four vials of holy water and missed with every single one. They fell short or went wide. The vials broke, seeping the precious liquid into the mud. Preacher pulled the shotgun from under the trench coat and took aim while running towards the demons.

He squeezed the trigger, and the sound was deafening. The kickback was so strong that it felt like it was going to dislocate his shoulder. He was still too far away, the rock salt may have touched clothing, but it didn't penetrate. He aimed the shotgun again but the Demon he was pointing at disappeared.

Hands grabbed the gun that were not there before. They ripped it to the right, the plastic clasp holding the strap broke and the gun was free. The Demon tossed it to the darkness. Preacher reached into his pocket and pulled out a vial of the goofer dust and slammed it into the Demons face.

The response was instant. It shrieked and pulled away clawing at its face, ripping the skin off its own skull. It took two steps back and started crumbling into dust.

Preacher straightened himself up in time to see Malik grabbing the tall, long-haired Demon and vanishing into a shadow.

Snyder was slashing away with his knife on the other Demon making quick work of the job. He turned to the shadow that Malik went through. He let the Demon fall and dove through the shadow, leaving Baba Doek and her humans alone with Preacher.

Baba Doek looked towards the hourglass then towards Preacher. She took a few steps backward and placed her hands on the two that stood motionless behind her. "Catch me if you can lover. But be warned, this is not a ride you want to go on."

Baba Doek stepped back and disappeared into a shadow.

Preacher saw the rippling and did not hesitate to follow. Without thinking he ran at top speed to follow her.

**

On the surface, Raz was deep in chant. The power of the spell was building. The bowl she was mixing things in was laid on a plain white sheet. Bobby was frantically handing her the next prepped container as soon as her hand shot out for another one.

It was a humid day, and sweat was pouring from their heads. The number of people in the square had grown considerably in the last half hour. People were standing shoulder to shoulder drinking and waiting to see something they may never see again in their lifetime. Everyone was so busy looking up they didn't bother looking at the group at all.

38.

The lights were off, leaving the room mainly in darkness. It was terribly hard to see. There was jazz music playing at a low volume, it was a foreboding sound. M.C. only played music low when she wanted to talk over it. That always meant Preacher had done something wrong.

Tables covered the floor in front of him. Table clothes of deep red laid on each table. A single candle was set in the center of each table, encased in a red candleholder that would toss shadows through the showroom.

All at once every candle lit causing the light to play tricks on his eyes. Preacher tried to see to the end of the room but the candles cast just enough light to throw shadows and obscure the view.

A familiar giggle came from the stage, giving Preacher at least a direction to travel in. Everything was familiar for him but still foreign. M.C. and Preacher had several of their most enjoyable dates here. He remembered everything about it, the pianos were off center of one another, leaving a large opening in the center of the stage.

Eight tables made up each row, three tables deep. Preacher made his way through the tables towards the front. He took a breath and allowed a calm to settle within him. He could see the empty club, the empty stage.

"Why did you come, Preacher?" The sound echoed through the empty club. It bounced off the walls and was impossible to follow back to its origin. "I told you to stay away, that it would cause you nothing but pain."

Preacher worked his way to the stage, saw steps up to the platform and walked up them to the stage. He searched through his new eyes. Being able to penetrate the darkness was both awkward and comforting. There was so much untapped knowledge running through his veins Preacher felt it hard to concentrate.

"She never loved you, Preacher. Not the way you thought she did, not in the forever way. You know that though, don't you?" Another giggle filled the air. Her voice bounced off the walls and played tricks not only with his perception but his memory.

"Think of it, Preacher. Think as you have over and over. Even after two years, you never met a single friend. They were all kept at arm's length. You were just a dirty little secret."

Preacher stood in between the pianos. He thought this would happen, he tried to harden his nerves in light of the Demons of the truth. There was some truth in her words, no matter how painful that truth might be.

He heard the sound of her shoes on the stage. The sound directed his attention to her position. He closed his eyes and remembered the way his M.C. looked the last day he saw her. He concentrated on the small things that he could remember. He focused on the softness of her skin and the shininess of her hair. He centered himself and opened his eyes.

She was wearing black high heels, which accentuated her athletic soccer player legs. She was still wearing the bone necklace she took the day she was Joined. Preacher looked at her shiny straight brown hair, it was just like he remembered. But the rest of her was strikingly different. Dark makeup surrounded her eyes, and a deep red lipstick covered her pink lips.

He could hear his lover's voice when the demon spoke, but it was not her. Different words were emphasized, a slight Creole accent that's found in the deep swamps of Louisiana was present where it shouldn't be.

"Demons lie. Even when they are wearing pretty skin." Preacher said. His voice hadn't trembled at all. Good.

The girl he loved looked at him, undeniably different yet still the same. She cocked an eyebrow, a sign of confidence that washed over Preacher like cold water in the shower. His hands began to shiver slightly.

Preacher continued. "The only reason you are in there is because she wanted to save me. It is my fault that this happened. There is no way for me to have her back after this, I know it. But that doesn't mean I am willing to let you keep her." Preacher looked at Baba Doek fighting back the wave of confidence with his own.

"There is no way for me to have her. Blah blah blah. You humans and your self-righteous attitude. She was never 'yours' to begin with Preist." Mockery filled Baba Doek's voice, M.C.'s voice. It cut Preacher to the bone.

"Demons lie, my M.C., my Doek, she's still in there. And I'm going to set her free." Preacher spat.

"Oh? Yes, we do lie. When it suits our needs. But I don't need to lie now; the truth is painful enough isn't it." She took a step forward her heels echoing through the empty club. Tattooed snakes slithered from under her dress and wound themselves around her arms, sliding under the skin as if they were alive and seeking prey.

"You were a plaything, something fleeting to hold her attention until something better came along. You were never going to grow old together. Was she to bury you? Try to move on once you were gone, after she was old and this body ravaged by time?"

She laughed cruel laughter, rejoicing in the truth laid bare between them. "So, you see I've done you a blessing, given you a greater purpose."

Preacher looked at Baba Doek, then somehow he looked closer into the Demon. He could sense the rolling hatred. It flowed over her skin like the snakes that were slithering there. It was like watching through murky water, you could see blurs but not objects.

Preacher pushed harder, looking for a sign of kindness, empathy, caring, some indication that M.C. was in there. Tearing through the illusion that the Demon presented was like peeling an onion. Every time you thought you may be at the center you had to yank one more time.

"Did you know, that there are a handful of times in every humans' life that they feel so much grief their soul literally tears into pieces? If a person doesn't choose to heal, parts of the soul dies. It dies Preacher, the beautiful gift that God gave to your kind and refused mine. It is squandered." Now there was anger in Baba Doeks voice.

"Some people turn to those they love for comfort when they need to heal. Love builds the soul back, a little stronger a little better. Others turn to hate, which twists the soul, turns it into something dark. You chose not to heal though. You kept the pain alive and tormented yourself. But even you couldn't stand that for long, could you? Now you try to drown it in Whiskey don't you." Baba Doek knew his weakness, and she was turning it against him.

"Did you ever find solace in the bottom of the bottle Preacher? Did it ever stop the dreams? You have let yourself go soft while throwing this pity party. Only when it was almost too late did you try to heal yourself. How many times did you have the barrel of your gun in your mouth? You've memorized the feeling of it against your tongue, wouldn't it be so much better if had just pulled the trigger?" Somehow it wasn't only Baba Doeks voice, but it was M.C.'s voice. It might have been Preacher own voice.

"You turned to vengeance to heal your soul. Against me. But you brought your precious Doek to me, didn't you? If it were not for you, I would have had to infest that trashy creature that summoned me. It's not me you want vengeance against, is it? It's against yourself." Baba Doek giggled. It had been so long that Preacher almost forgot how melodic it could sound.

"Even if you win here and drive me out, you know that you have lost her yes? I mean, really Preacher, how could she ever move past this. She finally knows how dangerous it is to be with you."

Preacher's thoughts turned to M.C., on a warm day in Savannah with Sinatra on the turntable. They were dancing in the kitchen, the sun beaming in the windows. They were in a place of peace, enveloped by love and peace of mind that comes with satisfaction with life.

And then he felt her. Still inside, fighting to get to him. He could still save her. Anger and fear washed over the thread he was following to her.

"NO!" Baba Doek growled. Sparks and flame burst from her hand and licked at Preacher. Only instinct made him dive out of the way. Heat washed over him causing sweat to break out on his forehead as he rolled to his feet.

From the darkness behind her came two figures. The two humans that were with her in the chamber.

"Do not kill him if you can help it, boys. Leave him broken, let him feel his failure." Baba Doek lifted her arm towards Preacher, one of her tattoos slithered down her arm and began puddling in her palm. She turned her palm over, and the inky blackness began gliding to the floor. The inky stream became a puddle, and from the center a snake emerged, slithering from the blackness into existence.

Baba Doek released the inky blackness of the snake. She stepped back in the darkness and was gone.

Preacher was watching her disappear when a flail landed on the piano, buckling the instrument in the center. As soon as it was there, it was gone again and flying at Preachers head.

Preacher ducked and rolled. Immediately he saw the problem in this fight, he needed to close the distance on the flail, but the guy with the baseball bat needed him close, so he needed to keep distance. Not to mention the time limit on saving the world from Baba Doeks spell.

Preacher slid to the right as the flail flew past his head. Castor was immediately there swinging the baseball at Preacher, aiming for a body shot. Preacher stepped into the blow allowing the shaft of the bat to hit his ribs but missing the spikes.

Muffled pain shot through his side as the bat made contact. Preacher wrapped his arm around the bat and trapped it close to his body. He spun Castor, putting his body in between him and Pollux. Preacher wondered if they would kill each other to get to him.

Preacher took the chance to look over Castor's shoulder to Pollux. He was standing still spinning his flail, looking for his opportunity to strike. Castor's eyes darted to the floor next to Preacher.

Preacher used his strength to spin Castor just as the serpent struck out. Preacher silently cursed himself. How could he forget about the Demon viper? The viper struck Castor in the leg instead of Preacher.

Preacher released one hand from Castor and pulled out his last vial of holy water. He threw it on the snake awkwardly, but with enough force for it to break. Where the water hit the snake it sizzled and boiled. The snake began to lose shape and dissolve into a putrid smelling smoke. It hissed like it was in pain and struck out again, hitting Castor once more in the leg.

Castor gasped in pain and became rigid in Preachers grasp. He tried to scream but no sound out. The veins in his forehead bulged, and tears welled in his eyes. The veins in his neck pulsed as a blackness took them over.

His mouth gaped open, and Preacher felt heat on his face. Flames burst through, close enough to singe the stubble on Preacher's cheek. Preacher pushed Castor back, watching as his skin blackened and cracked. Flames broke through his mouth, eyes, and cracks of the skin.

Preacher scooped up the baseball bat and turned to face Pollux. If he felt any remorse for the death of his partner, it didn't show. He threw the flail out again, but Preacher was able to knock it away with the baseball bat awkwardly.

The bat was severely off balance because of the spikes and Preacher had never had a chance to play the sport growing up. The flail came flying back towards him, again he batted it away awkwardly.

Preacher knew that he was running out of time, the eclipse would be starting soon and he needed to end this fight. His opponent didn't seem to be trying very hard to kill him. He was just taking up Preachers time.

The flail came back again, and Preacher sidestepped it this time instead of just knocking it away. He lifted the bat over his head with both hands and threw it at Pollux. It flipped end over end, making a whooshing sound in the air. It struck Pollux in the chest with enough force that he staggered backward.

Pollux looked down at the bat. The spikes penetrated deep enough that they were not visible. He tried to take a breath but couldn't. Pollux fell to his knees and collapsed over on his side, staring at the ashy remains of Castor and wondered who would be there to put them in a coffee can.

39.

Baba Doek returned to the chamber under the city alone. The last of the sand in the hourglass was falling through to the bottom. She walked to her position behind the table and smiled. The Fallen and Balisk's feeble minions teaming with Preacher was both unexpected and beautiful.

Even though there was limited time to enact her spell Baba Doek took a second to consider the situation. Many in the Church were sent after Demons, and those poor souls were taught that Demons were arrogant. It wasn't arrogance, it was superiority. Demons had existed longer than any human, they were smarter as a matter of experience. Not to mention the ability to use Celestial abilities, understand language and predict events that would take place in the future. Demons were the most sophisticated beings in existence.

She looked at the crates of Spiritus Vitae stacked behind her. She was going to have Castor and Pollux break these crates and vials for her. That was before she had to lead Preacher on a chase. She left him in a place that was special enough to fuckup his emotions and slow him down.

Baba Doek started building power from the area into herself. Bringing in the energy was slower than it should have been. It was like she was competing for the natural energy in the area. Someone was casting a spell that she wasn't aware of. Preacher's fucking witch.

A thud came from the collapsed wall. She ignored it and built her power, the cases that contained the Spiritus Vitae cracked but did not break. Another hit occurred, and dust was thrown into the air from the collapsed tunnel.

Another thud hit the cave in, and the fallen rock blew inward. Michael stepped into the chamber knocking the dust off his clothes. He looked about the room and saw only Baba Doek standing there.

"Glad to see I have not missed the party entirely." Michael stepped towards her quickly to close the gap between them.

Baba Doek turned and met him halfway. "I do not have time for this shit." She blocked Michael's right hook with her forearm. She drew in her celestial powers and forced them out and into Michaels' chest.

Michael flew backward into the chamber's wall. She struck out with her left hand and balled her fingers into a fist. Grabbing Michael by the collar with her power she lifted him into the air. She curled the fingers of her right hand as she summoned her demon-blade.

She pulled Michael towards her and thrust her blade out. His eyes went wide as it went through him and exited out his back. Michaels' toes scrapped the ground, blood pooled in his mouth as it filled his lungs.

Baba Doek opened her hand and released the demon-blade. The blade dissolved into nothing as Michael fell to his knees. Blood poured from the open wound. Baba Doek grabbed him by the collar and lifted him to his feet. She tossed him into the crates, breaking them and the vials of Spiritus Vitae.

Using her power, she tossed Michaels motionless body across the chamber. He landed in a sitting position against the wall, his chin resting against his chest. The Spiritus Vitae was seeping from the broken container in a blueish mist. Baba Doek concentrated on taking in the energy.

At first, it was a rush, something like what humans would feel when the adrenaline kicked in. It was euphoric and memorizing. She drew, and the mist flowed over her and through her.

She pushed the power to her necklace, charging it like a battery. It started to draw strength from her. The more power it took, the more it pulled Hell closer to the chamber. As it grew closer, she felt the effects on time in the room. It was time to begin her spellwork.

**

On the surface, Raz and Bobby were behind on their spellwork. Raz was near panic, the eclipse had started already. The crowd was getting rowdy and drunk, staring upwards at the sun through their special eclipse goggles.

Occasionally an almost empty plastic glass, can or bottle would fly. So far Josh and Gus did well at playing crowd control and keep people away from the spell site. Unfortunately the closer it came to the eclipse the more drunks showed up.

The moon covered the sun and Savannah was cast in darkness. The crowd cheered, all looking up except the members of the team. Someone pushed, then someone else pushed. They were all vying for the best position possible to see the eclipse.

Someone fell tripped over Bobby, who was on his knees opposite of Raz. He fell over Bobby's shoulder and on the bowl causing it to spill on the ground. He rolled off laughing and muttering an apology. The banishing spell was ruined, the energy that it had been collecting rolled free and evaporated.

**

From the mirror, M.C. watched in horror as her hands, and her voice worked the spell. She witnessed her hands place a heart on the table and slice it open. Her connection with the Damballa allowed knowledge to flow to her, now that she knew how to tap into it. The heart belonged to a middle-aged nun whose virginity was still intact. A mockery of the Virgin Mary that was removed during a full moon.

Inside the heart, she inserted the right thumb of an infant which was removed with an hour of the child's birth. Two viper fangs were dropped into the heart, followed by the tongue of a goat born with two heads. Finally, toes of a rabbit were added, even through the fog of shock M.C. wondered if these were for luck, like a rabbit's foot.

Once placed inside the heart, it was sewn shut and set in a bowl. M.C. watched Damballa through the mirror pour blood from a jar into the bowl. It was the blood of a Rabbi that had freely been given to the Demons. Jesus Christ, how did she end up here?

She had seen Preacher in the mirror, at the jazz club. He was truly alive, and he was trying to save her. But he wasn't here now, and that was a problem. Baba Doek reached down beside the bowl and picked up the hairbrush. The cursed artifact was the last ingredient needed for the spell.

A rustling sound behind her caught her attention. When she looked, she saw herself standing in the doorway.

"It is time." Her other stated it as a fact.

M.C. thrust her hands into the mirror. It felt like pushing through a slow running stream. It was cold on her skin, and she struggled through up to her elbows. There was a tingling running along her arms like they had fallen asleep and she was just getting feeling back in them.

She felt the urge to break the brush, the Demons influence and power was so strong that it felt like her own emotions. She wasn't sure where her feelings and desires ended, and the Demon's began.

She felt a surge of power from the hairbrush and heard it whisper to her in her own voice. "Resist," it said. M.C. looked down and realized that she was looking through her own eyes and not through a mirror.

She was in control. It felt, very different. It was so different from the dream world that she was in she wondered how she never noticed the difference.
"Focus, stay in control!" The voice hissed loudly.

She could feel the Demon struggling to take back control. It was howling silently in her head. It wasn't noise exactly, but it was a rush like a whirlwind in her head that made it hard to concentrate. She poured more of her energy into not breaking the brush in her hands.

The Demon pushed harder for control, and her vision swam. She started to doubt her ability to hold on. She forced all of her focus into holding the Demon's power at bay. It fought against her. It sent wave after wave of power against her. She felt her resolve start to slip slightly, and immediately she felt her hands tighten on the brush to break it.

She focused harder, concentrating all her efforts on not breaking the brush. She heard the urging of the brush, pleading with her to hold on. She felt sweat bead on her forehead as she strained to peel her fingers from the brush.

Suddenly Preacher was standing next to the wall of the cave. It was like he melted into the room. He was standing there looking at the body slumped on the wall next to him. He was here to help, she knew it. A wave of relief washed over her, she was going to survive this.

The relief broke her concentration. Numbness crept up her arm bringing a tingling sensation with it. Violently she tumbled back into the bedroom with the mirror. She rolled to her knees and looked at the mirror, but it was black. The radio that she had been using to listen to the real world produced nothing but static white noise. Panicking she turned to the door to flee the room, but there was no door, just four walls with no windows or door. No way to escape. M.C. screamed.

**

Michael's body was slumped over sitting next to the wall. Blood covered his shirt and pooled around his legs. He wasn't breathing, and Preacher couldn't see blood flowing from the wound. Michael didn't listen, he didn't flee, and now he was dead.

Preacher heard a sob and turned to see M.C., not Baba Doek but M.C. staring at him from the opposite side of the table. A tear spilled from her eye when she blinked and slid down her cheek.

When her eyes opened, however it wasn't M.C. anymore. Baba Doek was back. She was holding a hairbrush, and he thought that strange. It had to be part of the ritual; otherwise, she wouldn't have it. Their eyes met, and in one motion she bent, then cracked the brush. A thick deep red liquid seeped from the crack, and she held it over a bowl in front of her.

Preacher slid his hand into his pocket and pulled out the last weapon he had packed. Josh's spring-loaded crucifix garrote thing. He aimed for her neck and fired. The shot was low and right, it struck and wrapped around a table leg.

The first drop of liquid fell from the brush thick and viscus. It landed with a wet splattering sound in the bowl, and a blue fire ignited casting Baba Doek's face in an eerie light.

She wasn't looking at Preacher, she was looking at the bowl. Her smile was a thing to haunt your nightmares. Her smile was wide, pulling her lips over her teeth. The wetness of her mouth reflected the blue light.

Another drop fell, and the fire burned brighter. Preacher pulled with all his might. The table was pulled away and flipped onto its side. The now free-flowing liquid spilled on to the floor. The bowl crashed to the ground, and the fire went out.

Baba Doek screamed. The sound was more animal than human. Anger could be felt in the air as it traveled out through the noise. Her head shot up at Preacher, and he felt himself lift off the ground and hit the wall behind him.

He was inches off the ground, held firmly against the stone wall. He tried to move his arms, but they were pinned to the wall with an invisible force more potent than anything he had ever felt.

Blue sparks of Spiritus Vitae leaped between the teeth on her necklace. Preacher saw the broken crates and vials behind her. There must have been thirty vials broken and used.

"When I Joined with this soul and took this body it was on the agreement that I heal you and allow you to live. You, however, have become too annoying to let live any longer." She looked down at the bowl and its empty contents on the ground.

Preacher felt something grab his hand. He looked down, realizing that he could move his neck. Michael had grabbed his wrist, no it was Hashmal. The eyes were golden. Hashmal reached across his body with his other hand and touched the chains that he wore as a bracelet.

Hashmal pushed the bracelet upwards, the chains stretched as they moved over his wrist and their joined hands. He slid them upward further, onto Preachers' wrist and the world went white.

Power surged through his body, but not with force or aggression. It was a peaceful sensation power cascading gently over and through him. His strength grew with every beat of his heart.

When the world swam back into focus, he was standing on his feet. He was no longer being held in the air by Baba Doek. She was still staring at the remains of her spell that lay ruined on the ground.

She looked at him and their eyes locked. She leaped over the table laying on its side in front of her and landed with cat-like grace. In a fluid movement, she charged at Preacher. He knew that he shouldn't have been able to see her move, but somehow he could.

Preacher raised his arm, palm facing outward towards the charging Demon. He pushed with his mind, focusing his newly found energy and confidence to stop her charge.

Baba Doeks legs stopped pumping, they froze and her brow furrowed in confusion. Preacher pushed with a little more force, and she slid back towards the fallen table and wall. Her feet left tracks in the loose dirt as she slid backward. Preacher pushed harder towards Baba Doek. She slipped back further. She was resisting now that the element of surprise was lost. Preacher shoved harder, and she flew backward, off her feet and slammed into the wall. He held her against the wall, her feet inches off the ground. Her arms were spread wide, almost as if it were a mockery of the crucifixion.

"I command thee, unclean spirit, Damballa, who has taken possession of this handmaiden of God, that by the mysteries of the Incarnation, Passion, Resurrection, and Ascension of our Lord Jesus Christ, by descent of the Holy Spirit, by the coming of our Lord unto judgement, thou shall tell me by some sign or other they name and the day and the hour of thy departure!"

While it was not traditional to start an exorcism here, there was no one to say the responses. Baba Doek groaned against the wall, Preacher wished that he had not thrown all of the holy water already.

Preacher continued the ritual, allowing the calming power to flow through him. Baba Doek's face was frozen in a scream that was inaudible. He walked closer to her making the sign of the cross.

"I will kill you, Preacher, I will rip your entrails out and eat them while you're still alive. I swear the last thing you see will be your lovers face smiling at you while you die." There were layers to the voice, almost as if several beings were speaking at the same time saying the same thing. Preacher took at as a sign of separation between the demon and host, it was encouraging.

He opened himself up to the power and allowed more to flow through. Baba Doek gasp, black liquid filled her eyes and dripped down her cheek. Preacher said a prayer silently to himself then continued the ritual.

More black liquid came from the nose and ears of Baba Doek. Wounds opened on her hands and feet almost like signs of the stigmata. She lifted her head looking at him. The black liquid fell from her mouth staining her clothes. She spat at him, mocking him with her defiance.

As Preacher prayed, he could hear the separation in the screaming now clearly. Her mouth would move, and the sounds and words would follow but a fraction of a second later. She was in mid-scream and Preacher in the middle of commanding Damballa out when she suddenly fell silent. Her gaze lifted over his shoulder and a slight smile broke in the corner of her mouth.

Preacher started to turn but was too late. Something struck him in the side of the head, very hard. The power behind the blow was extremely strong. The blow caused Preacher to spin in a small circle causing him to trip over his own legs. He fell sprawling to the ground, his vision swimming.

With his concentration broken Baba Doek fell to the ground into a crumpled heap. Preacher groaned and rose to his knees. "Ugh." Preacher tried to shake the cobwebs from his head. "What the fuck was that?"

A slow tsk repeated itself from across the cavern. "That is not the right question." Preacher looked up to see Bolfry standing in the cavern. "You did better than I thought you would Preacher." Bolfry rolled his neck in slow circles like he was working out a kink in his neck.

Bolfry turned his head to Baba Doek, the look was a mixture of anger and disappointment. His tongue darted over his lips, maybe there was hunger in his gaze as well. "You let him interfere. It weakened the spell, it will take time to have its effect now. That is, very disappointing."

Preacher pushed himself up onto his knees and looked between Bolfry and Baba Doek. She was laying on her side, the skin that he remembered so well was wrinkling. It seemed dry and brittle to the touch. He knew that he could unjoin her on his own, he just needed more time.

Bolfry took a few steps closer to Preacher. "I wanted them! I wanted them all!" He reared back and kicked Preacher in the chest, causing Preacher to fall over and roll over and over until he hit the wall.

As he tumbled, Preacher felt something smack him repeatedly from the pocket of his coat. Something long and solid that he didn't remember packing, the black Demon blade. His vision swam again, and he wondered if he had a concussion.

Preacher shook his head several times to clear the cobwebs. It took a few shakes before he could see clearly. He used the wall to help him stand, and looked at Bolfry and Baba Doek. She was on her knees, using the wall to help her stand.

Bolfry nodded at her. "Flee, take your credit in a few months and take the office that should be yours." Baba Doek nodded at Bolfry. Preacher couldn't tell if it was out of respect or fear. Then she stepped into a shadow, and she was gone.

She was gone. Preachers mind went blank. Preacher screamed with rage and charged at Bolfry. He pulled out the black blade. When Preacher reached Bolfry, he grabbed him by the throat, lifting him into the air.

He pushed Bolfry to the wall with ease. Bolfry's eyes were going wide with surprise. Bolfry hit the wall hard. Preacher drove the blade into Bolfy's chest. Over and over he dove the knife home. Preacher drove it in hilt deep, feeling the blood pour out onto his hands. He pushed it in deeper and harder with each thrust out of anger, out of frustration, out of failure.

Preacher let Bolfry fall and screamed to the empty chamber he was in. Bolfry fell to the ground and coughed up blood. "See Preacher, I told you I would never go back to Hell." Bolfry's skin started to turn gray and Preacher turned away.

Preacher looked over to Michael's body, he noticed that nearby was the shotgun that Bobby had let him use. He grabbed the gun and walked to Michael's body. Michael was gone, and whatever was left of Hashmal was also gone. The body was a delicate shade of grey, ashy and fragile. Michael's features were cracked as lines ran through the face. Slowly he started to crumble, collapsing on its self. He was gone.

40.

The funeral for Michael was a small affair. It took place in Preacher's backyard. The entire team was there watching Preacher mourn in silence. Calling it a funeral was an overstatement, there wasn't a body to bury or photos laid out for others to see. There was just Preacher staring out over the marsh that his backyard ended in.

Preacher had grumbled a few words, even calling him a stubborn bastard at one point. It was clear to everyone that he was blaming himself. Josh and Gus were also feeling responsible for the loss. They were being hard on themselves for allowing someone to trip and fall on the banishing spell. It was their job to conduct crowd control, and they had failed. Miserably.

Preacher was sitting in a lawn chair looking over the marsh alone with his thoughts. A glass of iced tea lay at his feet. The sun was falling over the horizon behind the house, westward over the rest of the city.

It was a humid day. Sweat rolled down his head and soaked into his already wet shirt. The back door opened and Josh stepped out and sat next to Preacher in another lawn chair.

"You ok?" Josh asked. It was a simple question really, but one that was loaded and complex also.

"No." When in doubt keep it simple right.

"Okay. Sounds fair." Josh left it there, the silence fell heavy and thick just like the humidity. Preacher reached down and picked up his glass of tea.

"Looks awful light for whiskey," Josh observed the glass.

"It's tea." Preacher took a sip.

"I didn't know you even liked tea." Josh shifted in his seat.

"Your gadget saved the day, I'm not sure if I told you that or not." Preacher's voice was flat and distant. "If I didn't have that crucifix launcher gizmo I wouldn't have been able to disrupt the spell. Keep working on it and improving it. It will definitely come in handy in the future."

Josh shifted in his seat again. "Do we have a plan on needing it in the future?"

Preacher took another sip of his tea and didn't say anything for several minutes. Josh was starting to wonder if Preacher heard the question or maybe he thought it was rhetorical and wasn't going to answer.

"I'm working on one. If you have a suggestion, it would be welcome." Preacher put his tea back on the ground.

"I think I would like to stay here with Bobby and help with research and stuff." Josh let the idea float in the air. "I just really like this place, it feels more like home than I've felt in a long time. Besides we don't know where Baba Doek ran too. If she stayed here it makes sense for there to be two of us turning over stones and looking."

Preacher gave the slightest of nods. "It makes sense. Thanks, Josh."

Josh understood that this was the end of the conversation. He stood and went back inside leaving Preacher alone with his thoughts.

**

Preacher and Gus packed up the next day and headed back to Atlanta. It was a four-hour drive, and the two spent most of it in silence. They made it back to the house and quickly unpacked.

Preacher was taking the scrolls from the trunk and putting them on the dining room table. He would sort them and start going through them later.

Gus cleared his throat and Preacher looked up. He was leaning on the corner of the dining room wall. He had a sheepish look in his eyes when he was looking over Preacher.

"Got a second?" There was a wobble in Gus' voice that Preacher wasn't familiar with.

Preacher nodded. "Of course."

"I've been thinking that I haven't been much good to you in exorcisms so far. I need to be trained like you were trained. Through the Church with official title and status." Gus shrugged and put his hands in the pockets of his plaid shorts.

"I left the Church because of the bureaucracy and politics. I think you will have the same problems with the system that I did."

"Maybe I can change it from the inside over time. And even if I can't, I will have the backing of the Church and the power that comes with it."

Preacher nodded slowly. "So you have been selected already? When do you leave?"

"In two weeks. I applied months ago and found out just before we left that I was accepted. I didn't think that you needed any more distractions." Gus fidgeted a little under Preachers gaze.

"Congratulations are in order then." Preacher smiled at Gus and stood. "Have you told Raz yet?"

Gus shook his head no. "Not yet, I'll tell her when she gets back." Gus grinned at Preacher. "Besides I want to have my recipes in a book for her when she gets back. Cooking is like magic, follow the steps add the ingredients and voila, food."

Preacher let it go, but he thought that there was more to cooking than that. He could follow directions, but it never turned out quite as good as Gus' food.

"Speaking of food, I'm going to make some." Gus pushed himself off the corner and walked to the kitchen. Preacher watched him as he walked away. He could tell that Gus was proud of his decision and that truly made him happy, even if he didn't agree with the decision.

Preacher took a bottle of whiskey and glass and went to sit on the front porch. Two members of his team were distancing themselves from him. It was concerning since Michael died and Raz was still in Savannah for a couple of days talking with the local witches. He wasn't sure if she was coming back or staying.

Fighting against the self-imposed pity party Preacher swallowed some of his whiskey. The orange cat that had made its home under Preacher's front porch came bounding up the stairs. It hopped on the rail and stalked in front of Preacher.

Preacher gazed at the cat, it sat on the rail in front of him. He reached a hand out to pet the animal. He half expected the cat to lean into the hand and accept the affection. Instead, the animal swatted at him as soon as it was in striking distance. It let out a sound that was half hiss, half growl. The rules were clear, look but don't touch. It seemed fair.

**

It took Raz a week to get back to the house. Her arrival was a relief to Preacher, and just as the pattern of life started to normalize Gus packed and left for school. The absence of Gus and Josh was very noticeable, and it made the house seem very empty

Preacher filled the void with work. He was taking jobs that he usually would have refused or recommended others for. His exorcisms were slowly turning into interrogations as he searched for information about Baba Doek.

Raz filled her time by hanging out with other witches in the area. They discussed spell work, theory, and application. Sometimes they just drank wine and people watched. She found her ability to use magick rose the more time she spent with other witches. When the group cast spells together the power was almost strong enough to touch.

When she wasn't spending time with her friends, she was hanging out with the cat. Preacher didn't protest when she brought it inside, but she could tell that it annoyed him. The cat seemed just as annoyed that Preacher kept coming back home. He would stalk Preacher from one room to another, and if she and Preacher were in the same room, the cat was always between them.

Several months passed and Raz was working with her newly formed coven on a spell to levitate simple items. She was sure that there was a way to do it, and she was always partial to the scenes in the movies when characters could move things with their minds.

She was sitting on her bed, the cat curled up in her lap sleeping. She was concentrating on the task, wondering how the process should go. There was a power resonating from inside her, humming just under her skin.

There was more to it than that though. There was power in the world around her. It felt like a mosquito buzzing in her ear, a noise that was just loud enough for her to hear. Then there was a surge of energy from everywhere and nowhere at the same time. Power rushed in her and around her, it sounded like a snap of a rubber band. No, that wasn't correct, it was more like a crack of a whip.

The cat jumped to its feet, hair rising along its spine. The cat looked around the room frantically, then at Raz. "What the fuck was that?" The voice echoed in Raz's head.

"I don't know," Raz replied without thinking. The power of the world was vibrating, everything was more precise and also blurry at the same time.

The cat leaped from the bed and looked at her from the floor. "Did you just answer me?"

Raz came back to the present, knowing she was alone in the room she just looked at the cat. It tilted its head to the side like it was confused. Raz nodded at the animal.

"Holy shit. You shouldn't be able to hear me." The voice came into her mind but not through her ears.

Raz pushed herself towards the headboard of the house and away from the cat. Once she was far enough away that she couldn't see the cat, it jumped on her bed and looked at her.

"What's going on, what the fuck are you?" She said it louder than she intended. It came out as a scream.

The voice chuckled, a laugh mixed with a purr. "I am Stewie, I am a familiar. I am your familiar." The cat rolled onto its side, rubbing its scent onto the sheets. "This is wonderful."

The door opened, and Preacher stuck his head in. "Everything ok in here?"

Stewie looked over at the door with all the contempt he could muster. Cats are good at looking at people with contempt, but Stewie had mastered it. "It was better before you came in."

Preacher looked between Raz and the cat. He blinked in surprise. His focus went to the cat. "Did you just speak?"

It was Stewie's turn to look surprised. "What the fuck are you?"

The response made Raz laugh, which broke the tension that was building in the room. They were going to figure this out, and she could tell that it would be fascinating along the way.

Made in the USA
Lexington, KY
07 December 2019